A WIC...
WICKET

S. Terry Canale

ISBN: 1973972697
ISBN 13: 9781973972693
Library of Congress Control Number: 2017911812
CreateSpace Independent Publishing Platform
North Charleston, South Carolina

FOREWORD

I have written and edited many orthopedic textbooks, but I have never written a novel, which has been a lifelong dream. Although it is completely fictitious, many of the episodes were based on real experiences in my life. The episodes that aren't so real followed the old adage, "Never let the truth get in the way of a good story." To friends, relatives, and acquaintances who might recognize a situation or a setting or a character: don't worry; names have been changed to protect the innocent and the not-so-innocent. As all authors disclaim, "any resemblance to actual persons, living or dead, is purely accidental."

When I started this project, I had no idea how labor intensive it is to write a novel and how much effort is involved to make a story work. I owe a great debt of gratitude to my wife, Sissie, for her patience and encouragement. Thanks also to Renee Poe, Kay Daugherty, Pat Goedecke, Shawn Maxey, and Jennifer Perry for their assistance. A special thanks to Linda Jones, without whose expertise and perseverance this novel never would have been written. Finally, to MeMoe, my dog, who loved every minute of it.

All in all, it's been a great learning experience, as well as a fun endeavor. I have thoroughly enjoyed dredging up some old memories to weave into the plot, and I hope you find them interesting and amusing. Right now, MeMoe and I are going to try to find a croquet game we can get in on—but will stay alert for any suspicion of a wicked wicket!

1

I knew Simone Amstutz had been missing but hadn't thought much about it. After all, it didn't really concern me. I was just a passing acquaintance of the lovely Simone, estranged wife of local celebrity attorney Cooter Amstutz. When I heard that the groundskeeper at the Universal Club had pulled the tarp off the pool and found Simone's decomposing body riddled with stab wounds, I was shocked and saddened but not concerned—not my circus, not my monkey. How was I to know that Simone's murder would become my biggest concern and would send me running from Memphis to places I'd never imagined and from people I'd never met? I mean, seriously, how could the murder of the sexy Simone have anything to do with me? It was ridiculous. At the time, I already was a successful orthopedic surgeon, a rising star in my field, and I worked for one of the most prestigious clinics in the country. Since I was tall, dark, and handsome and in the prime of my life, the ladies did adore me—if you were a single nurse, or even a married one, beware—but Simone wasn't really among my core groupies. You might say this sounds vain and self-absorbed, and you'd mostly be right. But let me give you a little background about me so you can see just how ridiculous the idea of my having anything to do with Simone's murder was.

At the time, I had the world by the balls, so to speak, and practicing humility was just an act for me. I reveled in the glitz and glamour of being a top sports-medicine doc, at the center of the fanfare and fame associated with professional teams and all the perks that come with that. I'm not talking about being just a spectator but a participant. Thankfully for the world, however, I was growing into the mentality that it's not who you operate on but what you operate on that's important. Knees are my current preference.

All in all, my life's not been too shabby for a kid raised by a workaholic father and an alcoholic mother in a place called Yazoo City, a small town in Mississippi of maybe ten thousand people in a good year. Sure, some bad things happened in my life, but isn't it like that for everyone? My father didn't get very old. He died of a massive heart attack, something I blame my mother for—her brutal alcoholism was the death of him and, later, her, when she overdosed on rubbing alcohol. As a child, I spent some years in Clarksdale, Mississippi, having moved from Yazoo City, but didn't like it much. In the third grade, some of my classmates there told me I looked like a turtle. I didn't think I looked like a turtle, but one kid, Lance Mingledorf, kept calling me that. One morning in particular stands out in my mind. It was a hot, hazy Mississippi day. We were at break, all of us kids, playing softball. I hated break time, and we had a full thirty minutes of it too—thirty minutes to be harassed and harangued by my classmates.

"Turtle face, turtle face. Terry is a turtle face. Turtle Terry," Lance Mingledorf teased.

"I'm not either!" I recall shouting.

"Yes, you are. You're Terry turtle face—Turtle Terry. Ha-ha, Turtle Terry."

"You take that back, or I'll see you after school!"

Lisa Morgan was snickering into her hand, but Molly Langford was shouting to everyone to leave me alone. She couldn't stand to see people fight.

"Ha-ha, ha." Lance snorted. "I'm not afraid. We can fight now if you want. What? You gonna boohoo hoo?" The creep picked up a fist-sized rock from the dusty ground and threw it, hitting me dead center in the chest. It knocked the wind from my gut. I couldn't believe it!

Furious, I rushed him and clocked him a good one right in the schnoz. Unfortunately, that only made matters worse—after that all the kids started calling me Turtle Face. I remember going home asking my mother and my grandmother if I looked like a turtle, but they assured me, "Most certainly not." Bottom line is that I was so happy to move from Clarksdale to Memphis in the fourth grade, where I was considered a "normal" human being and not the offspring of a tortoise. Except to visit my grandmother in Clarksdale, I didn't leave good ole Memphis again until college.

At the present time, I work at the respected Camp Clinic, a large, renowned orthopedic practice in Memphis. It was a position I accepted after college, medical school, residency, and a short stint in the military. I haven't been stupid enough to marry and have done quite well financially, owning a condo in Memphis and a seaside home on the Gulf Coast. It's about an eight-hour drive, or forty-five minutes by jet if it weren't for the stop in Atlanta. I go there whenever my schedule allows. What I don't own, unlike most young studs, is an exotic car, preferring instead to cruise around Memphis in an old Ford Explorer. It suits me, and it *ain't* worth stealing.

Most of my free time, which honestly doesn't amount to much, is spent playing tennis and some handball at the Universal Club, an exclusive private tennis, athletic, and social country club. I had learned to play tennis back in high school and got pretty good at it, even though I had to play under the radar because of football. In my sophomore year, Coach Mix, my football coach, saw my picture in the newspaper after I'd won the Memphis tennis semifinals and hunted me down in class. I believe his actual words were, "Tennis is for sissies! If I ever catch you with a tennis racquet, I'll break it over your head!" Well, that ended my tennis career until way after medical school. The same football conflict-of-interest thing happened to me in college when I wanted to play lacrosse. One of the assistant football coaches told me to "throw that stick away, or lose your scholarship," ending my lacrosse career before it ever took off.

Running is something else I do on a daily basis to stay fit. It wasn't really my thing in high school or college, though. I always thought runners didn't look very happy, but it has its benefits for sure: one, it's good for your health; two, it's good for your psyche; and, three, it's good if you ever have to run for your life. Never did I dream that it might come in handy that way. When I first took it up, it was just to see if I could actually do a marathon. Not to brag or anything, but I actually ran the one in Boston, which almost didn't happen for me. I trained hard for that race, read all the books on it, and learned how to eat properly and what shoes to wear. The week before the marathon, I even wore a mask to the office for fear of catching the flu or a cold. I took every precaution and prepared for everything under the sun—except being slammed in the Achilles tendon by some guy's briefcase at the airport on the way to Boston. Fortunately it only left a big bruise, and I was still able to run.

I won't lie. The Boston course was grueling, especially the last steep incline they call "Heartbreak Hill." It's aptly named because it is heartbreaking to look up at that hill and realize that after twenty miles your legs just might decide not to play along. Once you reach the top, though, it's all the more awesome. Spectators line that section of the course to spur on runners. "Go, Terry!" I remember them shouting as I ran past. It seemed odd to me that they knew my name, but I didn't give it much thought considering my celebrity status. Later I found out that they have a roster of participants and yell out everyone's name. That's nice. Don't ask about the old guy who lied to me about finishing that hill a mile before it even started. I was never so disappointed in my entire life. In the end I finished the race in a little under four hours and received my medal, a proud accomplishment.

So, as you can see, I am a healthy, successful, content individual, and my social life is exceptional. I hang out with several young nurses at the various hospitals and some divorcées at the U Club. Most of the women there have had work done on some parts of their bodies, and most are exceptionally curvy and slightly top heavy, which makes for interesting afternoons and evenings. While one might consider me outgoing, for the most part, people don't, because I always try hard to paint a very conservative picture of myself and act as a part of the wall tile. Basically, this is where my story about the Simone murder begins—with me minding my own business.

2

It was late in the afternoon, and I was letting off steam in a handball game with three other U Club members after having seen some difficult ER patients. We were using a fat ball for the game. It's larger and softer than a regulation handball and not quite as hard on your hands, which is important to artists, musicians, and surgeons because it doesn't damage the soft tissues of the hand. Many consider the fat-ball game obsolete, a game only played by Neanderthals. Our game attire is, of course, totally *appropriate*—shorts, a jock strap, a black sleeveless T-shirt, and no gloves. Refreshments are lowered down into the court in a pail, and the participants do not leave the court until the match is over or the opponents are dead. My partner and I lost that particular game primarily because, being left handed, I missed a sharp right-handed shot. I worked out my frustration over the loss in a relaxing steam bath, and then I showered, shaved, and retired to the men's bar to catch some action. The bar is open only to men until six in the evening during the weekdays, but after that women are allowed. Historically, the club was an all-men's club, but obviously times have changed, and women are allowed to be members if they have enough dough and are socially acceptable.

I ordered my favorite drink at the bar, a Bloody Mary without the vodka, which I call a Virgin Mary, with a large stalk of celery and extra Tabasco. Because of my mother's *problem*, I try to avoid alcohol. Once I start drinking, it's hard for me to stop at one or two like normal people, and I continue to drink until there is no more or the next morning comes. Whether they are right or wrong, I follow the principles of Alcoholics Anonymous. It's not that I have a problem with others drinking or being around people who drink, but it's best for me to just not drink. When I was in high school, a frat brother and I got dead drunk at a New Year's Eve party at an illegal bar called A World Away and ended up driving all the way to New Orleans for the Sugar Bowl in our tuxedoes, with no luggage and just enough money to get tickets for the game. We sat in the stands in our tuxedoes and overcoats next to a couple of refugees from Cuba. We had no idea where we were going to stay or how we were going to get back to Memphis. Neither did the Cuban refugees. Fortunately, two men who were sitting in the seats in front of us took pity and gave us a key to their apartment in Metairie. We spent three days there before my New Orleans girlfriend, Georgia, whom I had met the previous summer, rounded up some food and enough cash for our trip back to Memphis. Unfortunately, my interest in the brew didn't diminish even after that experience, and I ended up drunk again at my senior prom. The punishment for that was not being able to go up onstage to get my diploma at graduation.

So far, I'd been lucky and managed to avoid trouble with the law and hospital authorities, but that was all about to change as I was sitting at the men's bar at the U Club drinking my Virgin Mary and munching on small cheese crackers, which I like to call "the fishermen's platter," while the sun set over the city of Memphis. I was stirring my drink with the celery stalk, when Lou the Jew slapped me on the back.

"Have you heard about Simone?" he asked, taking the stool next to mine.

"No. What should I've heard?"

"She's been missing. Her family has no idea where she is. They filed a missing person's report today."

"Really?" I popped another cracker into my mouth. I knew Simone casually, a thirty-something knockout, one of those curvy kind of women, married but estranged from her lawyer husband. She was a regular at the club who came in fairly often. I was not sure whether she had any children, but I did know her last name, and I guess it was better to have not slept with her and know her last name than to have slept with her and not know her last name, so we'll leave it at that. I vaguely remember making a pass at her one night at a downtown bar called Sleep-Out Louie's but then opting out of taking that conversation further when her date, a Mr. Atlas Thug with one too many buttons on his shirt undone, came out of the john. Ever vigilant of my visage, I thought better of a second pass at pretty Simone.

"She plays boccie ball here, doesn't she?" I asked Lou.

"Yeah, croquet's entirely too slow a game for her," he replied.

Simone was also an avid workout artist and had the body to prove it. I would know because I'm also one. We would run into each other occasionally in the gym. She would be taking spinning classes and body sculpting from Roberto, her personal trainer at the club, while I worked the elliptical or jogged on the track. Other than that, I actually knew very little about the woman but hoped she was OK.

"Well, I'm heading out. I'll talk to you later, Lou." With my Virgin Mary empty and having nothing left to add to the story about knockout Simone, I decided to call it a night and head to my condo, which is in the Central Gardens district, closer to the drugs-and-crime side than the plush residential area with the big homes. I like it there, and nothing's ever happened. If you watch yourself and keep an eye on those around you and have a security system, it's pretty safe.

I took inventory of my refrigerator to see what might serve as dinner. It was slim pickings as always, but there was a lone frozen dinner way back in the freezer behind the ice cubes. Weighing my options, I tossed it into the microwave and turned on the television. Joe Brown from the nightly news was giving the rundown on all that had happened in the last twenty-four hours—two murders, a robbery, a lost dog that found its owners after ten years—and then he mentioned the missing Simone. I turned up the volume.

"Mrs. Amstutz has not been seen or heard from since Friday. If you have any information on her whereabouts, you are asked to contact the Memphis Police Department." A number flashed across the screen under Simone's picture.

Studying her image on television, I wondered about the last time I had seen her—when was that? Two nights ago? Friday? I considered who else might have seen her that night and who might have taken her home or elsewhere. She was a lovely young woman, about five foot seven and full bodied. She had long blond hair, which she flicked back out of habit with every turn of her head. I thought about the rogue she had been with at Sleep-Out Louie's, happy we hadn't gotten in a tussle. It was too bad for Simone and her family, but none of this really had anything to do with me, so I went on to bed and slept great.

3

The following morning, there was a small article in the local paper about Simone being missing and that she was the wife of a lawyer by the name of Cooter Amstutz. Cooter had the reputation around town of being a ruthless ambulance chaser. I'd heard through the grapevine that the two were in the midst of a contested divorce.

I threw the paper on the table, downed my coffee, and headed to the office, which is about a mile east of the Mississippi River. It isn't that far from my condo, a few city blocks at most but far enough to have to drive. It's an old, gray brick structure built in the twenties by a visionary, they say. I never got a chance to meet the man because he was long gone before I was even born. Legend has it that he was one of the first bone carpenters of the time here in this area, a pioneer in the field. He was the first president of the American Academy of Orthopaedic Surgeons and the first chairman of the Department of Orthopedics in Memphis, two of the most prestigious positions in our field and ones to which I aspire. I've also set my sights on becoming the Camp Clinic's chief of staff one of these days and the chief of Pediatric Orthopedics over at the children's hospital, the latter of which will probably come first.

Dr. Camp's clinic was originally three stories, but two additional floors were later built. Currently, it has five stories and an outward appendage that we call the annex. That's where we see patients. Back in the day, before surgery centers and day surgery, they actually did operations in the old part on the fifth floor, and the two floors below were patient rooms. These days, the fifth floor belongs to physical therapy, and the fourth floor belongs to the foundation, which is responsible for the residency and fellowship programs and research. It is there that the bible of orthopedic surgery is created, of which I can proudly say I am one of the authors and basically the ghost editor. I say "ghost" because Kay Daugherty, a former high-school English teacher, is the person who does all the work. The second and third floors are the doctors' private offices, and the first floor belongs to the business office, the CEO, and a plethora of assistants, which works out well because he's close to the money. My private office is on the second floor just down the hall from the lunchroom. Glorious smells emanate from there, starting around ten in the morning. Kat and Jean, two very gifted cooks, serve country cooking between eleven and one, and it's gratis for the residents, fellows, and staff doctors.

I drove around back to the parking lot and took the elevator to my office. I would've taken the stairs, but Dr. Woo Woo was just coming down with his assistant; the doctor was railing about something going on over at the city hospital. He was always in a tizzy about one thing or another, and chaos seemed to make his day. His name wasn't really Woo Woo. That's just what the PTs called him behind his back—don't ask me why. He was a nice man, but I didn't feel like getting caught up in his commotion that morning. When the elevator dinged, I manually opened the door and the inner gate. Yeah, it's an original from the twenties, if you were wondering. We also have an old-timey dumbwaiter. I unlocked the door to my office, threw my bag onto the desk, and plopped down in my chair. There was a stack of insurance forms and charge tickets waiting to be filled out and signed.

I pushed the papers aside and yelled for my nurse: "Johnnie! Will you get me some coffee?" Her office was next to mine. We didn't use an intercom—too uptown.

Dr. Bailey's nurse, walked by and stuck her head in my office. "Get your own damn coffee!" she said spitefully and continued her pigeon-toed stroll down the hall.

That ticked me off. I know Dr. Bailey loves his nurse, but there's no love lost between her and me. We grew up across the street from each other. Their kids were told to stay away from us Canales.

Nurse Johnnie appeared with a cup of black coffee in hand and placed it firmly in front of me on my desk calendar.

"Do you mind having to bring me coffee?" I asked her, signing some of the charge tickets. I hated this part of my job but understood that it was all tied in to my remuneration.

"As long as my paycheck doesn't bounce," Johnnie answered curtly. The height of her eyebrows and the set of her lips let me know that she was in one of her moods.

I didn't reply and just kept working.

She stood there watching me for a full minute. "I'm heading over to clinic now," she said irritably.

Best to play dead, I thought.

She stopped at the door and sighed loudly. "We have over fifty patients today."

My shackles went up—those were fighting words in our world.

I stopped working and leaned back in my chair, hands behind my head, waiting for her to say one more thing. I was already fully annoyed at what Dr. Bailey's nurse had said and at the mountain of paper work on my desk.

Her eyes narrowed. "And just to let you know, I'm not staying a minute past four today. My son has a recital tonight."

"Have I ever made you work past four?" I shot back, now fully peeved.

"I'm just saying." Her eyes were throwing daggers my way.

I took to signing some more documents. "When did you put this stack on my desk?" I demanded, knowing full well I might be playing with my life.

"Last night before I left—why?" Her hands were now on her hips, and she'd grown a couple of inches.

"Don't leave paper work on my desk overnight; you know I don't like that."

"That makes no sense! What difference does it make when I put it on your desk?"

"It does to me. So don't do it anymore!"

She mumbled something unintelligible and stormed down the hall. By the time I made it over to the clinic area, she and I would be fine again. Regardless what you might think, Johnnie and I really get along well most days. She's a sweet lady, tall, with bright red hair on some days and jet black on others. She wears multiple earrings in her right ear. She has a young family, and she's very efficient in her work. In fact, Nurse Johnnie does most everything for me, including driving me to the airport, picking up my dry cleaning, scheduling all my trips, making sure I get a plate of food when there's a potluck—and that's in addition to taking care of all of my patients.

I finished my stack and headed over to the clinic, where things were in full swing. Dr. Carlisle, who'd just stepped down as chief of staff, was raising hell at eight in the morning—no telling about what. I hated the days we had to share our clinic space. We really needed to move to a bigger building. I'm as nostalgic as the next person, but we were busting at the seams. I passed Melanie, Dr. Carlisle's physician assistant. She was wearing a sign that said, "Shit Happens." Must've been what all the commotion was about.

All in all it was a trying clinic with many difficult patients, and at day's end, which was around three, I snuck out the back door, desperately needing to get away. I had a tennis match scheduled at the Universal Club.

When I arrived in the locker room at the U Club, there was more talk about Simone, who had not been found. They had located her car, however, evidently parked in the club parking lot. It had been there for the past three days. There are plenty of reasons for a person to leave her car parked overnight in the club parking lot, but almost always, embarrassingly, it's picked up the next morning. For Simone, that was not the case. A thorough search of the grounds—including the squash, handball, tennis, croquet, and boccie ball courts—had been carried out. Also, the clubhouse—including the gazebo bar, clubrooms, and locker rooms—revealed nothing suspicious and no evidence of Simone. Inside the club, the ballrooms, meeting rooms, and bars were all searched—again nothing.

While I was gearing up for my tennis match, my cell phone rang. Aggravated about the disturbance, I picked up.

"Dr. Canale?" It was Johnnie.

"Yeah," I acknowledged, trying to hide my irritation but letting her know to keep it short.

"A detective from the Memphis Police Department is on my other line. He wants to speak with you. Should I put him through? He says it's important."

"Oh, OK. What's his name?"

"Um, Reardon, Dan Reardon. Here you go. I'll transfer him."

I waited a second and then said, "Hello."

"Is this Dr. Canale?"

"Yes, it is. Can I help you?"

"This is Dan Reardon. I'm a detective for the MPD, and I was wondering if you would come to my office this afternoon."

"What's this about?" I asked, although I was pretty sure it had something to do with Simone.

"Do you know a Simone Amstutz? As you might know, she's missing."

"Yeah, I heard."

"We're looking to talk to anyone who might know her and anyone who may have seen her recently."

"Sure, I'll come by later, say around six? I have to be at a pathology conference at seven, but I can spare an hour." I didn't know much but was certainly willing to tell him everything I did know. I'd heard around the club that Detective Reardon had also interviewed Larry Allen, the prizefighter she had been with at Sleep-Out Louie's, but apparently he didn't know anything either. It was quite clear that they were suspecting foul play.

"OK, my office is at two oh one Poplar."

"I'll be there."

As promised, I met with the detective and answered his questions, letting him know at once that I barely knew Simone and never had an affair with her, although I'd tried. The interview seemed to go well and didn't seem like an interrogation. I was fairly certain he didn't consider me a suspect in her disappearance. Why would he? On several occasions during the interview, I told Reardon that Simone was not really my type. Truth is, I was probably not her type, especially on the day that she and I last spoke. It was after a doubles handball game, the one for Neanderthal men, when we were standing happenchance at the bar together. She wasn't in a flirty mood at all that evening, and our conversation was polite but minimal. I did tell Reardon about my problem with drinking and about how it was easier for me stick to the principles of abstinence than to squeeze out two to three drinks every night.

With that Reardon leaned back in his chair and studied me for a moment. "So you think you last saw Mrs. Amstutz at the Universal Club bar...what—three nights ago?"

I nodded. "I got there around seven. She was there at the bar having a martini or two."

Reardon raised his eyebrows. They seemed exceptionally heavy for his face, but that was probably because of his thinning hair.

"She had two glasses in front of her," I explained.

His eyes narrowed.

"She always leaves her olives, so I assumed they were her drinks," I added quickly.

"Always?"

"Well, yeah...I mean...I guess. She did on that night."

"What'd you talk about?"

"This and that, small talk, unimportant gossip. I don't remember exactly. Then I left and went to St. Jerome's Episcopal Church around seven thirty for a catered dinner."

"Do you know any of the people she hangs around with at the Universal Club?" he asked.

I thought about it and rattled off a list of names as he wrote them down. Sometimes only first names came to mind. "That's all I know," I said. "Sorry I can't be of more help."

The detective shrugged and stood up, offering his hand. "Well, thanks for coming by. I'll be in touch if there are any more questions."

"Sure," I replied and hurried to get back to the clinic for the conference.

When I arrived, the pathology conference was already in session. I took a seat in the back of the small auditorium, which seated about fifty people. We had meetings on Monday and Thursday nights and Saturday mornings before grand rounds. Dr. Sikes was reviewing a case of osteosarcoma of the talus in a young patient and asked one of the medical students who'd made a catty remark earlier to point out the tumor and differentiate it from osteomyelitis. Now, I am the first to admit that my grades weren't all that stellar, but I can say with absolute certainty that even in high school I knew the talus wasn't located up in the nether regions where this kid was searching the X-ray. As I sat watching the scene with Dr. Sikes and the medical student unfold, a strong sense of foreboding suddenly came over me. Dr. Sikes was purposely laying down traps, and the kid, probably nervous, was talking too much. Had I said too much? Detective Reardon had been pleasant enough during our chat; he was a Memphis Grizzlies fan, but his face and demeanor hadn't revealed much. I realized then that during the interview he'd mentioned not once but twice that I might have been the last person to see Simone before she went missing.

4

In the days to follow, gossip about Simone was rampant, and theories abounded. One of the rumors was that she had been seen at the Memphis airport on her way to Atlanta and then Costa Rica, but then it turned out that had been one of her friends. Someone else heard from someone who'd heard that she was planning to jump off the bridge into the Mississippi because she was depressed about her divorce, yet there were others who flat out suspected that her estranged husband had given her a helping hand over that railing. And then the inevitable happened—my name was mentioned. I was, after all, the last person to have seen her alive. At the club, people started giving me sideways glances, whispering to one another as they passed. By the night of the Universal Club's spring shindig, more than two weeks after Simone went missing, I was seriously considering not going because of all the gossip and stories floating around in the air like too much dandelion fuzz, most of it about me being the last person to see her alive.

As the night of the gala approached, I was still ambivalent about attending, but a small circle of devoted friends who knew I couldn't have had anything to do with Simone's disappearance persuaded me to go. Tony Petroli's band was going to play poolside at the newly renovated gazebo, and roasted pig, luau style, was on the menu. Besides,

Stephanie Palumbo, a new divorcée with old money and a body to die for, was going to be there—who would want to miss that?

My not wanting to go actually ran deeper than just all the talk about Simone. There's a lot of old money from well-to-do, old Memphis families at the Universal Club. My father belonged to one of these old Memphis families, but, unfortunately, thanks to my mother, we didn't have any money. In old Memphis terms, I was a roustabout, with a worthy name no doubt and the current ability to pay the handsome U Club membership fee, but the tether of acceptance was still tenuous. It was like being in private Catholic school all over again. The other families were rich and could afford to pay tuition for private school; their children were entitled to be there. I, on the other hand, was there on a sports scholarship assigned to pick up trays during lunch, work the popcorn machine, and help Brother "Candy Bar" sell candy behind the counter at lunchtime.

As poor as my parents were, though, my old Memphis name got me into a lot of places. During my second year of college, I pledged a fraternity called St. Anthony Hall. It was probably the most prestigious fraternity on the Virginia campus, a big-money fraternity, one that catered to anybody but athletes. It was a fun fraternity, but the problem was that it was filled with roaring assholes from first families of Virginia, all with too much money but not quite enough to get their kids into Yale or Harvard. I remember once being at a country-club wedding of one of my fraternity brothers. At the rehearsal dinner, his aunt, who was a member of the better half of the Virginia population, asked me, "What does your family do, Terry?" When I told her that my father had been a fruit peddler in Memphis, she immediately turned a cold shoulder and had no more use for the likes of me. And another time, after football season, when I tried to join the polo team (I'd found an old polo mallet and helmet), one of my fraternity brothers asked me how many horses I owned.

"I don't own any horses," I told him.

He smirked. "Well then, you won't make much of a polo player, will you?" Not only did that end my dream of becoming a polo player, but it also provided me clarity as to my social status.

In the end I decided to go to the Universal Club gala. Wearing a dark-blue blazer over a nice blue-striped, button-down shirt, jeans, and loafers with no socks, I showed up, trying to ignore some of the underhanded looks from those who saw me as a possible kidnapper or serial killer. "You know, Ted Bundy was handsome in his button-down shirts and blazers," I heard one elderly woman say as I brushed past her and her posse of white-haired buddies. The weather was mild for April, the crowd large and pleasant except for a few early drunks—the same ones, it seems, at each party. They usually turn out to be the late drunks as well. The talk was about Simone, of course, when you could hear it through the accordion music that Tony Petroli's band was pumping out at decibels equal to the noise of the crowd. Although the accordion in my view died many generations ago, my foot was tapping to the beat, keeping time, as Miss Elseworth, my accordion teacher, would say. Yes, I took accordion lessons. My mother made me. I was ten and hated it. Why not drum or guitar lessons? Those are cool instruments, but no, no, she liked the accordion.

"Ladies and gentlemen!" the disembodied voice of the club president said over the loudspeaker. "A moment of your time, please."

The accordion stopped, and the crowd quieted slowly, the inebriates being the last to comply.

"Ladies and gentlemen, thank you for coming to this grand occasion. As you know, we're gathered here to celebrate spring in our new gazebo, a work of art, no less. Thanks to Ann Mahoney, Bill Frank, John Farcas..."

He continued down an exhaustive list of do-gooders, but I had stopped listening and was watching orchids and floating candles on the pool cover, thinking how this was a neat idea. It was too early in the year to remove the cover, so someone had put decorations in the rainwater that had puddled on top of the black plastic cover.

Twinkling lights were strung from tree to tree surrounding the venue. The whole shining event reminded me of the Memphis Carnival, the Midsouth's version of Mardi Gras. It used to be called the Cotton Carnival. I don't attend anymore but used to back in high school. Basically, it was four to seven days of partying. The king and queen of carnival were socialites, old family names from Memphis, Memphis country-club types, such as Queen Phoebe from the House of Dent and King William from the House of Snowden. When I was a senior in high school, my good friend Clyde fixed it so that we could join the court of the carnival and meet the young princesses from all over the South for the week. We rode on the buses and floats, partying our way from town to town—Blytheville, Searcy, Clarksdale, Helena—trying to put the make on some sweet thing for the night and then move on the next day. I smiled inwardly at the memory of the carnival and of Clyde. He went off to Yale, and we spoke from time to time. Last I'd heard he'd moved to Highlands, North Carolina.

The president of the Universal Club was thanking everyone again and pointing to the buffet. The accordion man pumped his instrument back up and played a waltz. Aside from the talk about Simone, the gala was magical, and Stephanie Palumbo had not failed to impress, with her tight-fitting, bust-lifting red cocktail dress. The band packed it in, and the party finally broke up sometime around midnight.

Rain had started falling, and by the time I made it home, a major storm was crossing the Mississippi, knocking out the power as it moved east across the city. I didn't care. I fell into bed and was asleep before my head hit the pillow. April storms and power outages are run-of-the-mill here in the Delta. Back in '03 Hurricane Elvis flattened roofs and took out the power for weeks in Memphis. You learn to live around these inconveniences here.

As dawn broke on Sunday, it was as if the storm had never been. The sky was blue, and the sun was flooding into my bedroom; temperatures were mild. I stumbled to the kitchen, started the coffeepot, and stared out at the quiet street, wondering why I was feeling so low and anxious about this Simone business. There was an AA meeting on Union Avenue early that afternoon, so I decided to attend. AA had become my faith of choice, and I was beginning to believe in a higher power—maybe not a godlike higher power, but a power greater than myself that would make all things eventually turn out all right, although bad and evil may happen along the way. Regardless, I couldn't shake my anxiety, and the last conversation with Detective Reardon kept replaying itself in my mind even as I sat in the steam bath at the Universal Club later that afternoon. The club had survived the storm the night before, but the grounds were a mess, and the tennis courts were too wet to play on, so I settled on a barbecue plate at Sleep-Out Louie's and an early bedtime.

5

On Monday I was due in surgery at six thirty in the morning. Patiently I performed the ritual scrub on my hands and nails in the sink outside the operating room and allowed the OR nurse to help me into my gloves, gown, cap, and face mask before entering the sterile room. The surgery, a knee arthroscopy, was already underway with the fully anesthetized patient supine and the knee in ninety degrees of flexion. The nurses had already completed the preparation and draping part, and the residents had created the portals for the arthroscope. Everything was as it should be. My role that day was to observe and teach and to make sure nothing went wrong.

"All right, what do we have?" I asked.

The lead resident gave me the patient's name, affliction, and side of surgery. The nurses nodded their approval. This process ensures that everyone in the surgery suite knows what's going on and that everyone is on the same page.

"Good," I acknowledged.

The younger of the two residents spoke up. "Dr. Canale, we found the biggest loose body you've ever seen in your life floating around in a knee." A loose body is a fragment of bone that has become detached in the joint space.

"Really?" I asked, surprised. The man had some swelling and pain but nothing so severe as to indicate a monster loose body. My guess was that he had bad osteoarthritis or that the joint needed flushing.

"Yeah, we put a towel clip on it. We're trying to get it with this osteotome, but I'm not sure this can be done arthroscopically."

My eyes flashed to the screen where the joint was fully imaged. I hated having to open a knee. Watching the osteotome tug at a large white oval, I suddenly realized it was the kneecap they were trying to pull out. "No, no, no! That's the patella!" I shouted.

The young resident was so startled that he almost dropped the scope.

"Are you kidding me?" I reprimanded the residents but tried not to be too hard. They were only second-year residents, and this was their first week of rotation with me. I had to remind myself that it takes a lot of practice to know what you're looking at in a joint. To those who have never seen it, the inside of a joint resembles a moonscape.

Most people don't know how much pressure surgeons are under during surgery. They can't see it because we don't show it. As a surgeon you must always display confidence and capability even if you're not particularly feeling it that day, but it's important for a patient to fully trust the surgeon; otherwise, how else could one entrust one's life to a person wielding a sharp scalpel or saw, which are quite common in orthopedics? The worry is not so much about the success of a surgery but about mistakes and complications, of which there are plenty, I can tell you. One time, I witnessed a median nerve being removed from the forearm because the surgeon trainee thought it was a tendon that he could use for a graft. And not too long after that incident, I was doing a total hip replacement and had just gotten the hip prosthesis in place, when one of the residents bent over, and his glasses fell off his head into the large open wound. This presented a big problem because it meant the wound was no longer sterile. We did our best to bring the site back to sterile before closing it, but for the next procedure, that resident underwent a full Betadine scrub of his face and his glasses just to give him a lesson in sterility. Doing surgery on the wrong body part also is more common than you'd think. The "sign your site" program that has been initiated by hospitals was put in place for that very reason. It requires a surgeon to place his or her initials with an actual marking pen on the portion of the body or extremity to be operated on. Believe it or not, this simple technique has cut down drastically on the number of wrong-site surgeries performed.

By eleven thirty I had just finished up with the almost disastrous arthroscopy and did a second one all by myself, when Nurse Johnnie called. "Hey, uh, Detective Reardon from MPD is here to see you," she said tentatively.

"OK. Tell him I'll be there in a few minutes," I replied, not revealing to her the extent of my alarm. The most I had ever associated with the police up to that point had been for a speeding ticket or two and a highway patrolman who'd walked up to me on the sidelines at a U of M and Southern Miss game and threatened to take me to the Hattiesburg jail if I went out on the field and yelled at the officials again. I was the sports doc for that game and felt that the referees were making horrible calls. So did everyone else, but, needless to say, after the fine officer's warning, I kept my ass on the sidelines for the remainder of the game. The University of Memphis won, by the way.

I arrived a few minutes later at my office.

"Thanks for seeing me on such short notice," Reardon said without formality. He was a head shorter and probably fifty pounds heavier than me, something I hadn't noticed before.

I led him into my office, offered him a chair, and then took the seat behind my desk.

"Would you care for some coffee?" I asked, moving some papers aside and placing my Styrofoam coffee cup dead center on my desk calendar.

"No, I'm good; thanks," he replied, never looking away from my face.

This man unnerved me. "How can I help you?" I looked at my watch. This was a habit I had perfected to let people know my time was at a premium.

"I hate to tell you this," he said and shifted in his seat uncomfortably, "but we found a body this morning."

My eyes opened wide. "Really?"

"We're not sure yet, because the body was in pretty bad shape, but we're fairly confident it's Simone Amstutz's."

"Where?" I asked, cautiously—too cautiously, I worried.

"The Universal Club. Some workmen found her. I really can't give you any other information, but it appears that she's been dead for at least a week, maybe two."

It had been a little more than two weeks since I had last seen her alive. I felt my face flush and hoped he hadn't notice.

He had. The detective leaned forward in the chair, his eyes keen like a cat's that had just caught a movement in the bushes. "I need for you to remember everything that was said that night or if you may have seen or heard anything that was odd or out of the ordinary. I'll keep it confidential, of course," he assured me with a cat smile.

My immediate thought was that the detective had no reason to consider me a suspect, but on second thought, that was probably invalid, because the police consider everyone a suspect. Mostly, I reiterated what I'd already told him.

"Where were you between the night when you saw Ms. Amstutz and when we last spoke?" he then asked bluntly, taking out a little black book from his pocket and leafing through the pages. He clicked his pen and readied it for writing. He raised his eyebrows, waiting.

I wasn't ready for that question and had to think about it for a few seconds. Finally, I gave him a rundown as best as I could remember.

"Sorry, I don't recall exactly by the hour or anything."

The detective stood up, ending the conversation abruptly. "Well, I'll get back with you in a couple of days."

I nodded.

As he opened the office door, he turned and said, "Doc, I have to ask you not to leave town right now."

"What?"

"It's just a formality," he said before walking off without a good-bye.

Well, so much for not being considered a suspect, I thought, leaning back in my chair, alarm bells going off in my head. How did this happen?

With my stomach tied in knots, I went over to the clinic side to start seeing my afternoon patients. Nurse Johnnie met me in the corridor with a young blond woman dressed in scrubs. The woman—or, should I say, girl—looked to still be in her teens.

"Hey, Dr. Canale, I'd like you to meet Cheryl. She's doing the nursing rotation here with us for the next couple of weeks," Johnnie said. "She's a Rhodes scholar." Johnnie smiled proudly, and the girl looked down demurely.

I gave Johnnie a grumpy, puzzled look. My chest felt tight, and anxiety washed over me in waves.

"Remember, I told you about this a month ago? You agreed to have her work with you."

"No," I replied gruffly and brushed past them. "Let's get started!" Just what I needed today—a trainee nurse. I threw my bag into the dictation booth. "Hey," I said to the girl, who was standing quietly outside my door, adjusting her black-rimmed glasses, "get me some coffee, will ya?—half full, black."

Her mouth opened and then closed and then opened. "OK," she said, unsure of herself.

Nurse Johnnie intercepted my first bullet: "The coffee's right over here."

Pulling on my white coat, I watched the two of them whispering as they went to the coffee machine. The girl returned with a half-full cup of black coffee and handed it to me, obviously pleased with herself at having accomplished this great feat. I took a sip and then frowned. "Get my first patient," I barked at her irritably.

Her eyes flew open, and she frantically searched the hall for Johnnie, who was busily working her laptop. At Johnnie's instruction, the girl went to call the first patient. On patient number three, Johnnie received a call from her son's school and had to leave to pick him up, so that left me with the newbie. She was flustered, and I was mad and pretty sure she only had thumbs as digits. After two patient-chart flubs, she was totally rattled.

"Who's in here?" I demanded, pointing to the examination room.

"Mr. Humboldt," she squeaked.

I opened the door. "Mr. Humboldt." I held out my hand to a middle-aged woman sitting on the stool that was supposed to be mine.

The woman smiled, amused. "You have the wrong patient; I'm Mrs. Greenfield," she said politely.

"I'm sorry. I have the wrong chart. I'll be right back." I left the examination room, embarrassed and fuming, clicking the door shut behind me.

The newbie was feverishly working the laptop. "Hey, Rhodes scholar," I said loudly. The other nurses scattered.

She looked up.

"This is the wrong patient! There's a woman in there!" I hissed, the top of my head tingling as my blood pressure went up.

Her mouth flew open. "I'm so sorry. Let me see who that is." She clicked around nervously on the computer as steam began to build up around my person. "I'm sorry—that's Juan Gomez."

The top of my head was now full-on burning, and I began to scrub my scalp. "It's not Juan Gomez; it's not Juan anything. There's a woman sitting in there!"

"Oh, OK." She smiled nervously. "Just one second; I'll have it in one minute. Shoot, yikes…ooh…the screen just went blank." The girl looked at me with wide eyes.

My blood was now boiling. "Just answer me one question," I said, my voice high and plaintive. "We don't know each other from somewhere, do we? You don't have a vendetta against me for any reason, do you?"

"No, sir."

"Then why…why are you doing this to me?" I bellowed.

She bit her lip. "I didn't do it on purpose, you know," she stammered. Then she blurted out, "But had I known just how much pleasure it would give me, I'd have done it sooner!" She stared at me, shocked at her own belligerence.

I stared back and then sat down heavily in my dictation booth, rubbing both my eyes with my knuckles. Until that moment, I hadn't been aware of just how tightly wrapped I was after my meeting with Reardon, and I was unfairly letting it out on this girl. Sighing, I asked meekly, "Can you please make some fresh coffee?"

"Sure. I'll be happy to." Happy to have an escape, she ran off down the hall to the coffee machine.

Marti, Dr. Woo Woo's nurse, stuck her head in the booth. "Does she need some help?"

"Please."

By the end of the clinic, things had settled down somewhat, although I was still really upset at the knowledge of being a murder suspect. Why me? I wondered. Just because Simone and I ran into each other the night she disappeared wouldn't make me a suspect, would it? The idea was farfetched and crazy.

As I was leaving the annex for the night, I said to Marti offhandedly, "Thanks for the help, beautiful." She was a stick-thin woman with a lollipop head adorned with enormous bumblebee glasses.

She rolled her magnified eyes flirtatiously my way and smiled. "Why, you old smooch, I ain't helping you tomorrow, just so's you know."

"Bet no one's ever called you beautiful before, huh?" I teased back, trying to stuff my laptop into my bag and walk at the same time.

She burst into tears. Alarmed, I ran to her, my bag with the laptop falling from my hands. I put my arms around her. "I was just joking," I insisted. Jeez, I was two for two during this clinic, or three if you count the murder accusation. All I needed now was for someone to slap a sexual-harassment suit on me.

"It's not that," she said, sobbing. "It's my husband. He left me for a younger woman last night." She wept into my shirt for several minutes as I patted her on the back. "I'm so sorry," she said, pulling away and blowing her nose. "I'm such a mess."

"It's OK, and for what it's worth, Marti, I think he's a fool. He'll be really sorry."

"Thanks."

"You bet." I retrieved my stuff from the floor and hightailed it out of there. I've never done well with tears.

Man, what a day that was, and it wasn't over either. There was a news conference. The chief of police told the camera that a body that had been discovered in the Universal Club pool was that of Simone Amstutz. Further information would be forthcoming after an autopsy by the county coroner. No comment was made concerning the cause of death. Gossip spread within minutes throughout the whole Central Gardens area. The body had been found by the groundskeepers, wrapped in a tarp floating in the pool. Evidently, the storm on the night of the gala had ripped the pool cover, and when they went to replace it, they found the rolled-up tarp. Rumor had it that the U Club personnel had seen stab wounds on the body. Speculation ran wild.

On the six o'clock news, Handball Roy, one of the locker-room attendants at the club, declared that he had never seen anything like this in his twenty-one years at the Universal Club. He was present when the police arrived and witnessed the entire scene until the body was removed to the morgue. His exclusive interview with *Channel 6 News* was sensationalism at its best and included nothing of substance except that Miss Simone's ashen-gray body appeared to have multiple puncture wounds. The cameras zoomed in on the yellow police tape that enclosed the entire pool area, as well as the first two tennis courts.

My cell phone rang, and I picked up without checking to see who it was.

"Hello."

"Is this Dr. Canale?"

"Yes, it is," I replied.

"This is Christine Hulsaker from *Channel 6 News*. Your name has been mentioned in connection with Simone Amstutz, and I would like to ask you a couple of questions. Do you mind?" the newswoman asked, trying hard to contain her excitement.

"I do mind, actually. You have nothing to interview me about, because I don't know anything." I disconnected before she had time to respond. How in the world did they get my name and number, and why? I turned off my cell phone, not wanting to say anything to anyone until they caught a killer. My thought process at that point was, What the hell just happened? I knew that I was a suspect. The detective had made that perfectly clear. I didn't have a clue what to do, so when you don't know what to do, you just do whatever comes next, which for me was staying in my usual routine, telling myself over and over that they'd find the real killer any minute now.

6

The day after the body was discovered, you would think the local paper would have a national story as a headline, but, oh no, not the *Memphis Appeal*. Their headline screamed in four columns on the front page, "Prominent Memphian Socialite Body Found, Foul Play Suspected." While physically under no stress, mentally I was shot. The strain of being a suspect in a homicide was almost unbearable. The day passed for me in a cloud of panic and worry. In the evening I tried to carry out my normal workout routine, but upon arriving at the locker room, I noticed that people were uncharacteristically silent and would not make eye contact with me. Only if I spoke would they, on occasion, just nod. They really believe I'm involved with this, I thought in dismay.

While I was hitting tennis balls that the automatic ball machine was tossing to me, I saw the police talking to Mike, one of the grounds crew who had found the body. When they left, I walked over to talk to him. Mike and I had known each other a long time. He has a criminal record, but all in all, he's a good man. I had helped him get out of trouble once a long time ago.

"Mike, what in the hell happened here?" I asked, straightening my tennis-racket strings.

He took off his ball cap and scratched his head. "It's a hell of a thing, Doc; that's for shor. Hell of a thing."

"So you found her?"

"Shor did." He looked back in the direction of the pool area. "Storm tore up the pool cover over there by the shallow end, and me and the guys went over to see if we could fix it. When we pulled back the cover, there was this bundle floating right underneath, see, and Bob says, 'Hey, is that a hand?' Well, ever' blessed one of us scattered, as you can 'magine. It like to scared me to death. Old Eduardo took a stick and poked at it, and a whole arm fell out, up to the shoulder. We knew then there's a body in that tarp, and we called nine one one in a hurry. Eduardo held onto the hand, so it wouldn't float back to the middle, while I ran o'er the clubhouse to find Derrick." Derrick was the new club manager. "Then we waited till the po-lice came." He wiped some sweat off his dark eyebrow and replaced his cap, shaking his head.

"They made all of us get back while they unwrapped that poor gal, but we could still see. She were in bad shape, Doc, bad shape. It look like someone stuck her through, not just once but lots of times." He shook his head some more. "Someone had to be real mad or crazy to do something like that. The coroner say she dead and took her away. They had a time unrolling her out of that tarp, though."

I quietly listened to him recount these details, frowning, nodding, or shaking my head when appropriate, encouraging him to tell me all he knew.

"The po-lice put crime tape around the entire swimming pool and tennis courts and tol' us to come help take off the pool cover. We struggled 'cause it's a heavy bastard, more 'n thirty meters long. It's an official Olympic-size pool." He said this proudly, as if I had never seen the pool before. According to Mike, just to remove the pool cover took more than three hours. Finally, people from the pool service company had to come to help.

"Underneath the cover, the water was so clear and light blue, and they didn't find nothing 'cept for that widget and a ball," he was saying.

"What's a widget?" I asked.

"It's a metal thing that you put in the ground to hit the ball through when you play crocket," he said, wiping off some sweat running down his cheek with the back of his hand.

"Oh, a croquet wicket?"

"That's what I said, didn't I?"

"Well yeah…of course," I said and then changed the subject. "Mike, how many people actually play croquet here at the club?"

He thought for a moment. "Not many. Ten, maybe twenty, I reckon."

I knew very little of croquet other than it seemed to be a popular game. I thanked Mike for the information and handed him a twenty, which he took appreciatively. "Good talking with you, Doc," he said.

"Catch you later, Mike."

When I got back to the locker room, I found Handball Roy and two cops searching all the men's lockers in the athletic building. One of the women attendants and two cops were searching the women's lockers. My locker was number 437. My pass code was 2222. I reopened the locker that I knew had already been searched, not particularly worried, since there was nothing for me to hide.

Evidently, Detective Reardon was planning to interview all the people on the Universal Club list who possibly knew Simone, whether they were single or married, and me for a third time. This was really disconcerting. Surely they couldn't seriously be considering me a suspect. I called a friend of mine, Big Al, who owned a late-night bar called the Red Eye on Main just off Beale Street. He was called Big not because of his size, although he was hefty, but because that was what his mama had named him. Big Al kept up with all the who's who in Memphis, and I was pretty sure he knew Cooter and Simone Amstutz.

When he answered, I said, "Hey, man, how's it going?"

"Hey," he answered in a raspy smoker's voice. "What's happenin', my friend? I hear you got the law all over you these days 'cause of that pretty young thing they found dead in the pool. What's that all about?"

"Is that the word on the street? That I did it? I barely knew the woman!"

"Naw, not really. People saying her old man probably did it. He's the number-one suspect—till proved otherwise, of course."

"Yeah, well, they're interviewing me for a third time 'cause I was the last person to see her alive—so they say."

"Bummer, dude."

"You know anyone on the police force who might be interested in doing some snooping around for me? I'd make it worth his while."

"Gotta be careful with shit like that. I'll check around, but remember you didn't get his name from me."

"Yeah. Thanks. Later."

We disconnected, and I wondered where I should commission the "off duty" officer to search and for what. Was any of this even necessary? Why was I so wigged out? I was innocent.

The police interviewed several members of the Universal Club who hung around at the bar, but no arrests had been made. The members who were married kept their interviews quiet, but some of the unmarried young studs loved to talk about their male prowess. They didn't immediately interview me for the third time, which I took as a good sign and began to relax some. But unfortunately this was only short-lived when I was informed that Dan Reardon wanted me to come in for a *formal* interview at his office on Poplar. I put up as much fuss as possible, telling him that an office full of patients was waiting for me and surgeries had already been scheduled. He gave me three days and said that after that he would issue a subpoena.

To restate, I was innocent—I barely knew Simone. However, a couple of my friends thought an attorney should go with me to this interview, so I asked Pat MacBurney, a well-known defense lawyer in Memphis. They called him Mack the Knife because he had won a lot of big cases and had been able to successfully defend clients by cutting the prosecution off at the knees with damaging evidence. He returned my call and pleasantly informed me that if I was innocent, there was nothing to worry about, and even if I wasn't innocent, he would represent me at eight-hundred dollars an hour or any portion thereof.

Three days later, my attorney and I were sitting in a small, drab interrogation room at 201 Poplar, waiting for questions from Detective Reardon. The walls were steel gray, and there was a mirror, probably a one-way, on the wall opposite me. A camera hung in the corner, most likely filming and recording my testimony. My heart kicked up a notch, and my mouth was dry. A second, younger detective was present. He didn't seem particularly happy. It appeared to me that he would have rather been anywhere but there or that he couldn't wait for five o'clock to start drinking. His name was Benjamin something or the other. I tried calling him Ben, but he preferred to be called Benjamin. I let it go. I would have preferred speaking with Detective Reardon alone without Benjamin, who looked like he needed a drink, but no such luck.

Reardon asked if we would like a bottle of water, which I gratefully accepted, but to which Mack the Knife said, "No, thanks," making a show out of looking at his watch. Evidently he too had perfected this skill, or maybe he was just keeping up with his $800-an-hour fee, hoping this interview would take as long as possible so he could pad his coffers sufficiently.

The detective opened his little notebook and flipped through the pages. "OK, when we last spoke, you said you had last seen Simone around six o'clock at the bar, and that she had two drinks." He looked up at me.

I looked at Mack the Knife, who indicated with a nod that I should answer.

"Yes, that's correct."

"Do you know Cooter Amstutz, Simone's husband?"

Except for seeing him competitively on the tennis court, I knew very little about the man. I shrugged. "He's a lawyer. I think he does personal-injury cases, medical liability, class-action lawsuits, disability, or just about anything." I left out the part about him being an ambulance chaser and that I didn't think he had ever seen a dollar he didn't like. I just said, "That's pretty much all I know about him."

"You gave me a list of men who hang around the bar at the Universal Club," he said as he consulted his notes. "You know these men well?"

"I'm on a first-name basis with most, but some I only know by reputation."

"What about Lou Peroni?"

Lou the Jew Peroni was a character. He had been divorced and married more times than I could remember. He was a manic-depressive who did OK as long as he stayed on his medication. I didn't say any of that, though. Instead, I replied, "I know Lou through sports and the bar. He owns a commercial-roofing business."

"Did you see him on the night Simone disappeared?" Benjamin asked.

"I think so, but we didn't speak that night."

"OK." Reardon turned a page in his little black book. "Tell me again what you were doing the night you saw Simone."

I explained to the detectives that as an orthopedic surgeon, I'm a firm believer that to get a good result in surgery, you have to do the correct thing over and over until you're proficient. I'm like this even in the day-to-day stuff, so I lead a fairly rigid life. I go to bed after the ten o'clock news, get up around six, go to the office or the operating room early, and work until my day ends. Then I do paper work late afternoon and work out at the Universal Club or play tennis, take a steam bath, shower, shave, hit the bar, eat dinner, retire to my condo and wait for the ten o'clock news, go to bed, and then start all over. They were particularly interested in what I had done the night of the gala and several days before that. I gave them my exact routine again. Basically, all through the day, there were witnesses as to my whereabouts but none after dinner. I offered to give them my surgery and office schedules, but they didn't think it was necessary.

"What about telephone calls? Text messages? E-mails? Facebook?" Reardon asked.

"Facebook? I don't do Facebook. It's a huge invasion of privacy. I don't remember making any calls that evening; maybe I did. I may have sent some texts or e-mails. I don't really recall, but you can check my phone and computer anytime."

Mack the Knife harrumphed at this.

"I don't have anything to hide," I said to him and them.

Benjamin leaned forward in his seat and asked point-blank, "Did you kill Simone Amstutz?"

Startled, I shouted, "No!"

Mack the Knife put a hand on my arm to calm me.

"No, and I don't know why you would think so. I barely knew the woman."

"Would you be opposed to taking a lie-detector test and offering up a DNA sample?"

Mack the Knife interrupted before I had a chance to spit out an answer. "We are not inclined to do that at this point," he declared flatly. "Are we finished here, Detective? If so, I suggest you either charge my client with a crime or excuse us at this point."

I didn't like the sound of that. This was an either-or question, and I wasn't either-or guilty: I was not guilty.

"Just a couple more questions," Reardon told Mack the Knife. He then trained his eyes on me. "Doc, do you play croquet or boccie?"

The tone of the questioning had changed, and I had trouble keeping up. "Boccie? I played a French version once down at Gulf Shores, and I hit a croquet ball once or twice at the club when they first installed the courts." I stopped and looked at him in question.

"You wouldn't by chance have any boccie balls or croquet equipment, would you?"

"No, why would I? And what does this have to do with Simone's death?"

"We found a boccie ball and croquet wicket in the pool with her. Now, that might not mean anything, but we also found a croquet mallet in one of the men's lockers, which may or may not mean anything either. Just asking."

"I still don't know what any of this has to do with me," I said emphatically.

Mack the Knife said, "Well, if that's all, Detective, may we be excused?"

Detective Reardon closed his little notebook. "Sure, but stick around town, Doc."

Sure, I would stick around. Where would I go? Besides, I had nothing to do with Simone's death.

After we left Reardon's interrogation room, Mack and I stopped at a coffee shop downtown. He was still on my dime. I had them pour us both a tall cup of joe, caffeinated for him and decaf for me. My hands were shaky enough. Mack the Knife assured me I had nothing to worry about. They didn't appear to have anything on me, or they would have already pressed charges. However, he did say that he wished I had a better alibi like sleeping with a nurse or my best squeeze. "Me too," I agreed. "I'll try to do better next time." He laughed as he grabbed his coffee and left me sitting there to stare into the dark abyss of my cup and my life.

7

My patients and office had been canceled for the day, so I ventured over to the athletic building at the club. Before I could even get to the elliptical, Lou spotted me and came over. He was shirtless and wore a gold chain around his neck. He was quite smug and cavalier about his interview with Detective Reardon, oblivious to the fact that he might also be a suspect. Even though they had warned him not to say anything to anybody, he just couldn't keep his mouth shut.

"Wonder why they didn't interview me on TV?" He seemed upset about that.

"Lou, I don't think that's the way they do it when you're a suspect in a murder case," I told him.

"Suspect? But I'm innocent!" he proclaimed, incensed that I had even made such a suggestion.

"Yeah, you and me both, but who gives a shit, huh?"

"Did they ask you about a croquet mallet and boccie ball?" Lou asked, a little less smug.

"Uh-huh."

"Wonder what that's about?"

I shrugged. I had no idea how Simone was killed.

That night I skipped the men's bar at the Universal Club simply because there were some rowdy drinkers there, and I was in no mood to answer questions or be interrogated again. I called my best squeeze to see if she wanted to go out, to which she said no but instead offered to pick up a pizza and meet me at my place around seven thirty. Abigail and I had been seeing each other off and on over the last three years. We first met at the VA, where she worked as an occupational therapist. She was twenty-six years old, blond, beautiful, and sweet as apple pie. She also possessed a gorgeous, athletic body, to which I snuggled up every chance I got. Abigail arrived on time with a large "around the world" pizza, and all I could think of was how I'd like to go around the world with her. She was wearing a tight black-and-red workout suit with matching tennis shoes. Her long blond hair was loose, and her blue eyes shone bright through that natural tan she had from being a long-distance runner. I poured her a glass of stale wine out of the fridge and handed it to her and popped the tab on a Diet Coke for me. I was having trouble taking my eyes off her. She joined me on the couch, and we split the pizza.

"I guess you've heard about the dead woman they found at the Universal Club?" I said. She would have been too polite to broach the subject herself.

She nodded, covering her mouth with a hand as she chewed.

"They've interviewed me three times. I have no idea why they think I had something to do with any of this. Everyone at the club thinks I'm a murderer or something," I said, laying it all out there.

"I don't," Abigail said sincerely. She took a sip of her wine, wincing slightly.

What a relief! Until just then, I didn't realize how important it was that she was on my side. We spent the rest of the evening snuggling on the couch and then moved to the bedroom. I was still upset and distracted about the whole investigation and at one point wondered if I would be able to perform for her that night, but I needn't have worried. Abigail's an adventuresome sort and knows her way around the bedroom. Within five minutes everything but the feel of her body and the smell of her perfume evaporated from my brain as other parts of my body took over.

Later as we lay there, our bodies intertwined, Abigail asked rather timidly, "So, who do you think the murderer is?"

"I've no idea. I don't even know how she died. Her husband is the best suspect, I guess, but he's not being held. He must have an alibi."

At ten I turned on the news, and Abigail got up and started putting her clothes on as I watched by the light of the television. She bent over and gave me a quick kiss on the lips.

"Thanks for coming over," I said, wrapping her in my arms and pulling her back on top of me.

"You bet." She kissed me again in a way that said, "No more," and pushed herself up. With a slight wave, she was gone.

As the front door clicked shut, I pulled myself up out of bed and sat on the edge for a long while, wondering if there would ever be more than this between Abigail and me. It was doubtful. She was a looker, and I was smitten, but it wasn't the same as with Ginny, my first love. Is it ever?

Ginny and I dated during my junior year in high school. Those were wild and uninhibited days. She was the antithesis to Abigail. While Abigail is quiet and polite, Ginny was outgoing and exuded a confidence that only those with a true sense of self and social standing seem to have. Her father, a big-shot country-club member in the cotton business, didn't approve of me—his ire so great, in fact, that he ended up sending her to a private boarding school in Upstate New York. The final painful breaking point in our relationship still sours my stomach. I had gotten the bright idea around Halloween to leave a pumpkin on her father's doorstep, but it broke, and I ended up smashing it against his door instead and ran off. After that, we were strictly forbidden to see or talk to each other, and he confiscated my love letters to her. She finally cowed to her father's pressure and broke it off with me, leaving me more or less girlfriendless for my senior year. Even though I met another girl on a trip to New Orleans that summer, it wasn't the same.

I clicked off the remote, and the room went dark. Damn, if I didn't still resent the hell out of Ginny's old man.

8

S everal days passed with no further news about the murder. Nurse Johnnie was walking on eggshells, because she knew how tense I was over the whole ordeal. We had the usual cadre of patients in the morning—adolescent athletes, high-school athletes, college athletes, and then a busload of patients I would rather not have seen. To keep the books fluid, we all have to see our share of the nonathletic, slightly older than old, and at least two or three malingerers who don't want to return to work. A good percentage of these other patients are morbidly obese and come in complaining of joint pain—go figure. There is very little to be done for these types of patients except try to explain the morbidity of remaining obese, which runs across deaf ears most of the time. In some of these patients, arthritis is so severe that they would need total joint replacement, but because of their morbid obesity, most orthopedic surgeons won't operate on them for fear of a significant complication. I don't do total joints anymore, so I can't blame them. I guess it's a philosophical argument whether these patients are entitled to total joint replacement regardless of their obesity and regardless of the high rate of complications, but I digress. This is my day-to-day life, and on that particular day, my office was running as always, when all hell broke loose in the lobby. Two gentlemen from the police department were wanting to see me immediately. Nurse

Johnnie buffered the door and gruffly asked them to come back at another time. Both of them thanked Nurse Johnnie but informed her that they needed to see me immediately and that another time was not going to happen.

"It's OK," I told Johnnie, trying not to cause a scene in front of patients. "Gentlemen, come this way, please." I led them back into an examination room.

"Dr. Canale?" the older of the two uniforms asked.

"Yes?"

"We have a warrant for your arrest, sir."

"What? You can't be serious! On what grounds? I have an office full of patients!"

"You are under arrest for the murder of Simone Amstutz. You have the right to remain silent. Anything you say can and will be…"

I couldn't hear another word. My heart was beating so hard that all I heard was a loud drumming.

"Do you understand? Sir?"

"What?"

He had evidently finished his Miranda warning, but I could truthfully say I never heard it. I nodded, dumbfounded.

"This can't be happening!" I insisted.

They ignored that, and the younger one said, "We can use the bracelets, or you can come with us peacefully. I suggest we leave quietly," he continued, letting me know that they would drag me out of there by my feet through the front door if they had to.

Obviously I opted for a cooperative departure and asked them if I could contact my lawyer, to which they answered yes but down at the station.

"Johnnie, would you contact my lawyer, Pat MacBurney? And let him know that I've been arrested and meet me at two oh one Poplar."

She nodded, dumbfounded, her eyes fluttering wildly. "Do I cancel your office? What about tomorrow? What about your surgery patients? Should I cancel your surgeries?"

Shrugging helplessly, I followed the officers out.

At the police station, I demanded to see Detective Reardon, but the first thing they did was get my fingerprints. I told the policewoman that I'd already had my fingerprints taken several years ago in a routine matter, being on a small bank board of directors. She was unimpressed and continued to ink my fingers one after the other. I desperately hoped Johnnie had called my lawyer. Should I call someone else with my one phone call? I decided to call my lawyer, since he should've already been there. His snooty secretary informed me that he was out and she would let him know as soon as possible—and not to worry.

The policewoman led me to a room, where I was stripped, searched, and handed a new wardrobe, an orange jumpsuit with big black letters on the back indicating that this was the property of the Shelby County jail. Reluctantly I dressed in my new garb. My only alternative would have been to stay naked, because they took my clothes and other belongings, including wallet, watch, and phone, away in a basket. One of the officers told me to have a seat and that Detective Reardon would be with me momentarily, and he was.

"The prosecutor feels we have enough evidence to charge you in the Simone Amstutz case." He didn't look happy or sad when he said this. It was just a fact.

"What evidence?" I shouted. "I'm innocent! What reason would I have to murder her?"

Reardon was playing it close to the vest and said, unmoving, "I hope so for you. We'll see. The prosecutor's office is moving forward."

Mack the Knife appeared around the corner as if on cue.

"Where in the hell have you been?" I shouted at him. "When I need a lawyer, you're not around! I just talked to Detective Reardon, and he has evidence against me. I don't know what evidence. They won't tell me. You've got to do something to stop this, Pat! I'm innocent!"

"OK, OK." He grabbed my arm and walked me down the hall out of hearing range for Reardon. "Everything's under control, but you'll have to spend a night in jail. You'll go before the judge tomorrow, early, and no matter what happens, we'll post bail. You do have the money, right?"

Money? Money? What is money? "What are you talking about? I have patients to see. I have surgery tomorrow morning. I can't stay here!"

"You're going to have to stay for now. I'll get you out first thing in the morning." He patted my shoulder sympathetically and walked away. "Don't worry," he called over his shoulder.

My jailers were at my side and showed me to my new accommodations, an eight-by-twelve cell with a privy and sink in one corner and a bunk bed taking up most of the rest of the room. There was a man occupying the chair in the corner opposite the privy, who looked at me with interest but then returned his attention to a comic book without a word. I breathed in deeply to calm myself and to think of options. There didn't appear to be any. My only option at that point was to decide if I should take the top bunk or the bottom bunk, and since my cellmate looked the part of a hardened criminal, I offered him first choice. As expected, he chose the bottom bunk. I gave him no hassle.

Reclining on the top bunk, I wondered how in the world all this had happened. Why was I being accused of this heinous crime? It appeared that there would be plenty of time for me to think on it.

9

As I sat contemplating my situation in the jail cell, my anxiety levels soared into the stratosphere. This can't be happening to me! I can't stay here! I can't live like this! These were my thoughts as I jumped off the top bunk and paced by the door with the little barred window.

"I'm innocent!" I said to a passing guard, who ignored me.

My cellmate shifted on his bunk, throwing me a dark look that promised bodily harm if I decided to go off the deep end. Instead of banging my head against the door, which was what I really felt like doing, I took a seat in the chair in the corner of the room, bouncing my right leg up and down. This was an impossible situation. Bugaboos began to form in my mind again. What if I'm found guilty? What if I get life in prison? I can't live here the rest of my life without being able to move around and exercise. For twenty-three out of twenty-four hours, they don't do anything in this place: no elliptical, tennis, jogging—no handball. If a large man stretched his arms, he could touch both walls. Maybe I'd get the death penalty—that would be better, I thought wryly but began to sweat at that thought. The room was awfully narrow. Calm down, I told myself firmly. There hasn't even been an indictment yet. Someone will see that there's been a terrible mistake. The what-ifs began to take hold again, however, and I jumped back up out of the chair. My cellmate glared at me. I nodded my understanding at him and rubbed my five o'clock shadow. His five o'clock shadow looked menacing. What must my staff and patients be thinking? Or my partners? Angry and embarrassed at this thought, I felt shame licking at my heart again, just like when I was a kid, an old familiar torture.

I was born with a proverbial silver spoon to a well-to-do, old Memphis family, but it didn't take lifelong to yank it out back out of my mouth, taking some teeth along with it. I was a rebellious kid, and my mother was a brutal alcoholic. In retrospect, she probably did the best she could. She was a beautiful woman from the Mississippi Delta, a Chi Omega at Ole Miss in Oxford. It's been said that if you're not a Chi Omega at Ole Miss, you're just white trash, but that's never been my way of thinking. It really doesn't matter where you come from or what people think; it's what you do that counts. Unfortunately, my mother did alcohol, and that was what she did best. She was in and out of detox centers constantly. With no insurance, $30,000 a pop to enter a detox center got to be costly, and soon my father went broke. Things got so bad that we could no longer afford a private institution for her, and she ended up being admitted to a charity program and finally to a state psychiatric hospital for an indefinite stint. This was in the days before government funding went away for mental illnesses. These memories remain vividly with me, the shame and the embarrassment. I always wondered why my life couldn't be normal like my friends'. Basically, I hated my mother and my life, hated that we couldn't even celebrate normal holidays like Christmas or Halloween. Every day was a nightmare, a saga of not knowing what the next day would bring. Anyone who has experienced this knows what I mean. It's a feeling of being so ashamed that you don't want to communicate with anybody. You live an isolated existence to avoid somebody finding out about your *problem*. Corrine and Mable, our housekeeper and cook, took up the responsibility of raising me. They were strong, capable women who worked hard to provide some sense of security for me.

My father also suffered greatly under my mother's illness. In his younger days, he was a handsome athlete who played football for Notre Dame. He often spoke of the famed four players at Notre Dame who became known as the Four Horsemen and would recite their ode. I adored and idolized my father. Every day he would rise at four in the morning and work until dark, brokering and selling produce. He taught me everything he knew about football, how to play the game smart, how to be coy about it. I remember a confrontation he once had with my high-school football coach. Coach Mix had to take my father aside and explain to him that he was an outstanding football coach, but only one of them could coach me. From that day on, my father never interfered with my training by Coach Mix.

Dad died of a massive heart attack prematurely at the age of forty-four. He was stressed, overweight, and playing handball at the Universal Club when it happened. I was in high school at the time and had difficulty getting over my loss. We played a high-school football game the week after he died. We won the game easily, and the team dedicated the game ball to my father and me, but I was still reeling from shock. With my father gone, I was like a rowboat adrift at sea, trying my damnedest to stay focused but being totally unsuccessful at it. My mother continued to drink, and I tried running away, again and again. I would always come back home, or the authorities would bring me back. One time I ended up staying with a divorced woman and her two daughters. I was just coming into sexual maturity at the time. Well, when Coach Mix got wind of that, he ran me down at school and pulled me out of class.

"You better get your ass back home, and you better never let this happen again, or you're out of All Saints High School!" he shouted, so everyone could hear. That ended my running-away days.

My grandmother on my mother's side, whom I affectionately called Gran, lived in Clarksdale, and I was shipped between our home in Memphis to Clarksdale and then back to the Canale home at 620 South Belvedere in Memphis, a grand old house that cried affluence on the outside. On the inside, Grandmother Canale, my father's mother, lived there with three of her sons and their families. At one time there were probably enough kids living in that old house and an adjacent older house on Harbert to make up a football team. My father's mother was a wonderful person and possessed a mountain of patience. We called her Mama. I remember once when we were very young, a gang of about ten of us told Mama we wanted to build a large pool in the side yard of the old house.

Mama asked, "How big a pool you wanna build?"

"Really big, Mama. Two hundred feet long and fifty feet wide and at least eight feet deep."

She smiled, amused. "Well, all right, boys, go get your shovels; there's some lime in the basement. Lime out the field in the size you want to pool to be, and get to work. Start digging!"

It was a hot July day, and I distinctly remember the smell of freshly cut grass and mildew in the old basement. We dragged out the bag of lime and drew the outline of the pool in the side yard. It was huge and certainly not straight, but we figured it would end up straight and got to digging.

After about four hours, with about six by six by six inches dug out, which I'm sure is an embellishment, we stopped and went in to see Mama.

"Mama, I don't think we'll ever get this pool finished," I told her dejectedly.

She laughed. "Well, keep working at it. Nothing comes from nothing."

"I guess." My cousins and friends plopped down on the cool floor, their faces red and hands muddy brown. "I was wondering," I said, looking to the others for affirmation, "can you give us some money, so we can go to Wiles Drugstore and get a milkshake?" Wiles had the best shakes in town.

Mama forked over the dough with a sly smile, and that ended our pool-digging career at 620 South Belvedere.

Nothing comes from nothing. Sitting on the chair in the corner of my cell, I pondered Mama's words. If it was true and nothing comes from nothing, then what in the hell did the police have on me in the way of evidence in Simone's death? How did she even die? Stabbing?

Shooting? Choking? Stabbing, I assumed, but I didn't know for sure. What I did know was that someone had set me up to take the rap on this. Although irrational, I began to feel a lot less charitable toward Simone. She was the reason I was in this predicament. She should've been more careful, I thought, momentarily disgusted by her openly cheating ways. Picturing Simone's dead body came with a sense of loss. It was tragic. As a doctor I'm no stranger to death, and even as a child I understood on some level that where there's a beginning, there must also be an end. I used to watch the dead get embalmed at my uncle's funeral home, wondering if the dead were somehow still around or if they went off to heaven, like the Bible says, or in the other direction when they hadn't repented their sins.

Wondering how Simone had fared on judgment day, my mind traced the words THE LITTLE DIGGERS, a logo that was stenciled on the backs of our green-and-gold little-league football jerseys. My uncle's funeral home had provided the uniforms, cleats and all, so we could play the other little-league teams around Central Gardens and Midtown Memphis with dignity. Back in the old days, funeral homes took an interest in their communities, some even selling insurance along with burial plots and some running ambulance services. Rumor had it that when there was a wreck out on the highway, the funeral homes would race out to be the first to take victims to the hospital, a service for which they could charge, and if there was a fatality, they would race out to lay claim to the body even if it meant yanking it off someone else's stretcher.

My friends and I spent the night with all the corpses once at the funeral parlor, telling ghost stories through the night. If they minded, the corpses didn't complain. I wondered briefly if Simone was now a ghost living in the shadows at the Universal Club, roaming the many rooms, searching for justice or maybe absolution for her own sins. I cringed at the thought. Sin was also something I understood pretty well, having attended Catholic school from a young age. Taking one wrong step, doing one bad thing, would either bring on certain blindness or throw you into the burning pit of hell. I was one of the altar boys at our church—not the highest altar boy, mind you; that honor went to Lloyd, the priest's favorite pet. We were in the fifth or sixth grade at the time, and I was jealous because Father Euclid liked Lloyd more than me. Father Euclid wore clergy black, drove a big black Lincoln Continental, and carried a leather whip. His face always had two or three days' worth of hair growth. No matter what I did, I could never gain his favor. When we went to funerals, Lloyd always got to ride up front with Father Euclid. A few years ago, Father Euclid, obviously drunk, called me out of the blue and told me that he had left the priesthood, but he didn't tell me why. Maybe it was because of his alcoholism or drug abuse, or maybe something else. Priest-molestation accusations were running rampant in the Catholic church, and the Holy See had finally started cleaning house. Had something happened with Lloyd that I couldn't remember or didn't want to remember? I pushed that particular sermon on sin back into the recess of my mind from whence it had escaped.

With thoughts of Lloyd and what had become of him, I climbed back up into my bunk, trying hard not to disturb Godzilla, who was now fast asleep on the bottom bunk, snoring heavily.

10

I awoke with a start the following morning, a vague sense of shame hanging in the surrounding air. I had been dreaming of my high-school football stadium. It was our championship game against Central High. We were the obvious underdog, but we had been playing pretty well through the second quarter when the first-string center got hurt, and I was called to take over. Late in the fourth quarter, I snapped a punt to our punter, but the ball went way over his head and landed on the four-yard line, first and goal for Central High, and we lost. Even though we had been behind and numerous mistakes (not mine) were made, I still felt like the goat of that game. That was how I felt as I awoke from the dream, and scared. It was six in the morning, and a judge was waiting for me.

Promptly at nine, I was standing before Judge Peter Hoppenstein. He asked me some simple questions, such as "Are you aware of the charges against you? Are you aware of your surroundings?" I vaguely replied yes to both. He then let me know that the information and evidence would be presented to the grand jury for their consideration, and in three days he would make a decision about charges and bond. Three days? I remember thanking him, but for the life of me, I don't know for what. My lawyer informed me that this was not unusual and that he knew of several good bondsmen if we needed bail. He thought I might even be released on my own recognizance if I wore a monitoring ankle bracelet.

The three days went surprisingly quick in the jail. Good ole Nurse Johnnie visited and brought me some patient charts that needed dictation. I was given special permission to use my Dictaphone. She also brought the *Memphis Appeal*, the *Wall Street Journal*, a sudoku puzzle, and a new John Grisham book she had picked up for me at Johnson's on Madison. It had shot up to number one in the hardback fiction list. Other than that, no special consideration was given to my medical degree. I slept and toileted in the cell with a mute Godzilla, groomed in the community shower, and ate with the rest of the inmates on rows of cafeteria tables. The food was a mess of gray gravy over something rubbery, with yellow and green sides, a carton of milk, some white bread, and a minuscule amount of margarine.

"Hey, dude. What you in for?" A short kid of about eighteen put his hand on my shoulder in the mess hall. He had a pasty pale face and nasty-looking pimples all over his forehead; puberty hadn't quite reached his voice.

I looked at my shoulder where his hand was perched and didn't answer, getting my bluff in early.

He shifted his feet uncomfortably. "See, it's not me. It's Booger over there wants to know," he said, removing his hand cautiously.

Booger was a large, tattooed man who looked one girl short of having a harem seated around him. Scooping a spoonful of the yellow into my mouth, I ignored the boy.

My cellmate, Godzilla, parked two chairs down on the other side of the table, barked at the kid, "Boy, sit yo' skinny ass down 'fore they be havin' to feed you through a tube."

The kid shuffled back to Booger's table. Not sure of the protocol for thanking Godzilla, I focused on the gray sludge in front of me. The whole scene reminded me of my freshman year in college, when our football team played against Navy in Annapolis. Our team got to eat with the Navy team at Bancroft Hall before the game. As cadets, their team had to sit at attention during the meal, while our team slouched and scarfed up whatever was being served. As we were eating, one of their plebes came over to our table and said politely to our captain, "Sir, our midshipman would like to tell you that we intend to whip your asses tomorrow during the game. Thank you, sir." He returned stiffly to his table. Then, at the order of another midshipman, the next plebe would come over and deliver another harassing message. It was hilarious.

Lucky for me, Booger decided not to pursue further harassment, and I decided not to flip him the bird, which would have been the sequence of events in my early days, but I've since learned that being disrespectful can get you a twice-broken nose.

Walking in a line behind the other inmates to get to my cell, I was still having trouble believing that they had charged me for a murder I did not commit. My, my, how the mighty have fallen! I thought and shook my head at myself. In high school, I was in high cotton, hot stuff, really—cocaptain of the football team, secretary of the student body, president of the Upsilon Tau fraternity. And now? Now I was an esteemed member of the Shelby County jail, as the back of my suit advertised to the world. Don't get me wrong; my overall view of judges and lawyers is positive. In fact, a judge, Judge Hoffman, had done a great service to my fraternity in high school my senior year. We were having a party called the Seven Sins, an annual event for seniors, so named because seven of the best-looking high-school senior girls were nominated to wear their slinkiest outfits and parade onstage. Although quite sexist, it was still considered an honor to be asked to be one of the Sins. We'd booked Sam Klein and the Midnighters to perform at the party, but they were a no-show. Fortunately, the father of our fraternity's vice president was also the district attorney, and he had Sam Klein and the Midnighters arrested and their instruments confiscated. Good old Judge Hoffman made them return everyone's money. Fortunately, we had a jukebox the night of the party, and the Sins never missed a beat.

As Monday rolled around at the Shelby County jail, I was given a fresh shirt and tie and a pair of khakis brought in by Nurse Johnnie from my condo to wear to the court hearing instead of the orange jumpsuit. My attorney was present and seemed a bit too nervous. The judge and the prosecutor were also present.

The judge called the session to order. "You have been charged with first-degree murder in the case of Simone Amstutz. How do you plead?"

My breath caught in my throat. "I'm innocent!" I shouted.

Click, click, click went the court reporter's machine.

The judge asked, "Do you understand right from wrong?"

I couldn't speak.

"He's stunned, Your Honor," Mack the Knife said as he touched my arm.

"Yes," I said feebly, "but I'm innocent."

Click...click...click.

The judge then asked if I understood the bail-bond proceeding. I believe my answer was yes. He then hit his gavel and set bail at $3 million and told me not to leave the city and wear an ankle monitor. The judge then hit his gavel again and said, "Next case." He abruptly got up, left the bench, and retreated to his chambers just as another inmate was led into the courtroom in shackles. That was all for my court appearance.

The Shelby County corrections officers escorted me back to my jail cell. Over my shoulder, I said to Mack the Knife, "Will you take care of that bail?"

"I'll have you out of here in four hours," he replied, scribbling something on a legal pad.

With that I retired to a holding cell to await my freedom. The next four hours felt longer than the three days before. I was seriously considering my choice of attorneys. Mack the Knife was unsympathetic and seemed only half interested, and I wondered if he was really as good as they said and if he actually had a defense team like you see on television. Having a good defense would be the difference between winning and losing, between imprisonment and freedom or, at worst, life and death.

I've had the experience of being on a losing team with a poor defense. Being on a championship high-school football team, I was offered scholarships to play college football from Ole Miss, Tennessee, Vanderbilt, Notre Dame, Tulane, Virginia, and the Naval Academy. Notre Dame, where my father played football, is a great school with a wonderful football program, but my feeling was that I wasn't good enough and would be a small fish in a very large pond, so I decided on Virginia. Little did I know at the time that Virginia probably had the worst defensive team ever assembled in history. We called our unit the Green Maggots. I guess a maggot is about as bad a smelling larva as you'd ever want to meet, and our defense was that bad. We thought it sounded mean, hence the name, but unfortunately it didn't make us better football players; it just made us stink worse. What it boils down to is the quality of people on your team, how well you play together, and what kind of a coach you have. We had some great athletes on our high-school football team. But in my opinion, it was our coach who made the ultimate difference. He taught us smart football. He taught us not to face up an opponent but just move to one side or the other to establish a mechanical advantage. I see football teams today that still haven't learned those principles.

Contemplating Coach Mix's lessons, I reassured myself that everything would be OK. My plan was to review my own case, see what evidence they had on me, hire a second or new attorney with a team if necessary, and try to do some detective work on my own. I knew that I hadn't killed Simone, but someone had, and finding out who had would clear my name.

11

I guess I should have been happy that they didn't place me under house arrest, and I could move about the city freely, an ankle bracelet confirming my whereabouts at all times, but I wasn't. The judge evidently thought I might be a flight risk, and that was probably wise thinking on his part, because my first notion was to grab Abigail and take off to Costa Rica and never look back. On second thought it was a foolish idea, and it royally pissed me off. I was innocent! Why should my life be thrown topsy-turvy for something I didn't do? Besides, I wasn't all that sure that Abigail would embrace the idea—and they had confiscated my passport. As I let myself into my condo, kicked off my Weejuns, and threw my keys onto the coffee table, my cell phone rang. It was the chief of staff of the Camp Clinic.

"Hello?" I answered, not really wanting to speak to him, but I knew that sooner or later it would be necessary.

"Hey, Terry; it's Jim. Listen, I heard about all your trouble. I am so sorry." He was sincere.

"Thanks." I didn't know what else to say. I thought about telling him that I was innocent, but the words wouldn't come.

"Look, don't worry about anything, OK? You take some time off to get this business cleared up. You've got plenty of vacation and meeting time. I've had your assistant clear your schedule for the next ninety days."

"Thanks." It sounded hollow to my own ears.

"Terry, for the record, we all think this is a bunch of bullshit. You hang tight, OK?"

"I appreciate it, Jim, really. Thanks."

He disconnected.

Ninety days. What would happen after that was anyone's guess. I thought about going to the Universal Club to play tennis and blow off some steam and get something to eat, but even that seemed alien now. Where to start on all this? I flopped down on my bed and bounced an old tennis ball off my bedroom wall, back and forth, back and forth, until the old lady whose bedroom adjoined mine banged on the wall and shouted, "Knock off the racket, will ya? I'm trying to nap!"

A half-million-dollar condo, and the walls were like paper. Placing the ball on the side table, I decided to put in a call to Big Al and see if he had made any progress with getting me a private investigator.

"Hey, man, I been trying to get hold of you for three days. Where ya been hiding?" he said before I even had a chance to speak.

"I was in the slammer."

"Shit, man. Look, I got a fish on the line, a narc for the Memphis PD, but he's on unpaid leave and needs cash."

"For what?" I asked, exasperated—about what, I wasn't sure.

"Aw, he nailed some candy-ass who's beatin' on his old lady."

"Hmm."

"Does it matter?" Big Al was losing patience.

"I guess not. I just thought he'd be able to get info from the cops— you know, see what they had on me, but if he's not there…"

"He'll know." There was a pause; then he said, "Terry, he's good— very good. If there's anything to be found out, he'll find it, and that includes anything he finds out about you, my friend."

"I'm innocent!" I almost shouted into the phone.

"Hey, I believe you." I could almost see him holding up his hands. "He wants a thousand in cash to start. He'll give you a couple of days' work for that; then it's a hundred an hour plus expenses."

"All right. I'll go by the bank."

"Be here at the bar around eight. I'll introduce you."

"Thanks, Big Al."

"Sure thing."

Well, didn't that just beat all? Even Big Al was questioning my veracity. I was running out of team members. I still believed Abigail was on my team but sure couldn't count on many others. I picked up the tennis ball, ready to bounce it off the wall again, but instead picked up my phone and punched in Eric's number. Eric was the bartender at the Universal Club. As are most bartenders, the slight man with the little moustache was everyone's best friend. He was the barrel into which drunks poured their secrets. Eric picked up on the third ring.

"Hey, Eric; it's me, Terry."

"Terry, my man, how you doing? I heard all about that nasty business. I just can't believe it." He sounded genuinely concerned.

"Yeah, me neither," I answered miserably. "I guess the folks there are thinking I'm the killer."

"Naw, Doc, not at all. Most folks believe her old man's the one who did her in. They don't trust the likes of him for a skinny minute. 'Sides, most didn't even think you knew her. You know, that old Amstutz was having an affair with Monique is what I heard. Some of the folks seen him and her moving in and out of the club at odd times when hardly anyone's here," he confided quietly.

"Monique?"

"Hammond's ex."

"Oh."

"Well, Doc, I'm praying for you," Eric said sincerely.

"Thanks; I'll be needing plenty of prayers." I disconnected.

I'd met Hammond's wife once at a Universal Club party. She was an exotic woman, tall and lean, dressed to the hilt, with raven hair, eyes the color of topaz, red lips, and matching fingernails. She'd recently divorced the old guy, I'd heard. What was his first name? Jimmy, Jerry—no, Jake. She never hung around much at the U Club, but her ex, a bit on the rotund side, could always be found hanging around the lunch buffet and sometimes at the bar. If I stopped to think about it, I don't believe he was ever without something to eat in his hands. That's probably why she left him, I judged, but why on God's green earth would she choose to drop him in favor of Cooter Amstutz, of all people? He was a zero in the looks department, with knobby knees and a bad comb-over. Money, I guessed. He did have money, which Simone was saying was half hers. Was it enough to kill her over? Maybe. I'd have to remember to tell to my new private eye.

Nervously I looked around my condo, gravitating to the kitchen and opening the fridge out of habit. A jar of peanut butter, some suspicious-looking bread, an onion, and a half jar of mayonnaise (not totally sure how old) greeted me when the light came on. It sure wasn't promising, but it didn't matter, because I wasn't really very hungry. It would be a few hours before my meeting with Big Al's man. What to do until then? I could run. A long run would be just what the doctor ordered.

Back in the bedroom, I stripped all the way to my boxers and then decided to toss those into the hamper as well. It all smelled like jailhouse rot to me. I donned some running shorts, a T-shirt, and my brand-new Nikes, and then I hit the road down Belvedere, slowly building up speed until I reached Union, where I hung a right. My plan was to not stop until sunset except at the bank.

"Do you know what the best treatment for anxiety is?" my AA partner once asked me.

"No, what?"

"Live in the now, now. If you think about the future, you'll find anxiety. If you live in the past, you'll find depression."

It made sense, but my "now, now" consisted of a line of traffic all the way down Union to McClean. Some idiot trying to take a left where a sign clearly said No Left Turn almost ran me down. "Shit," I said under my breath. Had it not been for my quick thinking and evasive move, that Mercedes would have had a new hood ornament. Or I might've ended up like Ken and his bone box strewn all over Union Avenue. He and I were first-year medical students together at UT.

The bone box was something all of us first-years got from the medical school. It was filled with bones of half a real human body—one femur, one tibia, one fibula, and so forth. Poor Ken, having just been voted class president, was strutting across busy Union Avenue with his new bone box when he was hit by a car. He went through the guy's windshield, and his bone box was sent flying, a shower of bones landing all over the street. Luckily, he only suffered a fractured ankle and some abrasions. I'm not sure how the bones fared, but the shocked EMTs gathered them up and sent them on to the emergency room.

Knowing I was taking a chance running on Union, I decided to stop at the bank for cash first and then headed east, turning left on Tucker, where the traffic was quieter. I set my running speed at six miles per hour. My thoughts floated back to Simone and the elusive evidence against me. They had my fingerprints for starters, but how would they have ended up on Simone? Wouldn't two weeks in water wash those away? The police did get a DNA swab that I'd finally agreed to, but again, my DNA would not be mingling with Simone's, and the water would have degraded that as well. As my feet rhythmically pounded the pavement, my mind worked on other possibilities. The murder weapon? I had no idea how she had been killed or what had been used. Were the holes the U Club attendants saw caused by a knife or bullets? Maybe my prints had come up on something like a gun. I owned a gun, but it had been safe and sound in my nightstand just this morning. Shouldn't the prosecution have to disclose the evidence they had against me to my lawyer? I had an appointment with him in the morning and made a mental note to ask. As my mind continued to wander and one mile became two and then three, I found that there were just more questions.

"Angles. Tennis is a game of angles, just like pool. There are many different angles." Derrick Motron's voice penetrated my jumbled thoughts. I slowed just for a split second, contemplating these words. Derrick was the tennis pro at the Universal Club who gave me weekly lessons. He'd been an English Davis Cup player before he immigrated to the United States and got a job teaching tennis. He not only taught me the real game of tennis but also a whole lot about life in general, leaving me with thoughts like "I never beat a well man" or "The best part of my game is picking my partner." Choosing a competent partner was going to be key in all this. I hoped Big Al's private eye would be that partner. OK, so I could also consider the possible angles in Simone's death. That should be easy, right? I did major in psychology in college, after all. I had been taking other sciences, such as zoology and geology, jock courses, but actually became infatuated with the clinical aspects of abnormal psychology. What makes people tick? What makes them go off the deep end? Are they sick or just flat-out evil? These were questions that boggled my mind. I thought I knew everything, having read all the books, but things are different in the real world, and I was drawing a total blank on the Simone case. I couldn't see a single angle. Finding myself faced with real evil, I realized that I should have paid better attention in class.

Unfortunately, learning and grades weren't all that important to me in my first years in college. I was a partier. Even at Camp Greenbrier in Arlington, West Virginia, and at camp in Orange County outside Charlottesville, where we trained in the blazing heat my freshman year for the upcoming college football season, I could think of nothing but partying. Instead of seriously training as I was supposed to, I took up with the headmaster's daughter of the all-boy's prep school. She sneaked beer for my friends and me into the back of her house while we smoked and played cards. Come to think of it, it was quite the miracle that I ever graduated from the University of Virginia. I figured they were desperate for athletes, so I didn't worry about studying for exams, and my first semester ended with four Ds and an F, which landed me on academic probation. I spent the next three and a half years trying to get my grades over a 3.0 average, but only because my football scholarship was in jeopardy. I did love football in the beginning, and it may have ended up meaning more to me if our team hadn't sucked so badly.

I contemplated going into coaching and made overtures of being a graduate assistant and a freshmen coach, but my interests turned away from football, and that was when abnormal psychology became my thing. I often wonder if my football career would have been different if I had chosen some other school (not that it matters anymore). I made great friends there and partied with some of the great partiers of the decade in Virginia.

You know, the University of Virginia has a very strong honor system, and we had to be careful not to violate it with some of the shenanigans we pulled. I was placed on social probation once and had to beg the conduct committee not to suspend me. It was all because of the Sweet Briar incident. My fraternity brothers and I drove down to Sweet Briar College in Lynchburg, Virginia, which was a five-beer trip from Charlottesville, to pick up girls. Sweet Briar was an all-women's college at the time. When we left, one of my fraternity brothers shot out the lights at the entrance and exit to Sweet Briar. The security guard caught us red-handed. The student council banned me from visiting another college for one full year, especially an all-women's college. Sounds pretty benign, doesn't it? To me, it was a nightmare. It meant no more midnight calls to sorority houses at Madison College, no more setting off fire alarms, no showing off with fire extinguishers. My fraternity brothers got a real kick out of that. I was sort of famous, you might say (or maybe a better word is "infamous"), especially among the women, although I'm fairly certain they took me for a stud.

12

By the time I turned back west onto Vinton, I was facing the setting sun. It was time to head back, get a shower, and shave before I had to meet Big Al's guy. By the time I jogged up to my condo, I was in a great mood. Mrs. Habernathy, the old lady who lived in the adjacent condominium, was passing by with her furry little dog, MeMoe, tethered to a long blue leash. When she saw me smiling, she took it as an invitation to speak.

"Hello, Terry." She smiled big. Her lipstick had missed its mark and streaked away from her lips along her right cheek. She always called me by my first name and not "Dr. Canale," as I would have preferred.

I nodded politely, pulling a key chain from around my neck, trying not to stare.

"I was wondering if you could do me a great big favor," she asked amiably, her lipstick streak reaching her right earlobe.

My defenses went up immediately. This woman was never amiable.

"Sure, Mrs. Habernathy. What can I do for you?" If this was about that damn tennis ball, I was going to lose it for sure.

"Well, they're sending me to the hospital tomorrow, and I need someone to look after MeMoe, and I was wondering if you would be a sweet boy and see to him. It'll just be for a day or two."

"Hospital? What's wrong, Mrs. Habernathy?" She looked as healthy as a miniature horse.

"Oh, I'm fine," she insisted, fluffing her white helmet hair a bit. "I'm just going in for a little rest."

"Ah."

She continued smiling, one hand resting on a hip like Greta Garbo.

"What hospital are they sending you to?"

"Oh, a nice place." She grinned conspiratorially up at me. "Every time I tell Dr. Schmidt that I'm the missing Anastasia, he writes an order, and I get to have grand time for a couple of days. Well, I'm leaving first thing in the morning, so here you go." She handed MeMoe's leash to me without further ado and plodded off with her big black purse to her car, a gigantic white Lincoln Continental.

Stunned, the little dog and I stood staring after the Lincoln as it whipped out of the parking space and onto the street beyond, almost sideswiping a blue Toyota. The dog looked up at me expectantly.

"Good thing you decided to stay with me, buddy," I said to the dog.

He sneezed in agreement and hiked his leg on the side of the building, seemingly unconcerned about the recent turn of events in his life. Mrs. Habernathy had told me once that MeMoe was a Pomeranian, but I wasn't sure about that. If that was the case, he was the largest one I'd ever seen, weighing in at probably close to twenty pounds. Whatever breed he was, he was one white ball of furry energy. We let ourselves into the condo. MeMoe jumped onto my recliner as if that were par for the course, and I went to the kitchen to fetch him a bowl of water.

13

"Doc, you can't bring that dog in here!" Barry White exclaimed when he saw me entering the Red Eye. Not *the* Barry White—he's long dead. This Barry White was Big Al's bouncer. He looked just like him, though.

"Why not? He's my service dog."

"Come on, Doc."

MeMoe was tucked up under my right arm. He'd looked so pitiful back at the condo; I couldn't say no. MeMoe's eyes bugged out, and he flashed his canines at Barry.

"What kind of service do he perform exactly?" Barry wanted to know, stepping back.

Just then, a pretty little blonde walked by, and when she saw the dog in my arms, she downright purred, "How sweet is he!"

MeMoe went from pit bull to love muffin in a split second. She stopped and scratched his ear. His tail wagged happily.

"What's his name?" Her voice was a singsong.

"MeMoe," I replied proudly, as if I had anything to do with his name. I threw Barry a sly smile. He nodded knowingly.

"Come on, Doc. Look like you got a good racket goin' on there." He motioned toward Big Al, who was waving me back to a dark corner.

"Good to see you in one piece, my man," Big Al said, looking at the dog but not saying anything. He turned and introduced me to a large man sitting in the booth.

"Terry, this is Lloyd; Lloyd, Terry."

We shook hands, his grip crushing mine. Although he was sitting, I guessed the man to be around six foot four and about 240 pounds of pure muscle. Even his face had muscles. He had a crew cut and looked like a regular G.I. Joe kind of guy; he wore a thin, secretive smile, his blue eyes shining with amusement; about what, I had no idea. Nothing was too funny for me these days. I put MeMoe down on the bench next to me, and he sat at attention, sizing the man up just as I was doing. The man seemed vaguely familiar, but I couldn't place him. Was he a patient of mine? I hoped not. That would be uncomfortable. It was possible, though. With forty- to fifty-odd patients a day, it's hard to remember them all. If I got to see his x-rays, I probably could have identified him in a heartbeat.

"What'll you gentlemen have to drink?" Big Al asked.

"Ghost River draft," the man answered.

"The usual for you, Terry?" My usual was a cup of black coffee. I had quit drinking the nonalcoholic beers because even though they look like beer and smell like beer, they taste only a little better than sweaty gym socks.

"Sure, thanks."

Big Al left us to our business. The man continued to watch me, his blue eyes doing a jig.

"Do we know each other?" I finally asked.

"Yep," he replied but offered nothing further. The waitress set our orders in front of us.

"Are you a patient of mine?"

"Nope. Guess again."

I shook my head. "You look familiar, but sorry, I really have no idea."

"Saint Agnes? Father Euclid?" he exclaimed with a wide, happy smile.

It finally dawned on me who this man was. "Lloyd? Lloyd Williams?"

He nodded. "In the flesh."

"I was just thinking about you! How strange. Good to see you, man! When did you move back to Memphis?"

"Oh, been here awhile."

"You should've looked me up a long time ago."

We spent the next hour catching up and telling "do you remember" stories, but when I mentioned Father Euclid's recent defrocking, Lloyd's mood darkened, so I dropped the subject and got to the business at hand. He shared his reasons for needing cash. It was all a big misunderstanding, you see, and I did see because it was all a big misunderstanding that I was being accused of murder. MeMoe lost interest, curled up, and fell asleep as I gave Lloyd the rundown of all that had transpired, trying to not leave anything out. He took notes in a little book. I also told him the newest gossip about Cooter Amstutz and Monique Hammond, giving him her description as best I could remember. Last, I placed the envelope with a thousand bucks on the table, wrote my cell-phone number on it, and pushed it toward him. He looked at it reluctantly.

"Business is business," I told him, draining the dregs from my third cup.

"I'll call you in a couple of days," Lloyd promised.

Several women smiled at us as I toted a groggy MeMoe to the front of the bar. I was beginning to see the advantages of cute-pet ownership.

14

Nine o'clock the following morning found me fidgeting in a straight-backed chair in the waiting room of Mack the Knife's office. It was a rainy Tuesday, and my attorney was late again. I was beginning to understand that this was his modus operandi, which infuriated me to no end. As the minutes ticked by in the tastefully decorated waiting room into which horrible Muzak was being pumped, my blood pressure rose bit by bit until I was quite sure steam was coming off the top of my head. An hour and a half later, the secretary, a prim and proper woman of an uncertain age, informed me that her boss, my attorney, had been held up in court and couldn't meet with me but that if I were at home in the evening, he would be happy to swing by my condo.

With deliberation, I stood up and smiled at the sincere, puritanical woman. "Sure. Thank you," I said, taking my leave before my head exploded. I felt just like coach Rodgers from Georgia Tech when they were penalized fifteen yards for delay of game. He told me that they were playing Notre Dame in Atlanta when the Notre Dame band, two hundred men strong, used up almost the entire halftime, leaving the Rambling Wrecks, Georgia Tech's band of eighteen people in two jalopy cars, only a couple of minutes. The Georgia Tech coach yelled at the referee, "Oh no, you can't penalize us fifteen yards! Maybe five or ten but not fifteen. We can't help it that the Rambling Wrecks is the worst band in the country!" I too was being penalized at every turn, it seemed, for things that weren't my fault.

Not knowing what else to do with myself, I returned to my condo, put MeMoe's collar and leash on him, and took him out for a much-needed walk. As he trotted along the sidewalk, pausing here and there to have a sniff and to adequately reestablish his territory, my cell phone rang. It was Big Al.

"Hey, dude, got something that might be interesting," he said without preamble and continued without waiting for me to respond. "It's goin' round in here that your gal, Simone, was well known in Highlands."

"She's not my gal, Big Al," I reminded him. "North Carolina?"

"Yeah, folks seen her around town there."

"Alone?" I asked.

"I doubt it."

"Me too. Thanks." He had already disconnected.

Who did I know in the Highlands? Why, Clyde, of course—my good friend from high school. He'd made a small fortune after Yale and was already semiretired up there. I gave him a call. We spent some time catching up, and then I casually asked if he knew Simone Amstutz. He didn't, but he seemed to know everyone else in the neighborhood, and it took him a while to get to the bottom of the list. He'd always been that way, putting everything in long, tedious lists. Frustrated, I finally got a chance to thank him and say good-bye and pushed the end-call button, but it wasn't five minutes later before he called back.

"Terry, it's Clyde. Look, I just talked to Bud Merryman, and he said that Simone was dead. She was murdered!"

I didn't want to get into the "I'm innocent" business with him, so I didn't say anything.

"He saw her a couple of months ago. She was here with a woman, a pretty gal, a Monique somebody. Isn't that just terrible?"

Monique? "Terrible," I said.

"How did you know her?" he suddenly asked.

"Through the Universal Club. I knew she was dead. It's a big deal here. They're questioning everybody. I heard that she hung around up there sometimes and just wondered if you knew her." I hoped the news about my being charged hadn't reached the community in Highlands. If it had, he didn't say anything.

"No, I didn't know her."

"OK. Thanks. Well, good talking to you, Clyde. Give Melanie my best."

So, I knew from Eric that Monique was seen with Cooter at the U Club, and now I knew she was seen with Simone in North Carolina. Something was definitely afoot with this Monique person.

As promised, Mack the Knife showed up at my condo around seven. I thought we were going to talk about the evidence they had against me, but he wanted to talk about my honesty.

"Terry, I have to ask you this. No matter what your answer is, I will still represent you, but I have to know the truth. Are you being completely honest with me about your knowledge of Simone? Have you told me everything?" He sat, unblinking.

I averted my gaze.

"If you haven't, there could be all sorts of repercussions for us if we get to trial and they find out, or I find out, that you haven't been totally forthcoming. Perjury in and of itself is pretty serious."

I nodded and told him something that I had withheld on purpose. Simone had a friend by the name of Elizabeth. We'd had a short, half-evening romp a couple of days before Simone went missing. Nobody knew about it, including Abigail. The woman said she was married, so, trying to be discrete, I hadn't mentioned her to Detective Reardon. Other than that I had been totally honest.

He nodded. "Not sure that's anything of significance."

I agreed and changed the subject to something that was closer to my heart. "Pat, what do you think they have on me?"

He shrugged. "Don't know yet. The prosecution has to divulge all their evidence to us in due time, and we have to hand over anything we have also. I suppose they might have fingerprints, maybe a murder weapon. Possibly they've dreamed up some motive. You know you have a fairly disputable alibi. They'll try to match your DNA to something. I'll push them for information."

So they might have my DNA on something of Simone's, perhaps my fingerprints, a murder weapon, a motive, and I had no alibi. What a hell of a situation.

After Mack the Knife left, I sat in front of the television, flipping through channels mindlessly. I had to talk to Monique. Should I ask her ex—what was his name? Oh yeah, Jake Hammond. Was the Monique seen with Cooter Amstutz the same as the one seen with Simone? Reason would dictate that they would be one and the same. How many Moniques could there be anyway?

My cell phone rang. It was Big Al again. He started talking immediately.

"Hey, Lou Peroni just left the bar. He was going on and on about knowing all of Simone's friends, including some girl named Monique." He paused.

"Monique."

"You got it, friend."

"And?"

"No can do. You need to talk to Lou yourself." He disconnected abruptly.

I scrolled down the list of names on my contact list and found Lou's number. He answered on the third ring.

"Hey, Lou; it's Terry."

"Yeah." He didn't sound very friendly.

"Wondering if you could help me." I could feel him clam up as if he was expecting me to ask him for money.

"OK," he replied cautiously.

"Do you know a woman named Monique who hung around with Simone?"

"Know her or know of her?"

"Either."

"I saw her with Simone from time to time at local bars around town. Intriguing name and woman—you know what I mean," he said in his lewd way. He could make GiGi's cupcakes sound dirty.

"Does she live around here?"

"Would be my guess, but I've no idea what her address is or anything. Why are you interested in Monique?"

Not wanting to give him too much fuel for gossip, I replied, "What if she was the last person to see Simone alive?"

"Hmm. You know they were kind of an item," he said and chuckled. "At least that's how they behaved at bars."

"Really?"

"Yep, but you didn't hear that from me."

"Thanks, Lou."

"You bet." Lou sounded proud that he knew something that no one else did.

15

A t six in the morning, my cell phone rousted me from a dead sleep. I looked at the number. It was Lloyd.

"Hello," I answered groggily.

"Good morning." Lloyd was all business. "OK, here's the deal. The Monique you told me about, Monique Hammond, ex-husband, Jake?"

"Uh-huh." I rubbed sleep from my eyes and tried to pay attention.

"Well, his ex-wife is a fifty-one-year-old, overweight, gray-headed agoraphobic. Doesn't go out in public at all. Oh, and her name is Mary Edna. Whoever you saw with Hammond, this Monique, was not his wife or ex-wife."

"Huh." My vocabulary was still limited at this early hour.

"Anyway, there are four Moniques in this area. One of them lives in Millington out near the naval base, a really obese thirty-five-year-old with several young, illegitimate children. I think we can exclude her. One lives out east, and she's an exotic dancer; works at a club in Millington. Another Monique is a thirty-year-old female, married, works at the thrift store in Cordova but has been known to frequent downtown and mid-town bars without her spouse. The last one lives in Midtown. She's interesting because she's not currently married, has a child but isn't raising it. She works at Morgan Keegan and has frequented in the last month Sleep Out Louie's, Murphy's, and the Bombay Bicycle Club, which is a Midtown bar that Simone also has been known to frequent."

Lloyd had been very busy. All this he'd found out in a matter of twenty-four hours. Two of the Moniques we could exclude right off the bat—the fat one and the thrift-store worker. She wouldn't be affiliated with the likes of Simone.

"I think the last one would fit the bill. I bet she's the one," I said hopefully.

"Maybe so."

"Hell, I'm ready to move on this chick! Can we set up a sting?"

Lloyd laughed. "Man, you don't know anything about investigating. Let me handle this. I'll call you when I know something more."

Reflecting on what I had just heard, Simone and Monique both frequented the Bombay Club and were perhaps having an affair with each other. What could I do about it? Nothing. I could try to find this Monique from Morgan Keegan. What would I say to her? "Excuse me, is your name Monique, and were you involved sexually with Simone, who, by the way, was found murdered?" That'd sound crazy and would probably land me in more hot water. The woman I had seen with Jake Hammond a year ago at the U Club party was not his wife. Why had he introduced her as such? Why did Eric the bartender think she was? His wife, now ex-wife, was an agoraphobic; she never left the house. Then it dawned on me in a rush. Hammond had a rent-a-wife he could show off. Monique—a rent-a-wife—why not? The Morgan Keegan lady or the exotic dancer would indeed fit that bill.

Abigail dropped by that evening, bringing with her some fried dill pickles, catfish bites, blackened catfish, and fried shrimp from Soul Fish, a sticky-table, hole-in-the-wall neighborhood establishment that was packed at all times of the day. She handed the bag to me, and I placed it on the kitchen counter. MeMoe gave her two short barks and then wagged his tail furiously when she noticed him.

"Isn't this your neighbor's dog?" Abigail squatted to stroke his fur. He presented his belly for a rub.

"Yeah, I'm watching him for a day or two or three," I replied, watching her scratch his sweet spot, and then she put her keys on the counter and walked down the hall to my bedroom.

Abigail was beautiful tonight, dressed in a sports bra, shorts, ankle socks, and running shoes, which she discarded one by one on her trek to my bedroom. I followed, leaving the bits of clothing where they were.

"What sports have you been playing, croquet or boccie?" I asked as she finally began to peel off her shorts.

She didn't see the humor. "I'm training for the next ten K," she said irritably, yanking at her shorts.

I came up behind her and kissed her on the neck.

"And for the next marathon. I just don't have the time to get in enough exercise," she complained, shrugging off my advances, which just aroused me more.

I sat on the edge of the bed and pulled her to me, kissing the soft spot above her navel and then the place between her perfect, round breasts. Her panties fell to her ankles.

"I need to take a shower. I smell like sweat and fish."

Abigail is beautiful, and if I ever decided to settle down, it's possible that she could be the one.

"You smell like flowers," I said truthfully.

She kissed me tenderly and then with more purpose and then roughly as I pulled her hard against me, stroking the small of her back. I could feel her sweet acquiescence as we sank into our familiar, easy embrace.

Our lovemaking didn't last as long as I'd hoped—it had been a while, and besides, dinner was waiting, its tantalizing smells wafting into the bedroom from down the hall. Abigail jumped out from under the covers, and without putting anything on, she brought in the grocery sack. She spread the food out on the comforter like a picnic, handing me plastic utensils, a napkin, and a can of diet soda. MeMoe jumped onto the bed. He had been less than enthusiastic about our impromptu courtship, keeping to the living room as if he knew that three would be a crowd, but when he smelled the fried fish, he was pretty sure it constituted a party to which he was invited.

"What are you thinking?" Abigail asked, handing me the bag with the catfish bites.

"Oh, this just reminded me of something back in the day."

"What?"

I smiled. "I don't know why, but it reminds of the time when I was back in college. Some of my fraternity brothers and I went to Randolph Macon to party with some of their co-eds. We were out in the woods, sitting on blankets, eating, drinking, trying to make out. Well, the girls all went into the woods to use the bathroom, and while they were gone, we guys dropped our drawers and hid nude under our blankets."

Abigail took a bite of a fried pickle. "Oh, that's funny. What happened?"

"What do you mean what happened? They turned our asses in to the dean, and we got in big trouble." We laughed. "I warned you I was a badass."

"You did. You did. You gave me fair warning."

I stuffed some shrimp into my mouth. "Abigail, do you know any Moniques?"

She thought for a minute but shook her head no. "Isn't that an African tribal name?"

"Beats me. I've never been to Africa."

"Why do you ask? Is she your new lover?" Abigail teased, her eyes dancing playfully.

"No, there's a Monique involved with all this Simone business. It's an odd name. That's all."

After we finished eating, we decided to go for a swim in the condo pool. MeMoe didn't want to come with us. He wanted to sit in my recliner and watch *Zombie Apocalypse*, something we'd have to have a talk about at some point. For now, we left him to his monsters and rode the elevator down to the bottom floor to the indoor pool. Since the Simone incident, pools made me a bit nervous, but I jumped in anyway, swimming laps behind Abigail, who was in much better shape and was outpacing me by an arm's length. On our third lap, I caught her by the ankle and pulled her under, holding her there for a brief moment. We wrestled playfully until I had her corralled in the far corner. We were all alone in the pool. There were no people milling about. The lights were low. She wrapped her legs around me. It would be so easy, I thought, but suddenly, she let go, swam free, jumped up on the side of the pool, and motioned that it was time to take our business back to the bedroom.

"Have you ever heard of four by four?" I asked in the elevator, wrapping her almost-naked body in my arms.

"No, what's that?"

I smiled. "No worry."

It felt like a four-by-four kind of night—four times, four nights in a row. Back in my medical school and residency days, it meant four nights with four different women, but with Abigail that had changed. I wouldn't say we were exclusive, but we had a "don't ask, don't tell" policy. Back in the day, scoring with one of the nurses at the hospital was always a cinch; then there was this woman in my complex who was ready almost any time of day or night, so scoring on a second night was also easy. Then, of course, there was the girl who would come to the Jefferson Pavilion, and I could go three for three with her. The fourth was always a bit of a challenge and usually happened just from pure luck. I wouldn't say that I was a womanizer, just a normal man who liked women. Were other men like this? I didn't know.

Close to midnight Abigail got up and took a shower. "I have to leave," she told me as she was toweling dry.

"I have nowhere to be, so you can stay," I begged.

"Can't. I'm going to Destin tomorrow morning for spring break."

"What do you mean? Spring break's been over for a month."

"Spring break is secret code for going to the Gulf Coast with my girlfriends."

The secret code, in my humble opinion, meant that every eligible woman followed by droves of eligible men would be in Destin. "Well, so much for you caring about me, especially since I can't go anywhere," I pouted.

She laughed, patted my head, and left me alone with MeMoe.

16

The following morning I received a text from Big Al. He'd been asking around about Monique and Simone. Evidently, more people than Lou had seen the two of them around town, but it so happened that they had seen this Monique with lots of folks, mostly men, some in very high places, and that included Cooter Amstutz, Simone's now widower. Not only was she seeing him, but also some said the affair had been going on for more than a year. No one really knew who she was, though.

Love triangle? I texted back. *Simone—Monique—Cooter?*

Spot-on, said his text.

Makes sense, but who killed Simone? Monique, husband, or both?

Big Al returned with all question marks.

Hopefully, Lloyd could figure out which Monique this was. On that thought Lloyd rang in.

I placed the phone on speaker. "Yo."

"Spoke to one of my friends downtown about the evidence they have on you." He sounded dead serious.

"Yeah?" I answered carefully.

"Seems like they don't have much in the way of hard, hard evidence—a croquet stick they found in your locker at your fancy club, which they think was used to take out Simone."

"Really? I don't own a croquet set, and what was my motive? I didn't even know her that well."

"Someone said that you and she were having an affair."

"That's not true!"

"Someone else said that you and a Dr. Gower played croquet with Simone and some other folks at the Universal Club."

"One time, and that was ages ago when they first opened the croquet area."

"And someone else said that you were an expert boccie player."

I had played a French version of the game called *pétanque* on the Gulf Coast but never played the Italian version in Memphis. "That's also false. Besides, Lloyd, none of that constitutes an affair."

"I'm just repeating what I heard. I told you it was pretty flimsy evidence."

When I didn't reply, he continued. "Terry, what I would do if I were you would be to call Reardon and tell him about the Cooter-and-Monique thing. I don't think he has a clue about that. He's a good guy, and from what I've heard, he doesn't think you did it. I can't tell him because nobody knows of our arrangement—so don't mention my name."

"Of course I won't," I assured him. "You know that Monique has also been seen hanging around Simone. That's what Big Al told me last night."

He seemed to consider this. "Your girl, Monique, lives on Shady Grove…three two two Shady Grove. Her last name's Glazer."

After we disconnected, I rummaged through my wallet and retrieved Detective Reardon's card and punched in his number. He picked up on the first ring.

"Detective Reardon."

"Hi, Detective, this is Terry Canale."

After a moment of silence, he said, "What can I do for you?"

"I have to tell you something that I just found out."

"OK, shoot."

"Cooter Amstutz was having an affair with a woman named Monique Glazer. She lives at three two two Shady Grove Road. She was also seen hanging around with Simone."

He replied with more silence.

"I just thought you ought to know that."

"OK, thanks." He disconnected.

So that was that—not the response I had expected. My cell phone dinged, indicating a text message. It was from Big Al. *FYI. Your gal, S, played croquet with a fellow in Highlands…a lot. No name…sorry.*

After taking MeMoe on his morning walk, I decided to go on in to work. My schedule had been cleared for the next ninety days, so there wouldn't be any patients for me to see, but there were some open clinical-research projects with the orthopedic residents at the Camp Clinic. I also was involved in the educational process of training residents, and since a new academic year was coming around, I had to get with Renée, the residency coordinator, about selecting new residents. That day she was having a problem with one of the younger doctors who needed reprimanding. It seemed he'd hidden a cadaver part in one of the assistants' desk drawers. The woman was a horror of a human being who knew everything about everyone and had nothing good to say about anyone. She was a tattletale on steroids. I couldn't garner a lot of sympathy for her but had a talk with him anyway. The rest of my day was uneventful and mostly entailed me hiding out in my office, avoiding conversation whenever possible, and trying to focus on the incomprehensible words in my manuscript.

Around two my cell phone rang. It was Mack the Knife just calling to let me know that the medical examiner had released the official report on Simone. Not only had someone beat her over the head, presumably with a croquet mallet, but also had followed that up with stabbing her twenty-five times with a croquet wicket. That was really not nice. Who would do something like that? Whoever it was definitely wanted her dead, or he was crazy or insane—or *she*. All I knew for certain was that it wasn't me.

Upon disconnecting, my cell phone immediately rang. This time Detective Reardon was on the line.

"Terry Canale," I answered.

"Spoke with Cooter Amstutz this morning. He denies having an affair."

"Is that surprising?"

"No, not particularly," Reardon said, stifling a yawn. "I do have to ask you where you heard this."

"It's all over the Universal Club. I'm surprised no one told you."

"I guess they didn't want to go spreading rumors that might not be true."

"Or they might be true," I said. He thought I was just trying to save my hide, and he was right on that account. "Please, just check out his story with Monique what's-her-name on Shady Grove."

"We'll check out all leads."

"Thank you." My words sailed out into the empty airwaves, because he was already gone.

The day didn't improve much after that. This time it was my office phone that rang, and it was that damn reporter again, wanting an exclusive on Simone and why I had murdered her. This was my chance to defend myself in the court of public opinion, she insisted.

"Court of public opinion! I'm innocent!" I shouted into the phone and hung up on her. It occurred to me that whether or not indicted, my career in Memphis might be over.

On my way out of the office that afternoon, I opened the newspaper to avoid having to make eye contact with anyone in the elevator. To my horror, my face smiled up from the front page. Shit, here we go, I thought, hurrying from the building and jumping into my Ford Explorer before anyone had a chance to stop me. I threw the car into gear and hightailed it to my condo. With MeMoe as my only witness, I opened the paper and read the article. The writer had been very careful to always mention that I *allegedly* was the last person to see Simone Amstutz alive, and he quoted several people at the Universal Club who said nice things, such as "Terry is such a good guy. It's hard to believe he would ever do a thing like this" or "There is no way Terry could be a murderer. He is such a gifted surgeon." The newspaper writer had even gone so far as to interview the chief of staff at the Camp Clinic, who said, "We stand one hundred percent behind Dr. Canale. He is currently on paid leave, and we maintain his innocence until it is proven otherwise."

I kicked off my shoes; fell onto my bed fully dressed, mentally exhausted; and was asleep before my head fully hit the pillow.

17

Around midnight there was a ringing sound that I didn't know what to do about. I was back in my lab in medical school at UT Memphis, collecting a blood specimen from a corpse. Back in medical school, I had actually been involved in several notorious murder cases, collecting semen samples and other blood products from the morgue at night to send to the lab in the morning. Practicing on my own arm, I became quite proficient at drawing blood. This night I was drawing blood from Simone. She was stone-cold dead, but when the needle punctured her arm vein, she turned her head to me, smiled sweetly, and said, "Answer the phone." Puzzled that she could still speak with all her injuries, I said, "Hello" to the phone in my hand. Simone's smile faded into reality, and my cell phone rang again.

"Hello?" This time I'd answered for real, shaking off the dream of Simone.

"You killed my best friend!" a voice shrieked through the receiver.

"Whaaa…" Slowly I was regaining consciousness. "This is Dr. Canale," I informed whoever was sobbing on the other end of the line.

"I know who you are. You killed Simone. I hope they give you the death penalty! You deserve it!" the voice shouted.

"Monique?" I asked tentatively.

She disconnected.

How Monique, if it was indeed Monique, had gotten ahold of my cell-phone number was beyond my ability to comprehend at this hour. I sat up, untwisting my shirt and pulling it over my head without taking the time to unbutton it. As the fog of sleep lifted from my brain, it occurred to me that Monique might have received a call from Detective Reardon. Otherwise, why would she have called? Was she unnerved that the police were on to her? Or maybe she'd read the newspaper article. Either way I felt rather upbeat about this turn of events. At least the ice was broken—in a way. The question now was whether to leave things alone. If she was having an affair with Cooter or Simone or both, that might be enough to lead Reardon in another direction in his investigation, or he might just be lazy and not pursue anything. With that in mind, I looked at my most recent calls. The woman had not blocked her number. I thought about calling her all night long, tossing and turning, wondering what to say, wondering if it was even Monique who'd called.

At seven, I looked up the number in recent calls and hit send.

She answered just as I was beginning to lose courage. "Glazer residence." The woman's tone was cold.

"Miss Glazer, please don't hang up," I said, expecting her to slam the phone down.

"Listen, I really have nothing to say to you. You murdered my friend!"

"I didn't kill her. I barely knew her!"

"Well, I knew her well…and I loved her." She sobbed quietly on the other end.

"It wasn't me, I promise you. What possible reason would I have had to kill her?" The pathetic sound in my voice penetrated her anguish.

"What do you want?"

"Will you meet me for a cup of coffee? Look, someone set me up. If I get blamed for this, the real killer goes free."

She thought about it for a second. "I'm really not interested. I have enough problems as is."

"We can meet in a public place if you don't trust me." I was going to suggest University Coffee Shop, but so many medical students hang out there and do their homework without buying coffee; it wasn't a good idea, because someone might recognize me. "We can meet at Burger Barn at the corner of Cleveland and Union." I chose this place because the only people who frequented the establishment during the workday besides me were the "bird lady," who walked up and down Union flapping her arms; high-school Henry, the mentally retarded football manager of Central High School and sometimes the University of Memphis, depending on how they played the day before; Monk, who carried a baseball bat beneath the long coat he wore whether it was ten degrees or a hundred outside; and a punch-drunk prizefighter. If these people recognized me, they wouldn't care.

Monique was silent.

"If it wasn't you who killed her and it for damn sure wasn't me, there's a killer out there who butchered your best friend. We've got to do something," I said.

There was a long silence.

"OK," she finally agreed quietly, "I'll meet you at the Burger Barn on Union at three."

I described myself to her as six foot one and 180 pounds, with thinning hair, to which she replied, "I know what you look like. We met once."

Close to two in the afternoon, I called my assistant for messages and to let her know I wasn't feeling well and wouldn't be in the rest of the week. I had planned on leaving MeMoe at the condo but then decided to take him since he fared better with the ladies. Besides, maybe it would help break down Monique's defenses when she realized that a vicious killer would never own such a cute animal. We walked down Peabody and hung a right on Cleveland to the Burger Barn on Union. I ordered a cup of coffee, black, and a burger and fries, so they wouldn't say anything about MeMoe being with me in the restaurant. They didn't. The eight-bucks-an-hour workers couldn't have cared less, and their customers kept their opinions to themselves, obviously preoccupied with the voices in their heads. I sat at an orange-and-yellow table, took a sip of my coffee, pushed the burger aside, and offered MeMoe a French fry. He took it but was upset because he thought the burger was for him. Monk left with his baseball bat and overcoat, and the bird lady followed him out. I was just wondering if the two had a thing going when Monique walked in. Stupidly, I stood up and introduced myself even though we'd met before. She was quite lovely, not exotic lovely as she had been when I saw her with her pretend husband, Hammond. Today she was dressed in jeans and a T-shirt that hid her curves. Her breasts were ample, but her arms were thin, almost anorexic.

"Can I get you something to drink or eat?" I asked.

"Diet Coke."

I walked to the counter and ordered while she sat stroking MeMoe, who had jumped up onto the bench to get better acquainted.

Back at the table, I tried to make small talk. "I'm not picking up a Memphis accent. Where're you from originally?"

"Orange County, Virginia."

"Nice place. I went to college in Virginia," I told her. "Played football with a fellow named Dick Fogg from Big Stone Gap." She sipped her Diet Coke, unimpressed. "I also went to camp once on the Gulf Coast and met a girl named Penny Nickel from Money, Mississippi." She smiled at that. "How did you get to Memphis all the way from Virginia?"

"I married military and moved to Millington. Now I live out east, but I still work in Millington."

So she was the exotic dancer from Millington, not the Morgan Keegan lady. The conversation died again.

"How'd you get my cell-phone number?" I asked.

"A friend at the U Club," she answered immediately.

I nodded even though I really wanted to know who had parceled it out. "So, you said you loved Simone," I said point-blank.

"Yes, she was my best friend. We met at the Me-Oh-My-Oh Club."

I had heard of this club. It primarily catered to transvestites and lesbians.

According to Monique everyone loved Simone—except for the killer, of course.

"What about her husband?" I asked. "Did you know him well?"

She looked away when she spoke, suggesting a lie. "Only casually."

"Was Simone having a relationship with someone else that she told you about?"

"Simone saw lots of men, but she didn't talk about anyone in particular."

"Did she ever talk about seeing anyone in North Carolina?"

Monique looked down and then focused her gaze out the window, contemplating my question. "Some time ago she dated this guy who taught her how to play croquet and boccie. She never told me his name. I didn't want to know," she added jealously, "but she said he was from somewhere in North Carolina. I think the relationship ended some time ago, because she never mentioned him again."

"Can you help me find out who this guy is? I think it's important."

She stood up abruptly and slung her purse over her arm. "I'll see what I can do." She grabbed her Diet Coke and walked to the door.

I had a feeling that she knew the mystery man from North Carolina. I let it be.

I grabbed MeMoe's leash and the unconsumed burger, and we followed her out. "If you think of anything, please call me."

She walked to her car.

"By the way," I called out to her, "do you worry about somebody being after you, like Simone?"

She unlocked her car and looked at me uneasily. "You're damn right I do, and I'm still pretty worried it might be you."

"It's not me!" I insisted, but she was already in her car with the door shut and locked.

18

Now that the coroner had ascertained the cause of death, Simone's body was laid to rest at Memorial Park Cemetery. Because they expected a large crowd for her memorial service, they moved it outdoors to the Universal Club. I couldn't decide whether to go or not. If I didn't go, people would think I was guilty. But if I did, her friends and family might decide on a public lynching. I decided not to go. My good friend, Jack Meier, stopped by my condo and gave me the rundown after the service. Simone had drawn a large crowd. She had been very popular. They ended up having the memorial service indoors because of the rain, but Jack said it was very tastefully done. Three women gave testimonials. Cooter had been overcome with grief and could not say a word. There had been plenty of talk after the service around the buffet about who the murderer was. I didn't ask Jack what the consensus had been. At the end of the service, the rain had stopped, the clouds broke up, and the sun shined through. It appeared that Simone had peacefully been put to rest without any justice having been served.

As MeMoe and I walked Jack down to his car, he asked, "Are you entering your new pet in the U Club dog show?"

"They have a dog show?"

"Yeah, only every year, man."

"I don't have any papers on him," I told Jack. "I'm not even sure if he's a full-bred Pomeranian."

"It's not the Westminster Dog Show. He's a looker. You should go—it's only twenty-five dollars."

"When is it?"

"Day after tomorrow."

"I'll think about it," I told him.

As I watched him drive away, I wondered if I should call Abigail but decided against it, since she was probably having a grand time at the gulf with her friends, and opted instead to take MeMoe for another walk. It was walk number six today. My cell phone rang.

"Hello?" I forgot again to check the caller ID.

"It's Monique...Monique Glazer," a sexy voice on the other end said.

"Hey," I replied.

She was silent.

To fill the gap, I said, "I heard about Simone's service. I decided not to go. Did you?"

"Yes, I stood in the back and left right after. No one knew I was there."

"I heard that Cooter got pretty choked up."

"Yeah, he did." She breathed deeply. "Look, just so you know, Cooter and I did have a thing going. Mostly he helped me out financially, and I helped him out after they more or less split up, if you know what I mean, but that was it. Simone never knew."

"And so...now she never will," I offered.

"I didn't kill her," she said emphatically.

This time I was silent.

"I'm a stripper. That's what I do, and sometimes things go further. Sometimes I just need more money."

"You could try some other line of work. You're nice looking."

"Doing nails and hair? Believe me, the money's ten times better than doing hair." I didn't answer. "The work stinks, though."

"I bet" was all I said.

Monique cleared her throat. "You know, I really don't believe you killed Simone. I can't think of any logical reason why you would have. I got to thinking about the guy she played croquet with in North Carolina. She never mentioned his name. We didn't talk about it much, but I know he was married. Anyway, she said they played in cashews. Whatever that means."

"You mean like cashew nuts? Is that a croquet thing?"

"Beats me. Well, I'll call you if I think of anything else." She disconnected.

Cashew nuts? Well, that was no clue at all. I Googled croquet and cashews to see if anything came up. A lot came up about cashews and a lot about croquet but only one blog with the two words together, and it was meaningless. *They played in cashews*, Monique had said. I wondered if it was a place. Nothing came up under Cashews, North Carolina, either, but Google suggested that perhaps I meant Cashiers, North Carolina. I clicked on the map Google offered. The town was about ten miles east of Highlands.

The doorbell rang, sending MeMoe straight into orbit. He had been waiting for this moment, a chance to show me his grit. He barked ferociously at the unseen intruder. I scooped him up and answered the door. Mack the Knife stood in the hall, a wry smile on his face. MeMoe continued his earsplitting display of machismo.

"Come in," I said, holding the door wide open. "Let me put him in the back."

MeMoe was incensed when I placed him on the bed and shut the bedroom door behind me. It really hurt his feelings, I could tell, and I was sorry, but this meeting with my attorney was really important.

"Sorry about that." I motioned for Mack the Knife to sit.

"No, that's OK. I just stopped by to give you some good news." I waited. "Seems like they interviewed Cooter Amstutz again. There's some new evidence against him, so this may be the reasonable doubt we've been looking for."

"What do we do now?"

"Wait. Hopefully we'll know something before the week is out. Just thought it might cheer you up."

"It did. Thanks," I said as he walked out the door and to the elevator.

Well, how about that—sports fans? Out of the blue, I was no longer the most likely suspect or the *only* suspect in this murder. There were still a lot of ifs but not nearly as many as two minutes ago.

I made a few phone calls to acquaintances I knew who owned homes in North Carolina to see if they knew anything about Cashiers. Two had played golf there, and one played croquet, but, no, not one of them knew Simone or her mystery lover. It was very odd, though, that croquet kept coming up, especially since Simone had been bludgeoned with a croquet mallet. Something about croquet, Highlands, and a mystery-man lover made me feel I was on the trail of something important.

I decided to call Monique back. She picked up on the first ring.

"Monique, I just had a thought. Did you ever see that fellow from North Carolina with Simone?"

Monique thought for a second and said, "Dr. Canale." She paused.

"Call me Terry," I offered.

"Oh, OK, Terry. I did see her with him once. They had a rendezvous at my dance club one night. From where I was up onstage, I didn't get a good look at him and wouldn't be able to pick him out in a lineup or anything. That was a long time ago."

"If you had to give a description, what would you say?"

"Fortyish, distinguished, slightly graying hair. Sorry, but with the spotlight on me, it's hard to see out into the crowd."

"What'd they do there?"

"Talked for a little while and then left."

My phone beeped, letting me know that someone was trying to call through.

"Thanks, Monique. I'll talk to you later." I disconnected and went to my next call, without checking to see who it was.

"Terry?" It was Lloyd.

"Yo," I confirmed.

"Got some great news for you."

"What?"

"They're getting ready to arrest Cooter Amstutz for the murder of Simone."

"You're kidding."

"Nope. They found some threatening text messages he sent to her and a croquet set in his locker with one missing mallet."

"Hmm" was all I could think of to answer.

Lloyd picked up on my skepticism. "You don't sound happy."

"I'm happy that they're looking somewhere else besides at me," I told him, "but it doesn't feel right. Does it to you?"

"How do you mean?"

"It's too easy. First they find a croquet stick in my locker; then they find a whole croquet set in his locker with one stick missing. If he had been trying to set me up for this, wouldn't he have gotten rid of the whole thing or put the whole croquet set in my locker to begin with? Just doesn't feel right, you know?"

"Maybe, but for now I think you should count your blessings. Let Cooter Amstutz deal with his own defense."

"You're right." I had gotten lost in the mystery of it all. "Thanks for all your help, Lloyd. I really appreciate it."

Lloyd was silent for a moment. "Good luck, Terry. Maybe we can meet for a beer or something."

"Sure thing." We disconnected.

19

The morning headlines read, "Cooter Amstutz Arrested in the Murder of Simone Amstutz."

I rejoiced, and the first thing that came to my mind was entering MeMoe into the U Club dog show.

"Why, certainly, Dr. Canale. What category would you like to enter him in?" Bobbie, the dog-show coordinator, asked over the phone.

"Category?"

"Yes, our categories are cutest dog, shortest dog, tallest dog, fattest dog, best behaved, dog with the longest tail, dog that gives the most kisses, and, of course, best in show."

"Hmm." I thought about this for a minute. "Definitely the cutest dog and the dog who gives the most kisses." He'd do well in those. "How many dogs are signed up?"

"Around thirty."

"Great. What time?"

"It starts tomorrow at six out on the south lawn."

Next I punched in Abigail's number and then remembered she was out of town having *fun* on the beach. I scrolled my recent calls and hit Monique's number. She answered on the first ring.

"Did you see the headlines this morning?" I asked.

"Saw it on the news. The police came by to question me. I feel like they're trying to build a case against Cooter and me. I don't know why they would think I had anything to do with her death."

I didn't say anything. They no doubt thought that because I had given Reardon the information about her and Cooter. I didn't have the balls to tell her about that right now.

"I don't like Cooter," Monique said. "He's a prick, for sure, but he's not a killer."

"How do you know?" I asked but also felt that he hadn't done the deed.

"Well, he's not a violent person. He doesn't even kill spiders—just gently puts them outdoors. He owns a chinchilla, for Pete's sake. He gives it the run of his house."

"People can do some surprising stuff though when they're under duress," I said.

"I guess," she conceded.

I too conceded something. "Monique, I don't think he did it either. That North Carolina man who played croquet with Simone bothers me, and I don't know why."

"You and me both," she said.

"Well, I've got to put a call in to my work and see if they'll let me come back. I'll talk to you soon."

When we disconnected, I called Hap Herndon, the CEO of Camp Clinic, and informed him that I was ready to get back to work.

Hap hesitated—no, more like stalled. "Wonderful, Terry, wonderful. I'll get with the board of directors this week and see if we can put you back in business."

Taken aback by his hesitancy, I said, "Now, listen, Hap, I'm on the board of directors. I'm coming back to work on Thursday. Tell the others on the board that I'm innocent as new-fallen snow, and I put big bucks on the books for Camp Clinic! This is Monday, and I'll see the first patient Thursday. Thanks." Click. I hung up worried. Hell, knowing what goes on behind closed doors at those board meetings, this was troublesome. When a board meeting is called, you always make sure to attend, even if it means having to fly in from wherever you are, because if you don't, you're liable to get stuck on some crazy committee that has to oversee something inane, such as cleaning out the cafeteria refrigerator. Also, I'm not the most beloved partner due to the fact that I don't let people run over me. Nary a meeting goes by that I don't get into it with Dr. Sikes or Dr. Carver about something or the other. More than once the offer to "take this outside and settle it like men" has been thrown out there as an option.

The next call was to Mack the Knife. Amazingly, his secretary put me straight through.

"Hey, Pat, this is Terry."

"Terry. I guess you saw the news?"

"I did. When can I get this ankle bracelet off and get my passport back?"

My attorney snorted. "It doesn't work quite that fast. They still haven't released you yet. My guess is they'll drop the charges some-time today."

"OK, will you let me know?"

"Sure. I'll call you as soon as they let me set up a time."

I didn't tell Mack the Knife that the ankle bracelet was hanging on the key holder next to my front door. Evidently, when they first placed it, my ankle had been severely swollen, which it sometimes does because of an old injury I got during a freshman football game against the Naval Academy. A plebe named Lamar clipped me during the game, causing me to sprain the ankle, and later an opposing line-man stepped on the back of my heel and fractured my fibula because the coaches had my ankle taped too tight. At any rate, after the swell-ing had gone down in my ankle, that bracelet slid right off. My plan was to slide it back on before going to the courthouse.

Ten minutes later Mack the Knife called. "Terry, meet me at two oh one Poplar in twenty minutes—with your ankle bracelet on—so they can take it off properly."

He'd noticed that I wasn't wearing it. "I'll be there in ten," I told him, and then I slid the ankle monitor back on and grabbed my keys.

Twenty-four hours after my call to Hap Herndon, the chief of staff of the Camp Clinic called. "Terry, this is Jim. I just wanted to touch base with you. Hap said you called. I'm so glad you're not in jail and ready to go back to work." He sounded reserved.

"Thanks. I told Hap I'd be back in the office on Thursday."

"Terry, I called a meeting of the board of directors last night. Now, I realize you're on the board"—he was hurrying along before I could say anything—"but I thought it would be better to have this conversation without you being present, so others could speak freely."

"Uh-huh." I wasn't happy about that. Who knew what had been said about me behind my back.

Jim went on. "It was a unanimous opinion that we want you to come back to work as soon as possible, but everyone believes this needs to settle down and blow over a little before you start back. You need some time, and these court things can drag on until they're fully resolved. It's now the fifteenth of May, and we thought you might return first week in June?"

"Jim, that's a bunch of rat shit. I know things have to be finalized, but why can't I come back to work this week?"

He replied calmly, "We believe that PR-wise, it would be better this way—make sure all the formalities are taken care of, you know?"

Here was the funny thing: I actually agreed with him. If it had been someone else on staff, that would have been my decision also.

"OK…OK. June, then. I'll be there first clinic day in June."

"Good. Now you go and take some time for yourself, you hear?"

"Thanks, Jim." He was a good friend, and I knew he was my strongest advocate at the clinic. I was thankful they were paying me even though I wasn't putting any money on the books. They were a decent bunch—that much was for sure.

As I disconnected, strangely my only thought was that I had sixteen days—eighteen, if you counted the weekend in between—to solve Simone's murder. Now, anyone else in his right mind would have dropped this nonsense about solving murders and left well enough alone, but I couldn't. Maybe I wasn't in my right mind. In retrospect, I think I was really angry because someone had tried to pin this murder on me, and I didn't think for one minute it was Cooter. My first instinct was to jump on a plane and fly to Asheville, North Carolina, get a rental car, drive to Highlands, find that bastard who'd killed Simone, and rattle his brains, but I'd no idea how to go about finding him and had no idea who he was.

I called Nurse Johnnie at the clinic. "Hey, Johnnie, what's going on there? Any calls?"

"Nothing's going on."

I could tell she was pissed.

"What's up?"

"Oh, Ginger called in again and said she couldn't come in today."

"Ginger?"

"Ginger, Dr. Frohse's nurse," she said, annoyed at my lack of attention to these details. "Oh, and Mr. Hickerson called, wanting some more pain meds. I told him, no way! If he's in that much pain, he needs to make an appointment."

"Good girl." Our office mottos are that lunch is for sissies; only babies sit down; we work until we're done; the quicker the better; and we will see any patient, any place, and anytime. They often called Nurse Johnnie Nurse Yes, because, even if I get mad, she will allow any patient at any time to come in to see me, even if we're overbooked and understaffed. What she won't do, however, is dole out medications and narcotics willy-nilly to people who call on the phone. If they're that bad off, they need to make an appointment.

"I don't know if you've heard, but I won't be back to work until after June first," I said to her, checking my watch.

"Taking some time off after all that?"

"Yes. Can you call Terri Harmon at Regency Travel and have her get me a list of good hotels in Highlands or Cashiers, North Carolina? Also, find out where I can play golf and croquet. I'll call you before four."

"Did you say golf and croquet?"

"Yeah."

"OK."

"Thanks."

I called her back promptly at four, and as promised, Nurse Johnnie had the material I had asked for, including possible flights. Apparently it was better to fly to Greenville, South Carolina, through Atlanta and rent a car and drive to Highlands than to fly into Asheville. Regency Travel had recommended the Sir Henry Inn in Highlands, a boutique hotel with a small number of rooms and a workout facility. Highlands is a very small community in the mountains of southwestern North Carolina, but in the spring and summer, the population doubles, and that's why there were so few vacancies. I opted for the Sir Henry Inn because all the other decent hotels and resorts were taken, and I booked a flight to Greenville, where I would get a rental car. Getting to play golf in Highlands and Cashiers was not going to be easy either, the travel agent had said. Use of the golf courses is limited to members and likewise for croquet, unless I wanted to play on a public course. Figuring I could work on that later, I booked a room for a week.

MeMoe barked at me. Surprised, I looked down at him, having forgotten all about my charge. It had been a lot more than a couple of days since Mrs. Habernathy had given him to me, and we had seen neither hide nor hair of her since. Either the Russians had decided that Anastasia didn't die with her family and that she was alive and well in the United States at the age of 115 and reclaimed her, or Dr. Schmidt had decided she needed more than just pampering. Either way, it didn't really matter, because MeMoe was now my best bud, and I had no intention of giving him back. I called Terri Harmon at Regency Travel and told her to book a room that would accommodate my pampered pet; then I ran a bath for MeMoe. We had a trophy to win in a couple of hours.

When MeMoe and I arrived at the U Club lawn, it was packed with four-legged creatures in all colors, shapes, and sizes. MeMoe stood out like royalty. We were second in line to the review stands. I paraded MeMoe proudly around the judges and up onstage. With a dog treat, I bribed him to sit, which to my surprise he did without hesitation. He had not done that once since I'd had him, but he knew there was an audience and that this was the real deal. Everyone clapped politely, which signaled some kind of ending to MeMoe, who then took it upon himself to be the grand sniffer of all the other contestants. According to him and me, there were no winners in this bunch, but the judges didn't agree and awarded eight other dogs the prizes. I told Dr. Gower, who was a veterinarian and one of the judges, that I was not happy and was pretty sure the whole gig was rigged against us. If MeMoe couldn't win in this dog show, who could? MeMoe was worthy of best in show. Dr. Gower must've agreed, because he disappeared for a little while and came back with a small plastic dog statue. The inscription read, "The Greatest of Dogs." He presented it to MeMoe, who was ecstatic over his win and carried it out to the car all by himself. When we packed for the trip to Highlands, he insisted on taking the cheap toy with us.

At one point during packing, I did wonder about my motive for going to North Carolina, but as is true for me in everything, I refused to travel down that road of thinking. Shoot, at this point in my life, I could afford to fly to the Cayman Islands; or Easter Island in the Pacific; or Machu Picchu in Peru; or Portofino, Italy; or Cape Town, South Africa; or anywhere, really. A trip around the world with Abercrombie and Kent, *National Geographic*, or Four Seasons on a private jet at the cost of $120,000 was something MeMoe and I deserved; but, no, instead we were flying into Greenville, South Carolina, so we could chase a ghost up to Highlands. I Googled to see if there was something interesting for us to do in Greenville, so we could combine work with pleasure, but all the Internet produced was Bobby Jones University and revival tents where you could be born again. Instead of making a bucket list, why not make a gratitude list, since I was not being charged for murder?

20

The following day, having packed a couple pairs of khakis, T-shirts, swim trunks, and a dress shirt and jacket, MeMoe and I were off. The flight from Memphis to Atlanta was uneventful except that the ticket was way too expensive.

A small, frail elderly woman occupied the window seat next to MeMoe. She gave him an inordinate amount of attention, and he accepted her kindness with grace. What a man! I thought.

The woman smiled at me. "It is so wonderful to sit next to an animal lover. I'm one too." She poked her fingers into the cage. MeMoe allowed her to stroke his ear.

I'd never thought of myself as an animal lover overall, but I could say with confidence that I loved MeMoe and was so proud that he didn't bite her knobby little fingers.

As we were taxiing out to the runway, the pilot announced that we had a ground traffic-control delay and that our flight would be delayed for thirty-eight minutes, but with luck he should get us into Atlanta only a few minutes late. Is there ever no delay when it comes to flying these days? Why don't they just move the flight to a different time? I wondered. I then felt guilty that instead of being grateful I was inwardly bitching.

"Oh dear," the woman next to us fretted, "I bet I'm gonna miss my connecting flight."

"Maybe it'll be delayed too," I said by way of reassurance, because she was in obvious distress about it. "How long a layover do you have?"

"Thirty minutes. I'm on a connecting flight to Boston." I couldn't help but wince. "They did say they would have a wheelchair waiting at the gate for me."

I didn't say anything but was pretty sure she still wouldn't get there on time.

As we landed, the pilot's voice crackled over the intercom. "Thank you for flying with us. We apologize for any inconvenience our delay may have caused."

"That should be the airline's tag line: 'We apologize for any inconvenience,'" I said to the woman, who just nodded. MeMoe's little bug eyes told me that he also fully agreed with my assessment.

As I exited the plane, an attendant with a wheelchair was waiting as promised for the elderly woman but at the top of the ramp. I checked the departure schedule on the wall. My connecting flight wasn't there yet, so we had plenty of time. The woman's flight to Boston was delayed, but they were already boarding. I looked back. The woman was making only slow, painful progress up the ramp to the wheelchair. What the hell, I thought, and jogged to the gate where the Boston flight was just about to close the doors.

I ran up to the attendant, MeMoe in hand, and looked her straight in the eye. "There's an old disabled lady on this flight coming in a wheelchair. Don't let her miss this plane!" I said importantly.

"Yes, sir," the attendant replied as if I were some kind of airline dignitary who had a say-so about something. I turned and headed off to my own gate, passing the old woman on the way. I wanted to tell her about my heroic deed and receive accolades that she wouldn't be missing her flight, but I didn't. Even though I feel that most things I do are conditional, sometimes they aren't, and I just want to do good just for the sake of doing good.

Despite the delay and mile-long hike up and down escalators in the Atlanta airport, MeMoe and I ultimately made it to Greenville and the rental-car place, where I demanded an SUV with satellite radio.

MeMoe had to use the outdoor privy first, but soon we had settled back in the rental car with plenty of sunlight left. Tuning to channel 33, I pulled out into traffic with my favorite song, "Mambo Man," blaring through the speakers.

After two days in Highlands, MeMoe and I still had uncovered nothing. The weather was gorgeous, and I felt rested—and bored. Should I stay here longer? I didn't know. Maybe there wasn't anything to uncover. After all, it was possible that Cooter Amstutz was guilty and maybe Monique too. Maybe she was just playing me. Not wanting to go down that road because I liked her, I kept telling myself that it was necessary to find the real murderer so my name would be completely cleared. That worked for the time being, but Simone's mystery man never materialized and probably wouldn't because, frankly, I didn't have a clue what he looked like, and asking around about him and Simone had been fruitless. Most rich folks are closemouthed.

I called Monique. "Hey, Monique; it's Terry."

"Oh, hello. Long time no hear." She sounded winded. "Sorry, I'm working out on the elliptical."

"I'm desperate," I told her.

"Oh?"

"I'm in Highlands looking for Simone's ghost man. I'm coming up with zilch. Can you remember anything else at all? Anything?"

She was silent for a long moment. "No, Terry, I told you that I'm not even sure I could pick him out in a lineup."

"Would you consider coming to Highlands? Maybe you could recognize him."

"I doubt it," she replied. "You know I'd do anything to help find Simone's murderer, but I think what you're doing is useless. Besides, I have to work the next three nights, and, you know, once a table dancer, always a table dancer."

"Don't put yourself down like that. Please come. Let's find the killer together, and then we can work on that inferiority complex you seem to have. I'll check flights through Atlanta to Greenville and call you back. And don't worry; it's on me." It was an invitation to which she didn't answer yes or no, so I assumed it was a tentative yes. There were early-morning flights from Memphis to Greenville through Atlanta, and it was an easy ride in a rental car from there. Monique finally said she would be there the next day.

That afternoon, with the aid of GPS and our cell phones, Monique and I met in the middle of town next to the Sir Henry Inn and got her a separate room. MeMoe was very happy to see her and strutted about like a rooster.

Monique, dressed in hip-hugger jeans and an extra-tight Grizzlies T-shirt that showcased her outrageously beautiful body, handed me her purse. She scooped MeMoe up under her arm. Her topaz eyes looked skeptically at me from beneath mile-long lashes. "OK, Terry, I'm here. Where to? I don't see anybody I recognize and seriously doubt I will."

"Let's start by going to the high-end country clubs and see if Simone frequented any." I had already picked out three clubs: the Loblolly Pines Country Club, which had a golf course; the Cashiers Country Club, which had oodles of big Atlanta money and a croquet court; and the Mountain Way Country Club, which was the most prestigious and oldest club that boasted a golf course and boccie and croquet courts.

We dropped off her suitcase in the room and then set out to visit Loblolly Pines, where we were immediately turned back at the gate by those in charge of the little booth. We did get into the one in Cashiers on the pretense that we were going to have lunch with a Mr. Norfleet, whoever that was, and once inside, we snooped out every-thing from the golf shop to the dining facility. But Monique didn't recognize anyone, so we headed back to Highlands.

I put in a call to Clyde, pretty sure he had a membership at the Loblolly Pines Country Club.

"So you being here in Highlands doesn't have anything to do with running from the law?" he asked, evidently having heard about my recent incarceration.

"Nope." I laughed. "My name's been cleared."

"Good to hear," he roared jovially. "I knew that was a bunch of bullshit anyways. You just go on out to the Pines and tell 'em old Clyde sent you for some drinks at the bar on me. I'll call ahead."

"Thanks, buddy."

We drove over to Clyde's country club and took advantage of the comps as Monique checked out the few members wandering about, but nothing rang a bell. Unfortunately, their staff was highly efficient, and we didn't get to see their golf course. They didn't have a croquet court, but the maître d' did inform us that there was a boccie court and a workout facility, all of which we were not invited to see. Apparently this place checked out your financial statements before they actually invited you to become a member. The man looked down his nose at us, obviously convinced we weren't up to snuff. On our way out, we stopped to take a quick look in the dining area—again, no luck. We got back into the rental and drove out the main gate, waving to the attendant as we left the grounds. We hung a right and then another and parked just out of sight of the main gate.

"What are we doing now?" Monique asked.

"We're going to walk down that dirt road and climb over their fence to check out the folks on the golf course."

"Are you nuts?"

"Where there's a will, there's a way. Come on!" I urged.

Monique unfastened her seat belt and got out. We walked a ways down the dirt path, past the No Trespassing sign, until we reached an area of fence hidden behind a screen of bushes on the other side. I stooped low and clasped my hands to give Monique a boost. She was a lightweight, probably not more than a hundred pounds. It was easy getting her over the fence. I climbed over after her, receiving nasty scratches from the bushes. There was no evidence of cameras or security out back, but we kept a low visibility and then casually walked the grounds to the golf course, nodding courteously to the people we encountered. Monique checked out everyone.

Finally, she shook her head. "I don't see anyone who looks like him…I guess. Like I said, I probably couldn't pick him out of a lineup."

With that, we ambled back to our secret place, scrambled back over the fence, and walked to the vehicle. When we were on the road, I called Clyde and thanked him again for the comps.

"How'd you like the place?" he asked, evidently under the impression that I was scoping out country clubs to join.

"Nice!" I said enthusiastically. "I'd like to check out the Mountain Way Country Club while I'm here."

"Oh." He sounded disappointed.

"It's not for me. It's for a friend," I lied. "She's thinking of moving here."

That seemed to smooth over his hurt feelings.

"I know the maître d' at that club. His name's Delmár. Used to work at the Universal Club years ago before he moved to Highlands. I'll give him a call. By the way, Terry, is that honey you're hanging out with attractive? If so, let me know."

"This is official business, Clyde. You know better than to come to me like that. Don't you dare tell your wife that I'm traveling with a woman. She's been trying to get me married off for years."

"You got it."

"Thanks, Clyde." I disconnected and looked at Monique. "I think we just hit pay dirt. Let's go back to the hotel and call it a night. Besides, I have to let MeMoe out."

We drove to the hotel in silence, with me wondering whether I should make a move on Monique. I tried placing my hand on her leg, but she moved it out of reach, sending the message loud and clear that she was here on business, and that was that. What the hell are you doing anyway, Terry? I chastised myself. We're looking to find a murderer, and here I am trying to get lucky. And what about Abigail? That thought brought both hands back to the steering wheel. At the Sir Henry Inn, we parted ways to our separate rooms for the night.

The following morning, I saw Monique in the breakfast area and sat down at her table without invite. "Morning," I said.

Today she wore only a minimal amount of makeup, if any. She was still stunning.

"Where do we go from here, Sherlock Holmes?" she asked skeptically, continuing to read the morning paper, taking a bite of her bagel.

"I dunno. My friend Clyde called. He spoke to the maître d' at the Mountain Way Country Club, and he's expecting us for lunch there today—the maître d' is. Maybe he'll know something interesting."

After breakfast I went back to the room to get ready for the day and to check on MeMoe. He had seemed out of sorts earlier, so I put in a call to the doggie day-care center. Miss Mamie, the day-care teacher, assured me that he would have a grand time with all the other pampered pets, and they had plenty of activities planned. MeMoe wasn't sure about the whole thing, but I was finally able to convince him that it was better than sitting in an empty hotel room or, worse, in a hot car. Reluctantly he agreed.

Monique and I left the hotel shortly before noon, and at twelve thirty, we were admitted through the golden gate of Mountain Way Country Club. I wore my button-down dress shirt with khaki pants for the occasion, and Monique wore a tight-fitting, light-blue knit dress that accentuated her perfect curves in just the right places. It was a tad short but didn't cross the fine line to indecency. I walked a step or two behind her, enjoying the view.

Delmár, the maître d', greeted us and led us into the dining area. He was a big man with mocha skin, impeccably dressed, with manners to match.

"It's good to meet you, Dr. Canale. I remember your father from the Universal Club," he said in a quiet voice. "He was a fine man."

"Thank you," I said politely. "How long have you been here in Highlands?"

"Oh, probably going on ten years or more. I love it here. I was glad to get away from Memphis." He stopped himself. "Nothing bad about Memphis," he continued apologetically. "Just the weather's nicer here in these parts."

I agreed.

"How 'bout you?" he asked Monique.

She smiled sweetly at him. If you didn't know better, you'd have thought she was a billionaire's wife. "Just looking to get to a place with better weather."

"Well, you'll really like it here then," he said warmly.

"It's even prettier than Germantown," she continued in a heart-warming voice.

"Oh, I reckon it is." He let the conversation go and waved over a server.

I didn't want to tip my hand and ask Delmár directly if he knew Simone Amstutz or her mystery man or even whether he knew of her murder. We ate an incredible lunch, and I felt just a little guilty about our deception—but not guilty enough, evidently, because I still let Delmár give us an exhaustive tour of the facility, while Monique searched for the mystery man.

Back in the car, I asked, "What do you think?"

"It's lovely. I wish I had the money to join a place like that, and Delmár is a great maître d'. Other than that I think you're barking up the wrong tree."

"I think you're right," I said dejectedly.

After a bit I asked, "Did you bring your swimsuit?"

"I did."

"Well, when we get back to the hotel, we could go for a swim, maybe work out a little bit, and then get an early dinner and see when we can get a flight back to Memphis."

"Sounds like a plan," Monique said.

We followed our plan, and when we had finished working out, Monique went to her room to do her hair and freshen up for dinner, and I picked MeMoe up from the doggie day care. He reeked of perfume and was utterly exhausted. A little blue bow adorned each of his ears. What on earth had those hussies done to him? He gave me a self-satisfied yawn and stretched out on my bed. "Just look at you!" I scolded. "I'm so disappointed." I reached for his bows, but he jumped out of my reach. He liked those bows!

21

I looked up the airline's number on my smartphone and called for reservations. There were no flights to Memphis until the next evening, so I booked us on those and then went to meet Monique in the lobby. We drove out Highway 72 to a barbecue place that the hotel manager had recommended. We arrived at sunset, the bluegrass music in full swing. The barbecue was good but no comparison to the barbecue in Memphis. The North Carolina barbecue was unfortunately dry, and the sauce was different. In Memphis, if your clothes aren't messy after eating barbecue, you really haven't eaten barbecue. We ate the North Carolina barbecue anyways and stayed around long enough to listen to a few bluegrass tunes. Around ten we headed back to the Sir Henry Inn and parted ways back to our separate rooms.

MeMoe was still zonked from his day's adventure with ladies, so I retreated to the balcony alone with my complimentary bottle of Perrier and gazed out over the dark silhouette of mountains against the moonlit night. Lights from houses shone here and there through trees on the mountaintops, blending with the stars and the twinkling lights from downtown Highlands. It was serene and peaceful, something I fully embraced at this time in my life, especially after the ordeal over the past several weeks. Back in the day, though, when I was in college, this would have been pure torture, because back then I craved excitement and beer. Once in my freshman year in college, three of my fraternity brothers and I went to Manhattan during the Thanksgiving holidays and stayed at the Roosevelt Hotel. I promised to meet a former girlfriend underneath the clock at the Biltmore. She showed up but only for a little while, until the drinking started. We never saw each other again after that. I ended up getting so drunk that night, my buddies locked me in the hotel room to sleep it off. Our room was on the thirteenth floor. Sometime in the middle of the night, I stumbled out of the bed and found the door locked and couldn't find my phone or the hotel-room phone, so in my stupor I thought I was trapped. Sober, it would have never occurred to me to go out on that ledge, but in my condition, it must've seemed like a good idea to climb out on all fours and crawl across the three-foot ledge to the next room. If I had fallen, it would have been thirteen stories down to Madison Avenue pavement. By a miracle I made it to the next room and beat on the window. A surprised Wally, an old buddy of mine from Memphis, was the one who let me in. Too drunk to remember that incident clearly, it wasn't until I read the reviews of the movie *The Ledge* in the *Wall Street Journal* that it all came back to me—well, parts of it anyway. "Hey, I've been there and done that!" I told everyone at the office, but no one believed me, because they knew of my fear of heights. A week after that article appeared in the *Wall Street Journal*, Wally sent a postcard of the Roosevelt Hotel, stating simply, *"The Ledge*...do you remember this?" We got in touch, and he was able to fill in some of the missing details of that night. I painted an original acrylic of the hotel for Wally, highlighting the thirteenth floor.

Around midnight, I poured out the rest of the mineral water, slipped out of my clothes, and crawled under the covers, immediately sinking into a deep sleep. It wasn't too much later, though, when something woke me in the middle of a dream. My eyes flew open, scanning the room. It was dark, and my watch showed two o'clock People were shouting outside and running up and down the steps. MeMoe growled and then whimpered, jumping off the bed and scratching at the balcony door. I slipped out from under the covers and grabbed my pants, still fiddling with the zipper as I stepped out onto my balcony. Someone was lying on the ground by the pool.

It was Monique!

I grabbed my shirt, slipped my sockless feet into loafers, and raced downstairs. She was on the ground, bleeding from her arm, and her femur was badly fractured. It was obvious she was in shock. A woman handed me a blanket to cover Monique's shivering body. Having worked the trauma unit many, many times in Memphis, I knew a bullet hole when I saw one, and that was definitely a bullet hole in her upper arm. Someone said an ambulance had been called, and it arrived within minutes. The paramedics also immediately knew what they were dealing with and radioed for the police.

In the ambulance, I held traction on Monique's humerus and femur as the paramedics worked to stabilize her. She mumbled incoherently about being shot and thrown from her balcony. By the time we made it to the Highlands hospital, it was obvious to me that she was going to need the humerus and femur fixed internally. The hospital had no provisions for skeletal traction, and the debate was whether to admit her for the night or transport her to Asheville immediately. I called an orthopedic surgeon, Peter Markola, in Asheville but got his answering machine, so I left a message that my nurse was in dire need of emergency surgery. It was the ER physician who made the final call to transfer Monique to the trauma center in Asheville, but he told us that the police were waiting to speak with her first.

Out in the lobby, I had already told the police all I knew, but they wanted to question her. She rambled about a large African American man who had broken into her room and shot her, aiming for her head but missing and hitting her arm instead. She was able to get to the balcony, where he caught up to her and threw her over the railing, and she landed on the ice machine. She had no idea who he was or why he had attacked her. Luckily, he didn't shoot at her again. The police were still searching the facility, but so far no one had seen or heard anything.

It was a long ride from the small hospital in Highlands to the Asheville Mission Trauma Center. Monique slipped in and out of consciousness, probably because of shock and the pain meds she was being given.

During a period of lucidness, I whispered to her, "Was it Delmár?" He was the only African American man in Highlands I could think of.

"No...no," she moaned, "he was large...not fat like Delmár...and much younger. He was young and strong."

A million thoughts paraded through my mind, the first being about Monique's condition, as we sailed, with blue strobe lights, down the winding roads from Highlands. I knew she would have to have the humerus washed out and properly plated. Luckily, her femoral fracture was a closed injury, but it was comminuted. For now the leg was in traction. She was young; she would manage, I thought, but my next thought was about how in the hell I was going to get her back to Memphis. What in the world had I been thinking trying to solve a murder of someone I barely knew—and now what? Someone had attempted to murder this table dancer, and it was my fault.

"Terry?" Monique called out, and I took her hand. "How're we gonna get back to Memphis now?"

"Don't worry about it, sweetheart. I'll take care of it," I told her. The only problem with that was that I had no idea how. An ambulance trip from Asheville to Memphis would have all sorts of problems and complications. Furthermore, she was at high risk for a pulmonary embolism. A commercial airliner would require two seats for her and a long convalescence before she made the trip. To me, the easiest but costlier option would be a private jet from Asheville to Memphis. Regardless of the price, I decided on the private jet. After all, I was a young, successful, unmarried orthopedic surgeon with a sizable income and a great expense account. I could afford it.

When we arrived in Asheville, the sun was just coming up. It was going to be a beautiful day for most people in the Asheville city limits, just not for us. I'd been to Asheville under different circumstances, to an orthopedic medical meeting. It's a wonderful place to be, just not that morning. The Mission Trauma Center was located in the heart of Asheville in a less-than-desirable neighborhood, but no matter, Dr. Markola and the rest of the staff were waiting for us. Monique was immediately whisked off to the resuscitation-and-critical-care unit. There, numerous vital signs were taken, and she was stabilized with a large amount of intravenous fluid and catheters placed in appropriate areas. Her radiographs revealed a transverse, slightly oblique, minimally comminuted fractured femur on the left and a right three-part fracture at the surgical neck of the humerus. An MRI of Monique's brain was obtained and showed no fractures or bleeding, but she did have a slight concussion.

Monique's leg was placed in skeletal traction, with weights added to relieve some of her discomfort. I spoke to the orthopedic surgeon, Dr. Markola. He thought that the gunshot wound would require debridement and internal fixation, and the femoral fracture would require an intramedullary rod. He was anxious to proceed for fear of complications, pulmonary embolism, pneumonia, and infection.

Monique was bedded down for the rest of the day in the ICU, and I was relegated to the waiting room. So this is how it feels to be on this side of health care, I thought somberly, looking around at the faces of those in the waiting area. People who had been there all night were asleep across several chairs, and some old guy with an incessant smoker's cough had taken off his shoes and made himself at home in one corner of the waiting area near the television. The coffee was old, Cokes in the machine cost a dollar, and the peanut-butter crackers were all sold out in the snack machine. All in all it was an unhappy experience. Suddenly I remembered MeMoe back at the hotel with the blue bows still in his ears. I called the front desk of the Sir Henry Inn and made arrangements for him to be placed with the doggie day-care ladies until I knew how we were getting back to Memphis and when. The polite lady said she understood and that it would be no problem at a hundred dollars a day plus food. I then called the airlines and canceled the flights booked for that day. They balked on the refund at first but then agreed when they saw the number of miles on my perks card.

22

With nothing left for me to do, I sat back in the chair on the opposite side of the room of the man without shoes, taking in the state of our health-care system and watching the reactions of family members as the doctor or nurse would come in and give an update on their loved one. I wondered what gave people the selfless desire to become doctors and nurses in the first place. What drove them to want to help others, to work impossible hours, and deal with the impossible challenges of trauma, sickness, and death? I thought about my own reasons for entering the medical field. Was I one of those people who just had to help someone? Maybe. I am a people pleaser and want to help people, but to be honest with myself, it's not unconditional. It might seem so at first glance, but it's really not. I want a patient to get a good result, I do, but is it more for me or for him? If a patient gets a good result and likes me, he will talk to other people who may become my patients, and hence I build up my practice. See? It's conditional. The sentence is not "I hope the patient gets better"; it's "I hope the patient gets better, so I can have a better career." When you start talking about conditional or unconditional acts, you are suddenly talking about humility, and as I mentioned previously, practicing humility is just an act for me, and it's really hard to define anyway, for anyone. One of the better definitions is knowing who you are, no less and no more. It's riding in the middle of the road and do-ing the next indicated thing. If you go around wondering if you're humble, you're probably not. Humility is doing something for some-one without that person knowing and without you patting yourself on the back for your good deed. That's a hard thing to do. So you see, the good any of us do is usually conditional.

Regardless of all that, none of that really even crossed my mind back in college. As strange as it may sound, one day I woke up and de-cided I wanted to go to medical school, and that was that. Since tak-ing premed classes and continuing football at the same time would have been impossible, I gave up the idea of coaching football as a career, which was probably a wise decision. Coaches are fired all the time, not for any fault of their own but because they have to tutor and care for eighteen-year-old prima donnas who can play a little football. Coaches' lives and careers are at the whims of these players, whether they realize it or not. If the players don't play hard for them and win, heads roll, and not the players' heads.

I looked into taking premed courses at the University of Virginia and actually signed up for organic chemistry and physics, until some of my fraternity brothers flunked out and couldn't make the cut into medical school. Reasoning that it might end up being the same for me, I decided to leave Charlottesville and return home to Memphis, leaving my friends and all the girls who had broken up with me be-hind. With no job and no money of my own to speak of, medical school seemed out of reach, but I still wanted to go. It wasn't too long after I returned to Memphis, when one of the local hospitals hired me as an oxygen therapist at a low wage and allowed me to work my way up to lab technician and then head of the night lab. Finally, one day I got up enough courage to fill out an application for the University of Tennessee and went to talk to the dean of admissions, Dr. Carmichael. The dean was a no-nonsense kind of guy who sugar-coated nothing.

I sat nervously in his office as he perused my application with a frown on his face, his eyebrows touching. "So you want to go to medical school; is that right?" he asked, leaning back in his chair and eyeing me skeptically.

"Yes, sir," I replied.

"Is this a joke?" he asked without a smile.

"No, sir, I want to go to medical school."

"Son, you don't have the courses to go to medical school. What the hell is this? Geology?" He shoved my transcripts across the table to me.

"That's the scientific study of rocks," I answered naïvely.

He laughed out loud. "Yeah, I know what it is."

My face reddened over the truth laid bare. I had done nothing to prepare for medical school—no chemistry or physics or anatomy; none of the heavy stuff. I'd gone the jock route and taken courses such as geology and psychology.

He leaned forward in his seat, placing both elbows on the desk. "The only saving grace for you, Canale, is that you haven't taken any of the tough courses you need for medical school. You can go ahead and take those courses now, and if your grades are good, I'll consider your application. If they're not, you aren't stepping foot into medical school at the University of Tennessee."

It was an eye-opening experience, but I took the dean's advice and started taking the science courses at the University of Memphis, passing most with flying colors, although physics was my undoing. I had trouble with Professor Imes's tests, so I dropped the course and took it during the summer, sliding by with a C. Finally, Dean Carmichael agreed to give me a try in medical school, not because of my stellar grades, mind you, but because two of my uncles who had political clout were putting pressure on him, something I'm not proud to admit.

My first semester in medical school was by far the hardest. I continued to work at night and took physiology and biochemistry among other sciences and math during the day. My grandmother from Clarksdale helped me with the tuition, but for the most part, I paid my own way. Anatomy, for me, was very tough. I spent long hours in anatomy classes, trying to understand and memorize the parts of the human body and the bones in our bone boxes. The smell I most associate with medical school is formaldehyde. The cadavers we used for dissection were filled with it. Within ten minutes of working on a cadaver, you smelled like the stuff for months to come. No matter how well you washed or how much shaving lotion you used, you'd still smell like a cadaver. As a matter of fact, I had difficulty getting dates back then because of the smell.

We had a professor, "Hatchet" Harry Wilcox, so named because he took shit from no one in his classes and would fail you just as quickly as not. He held a PhD and not an MD, which I think is why he was so crotchety. He worked with us in the cadaver lab. I can still hear him say, "If you cut something deep, it's probably the cadaver; if you cut something and it bleeds, it was probably your lab partner; if you cut something that bleeds and hurts, you just cut yourself." One time, Hatchet Harry caught a student throwing cadaver parts out the window so he could study for an exam the next day at his house. As the body part fell to the ground, Hatchet Harry walked up to the guy and said, "Young man, if you can catch that hip joint before it hits the ground, tomorrow you will still be a medical student at the University of Tennessee. Otherwise, pack your bags." I think the student went ahead and packed his bags that night.

I got through that first semester but ten in my class did not. The failure rate was pretty high. After a year and a half in medical school, we had to take our part-one boards. If you didn't make a high-enough grade, you couldn't continue on to clinical medicine. Fortunately, I passed but many did not, and some had to leave medical school.

Graduating from medical school and doing an internship and residency and eventually making big bucks was something to look forward to. I actually got to go up onstage to receive my diploma at graduation, unlike in high school. My grandmother and mother showed up, my mother sober for once, but it wasn't long after that she took her own life. To this day, I don't think it was intentional. She just had nothing else left to drink in the house but rubbing alcohol.

With a medical degree in hand, I elected to do my internship at a city hospital in Philadelphia that had a large emergency ward. They had a large sign posted on the emergency-room entrance that said, "The Shit Stops Here," and the one in the autopsy suite said, "This is Where the Dead Teach the Living How to Live." Funny the things we remember. It was a year of hard work—on call every third night, living in the intern quarters. The only things that made it bearable were the single nurses.

23

A large black man walked into the ICU waiting room and sat across from me; he pulled a phone out of his pocket and embarked on some fantasy game. His face became animated each time he took down a pretend perpetrator. I thought about the man who had shot Monique. Really, only Clyde and Delmár knew that we were in Highlands. Did either of them say something to someone about Monique? How would anyone have known where to find her? Was she being followed? Did someone recognize her at one of the country clubs? Most likely the person who shot Monique was the same person who'd killed Simone. Maybe he was worried that Monique could identify him. She couldn't. She didn't know the man who had shot her. It was like a puzzle, and we only had a couple of pieces. Could it have been a friend of Delmár? A friend of Clyde? I wondered whom Monique had confided in about going to Highlands. At that point, I was drawing a complete blank.

A midget-sized woman with bouffant hair entered the waiting room, the heels of her pumps clicking hard on the tile. Without the hair and shoes, she would have been six inches shorter. Freckled arms held a clipboard close to her chest.

She approached with a wide, practiced smile. "Dr. Canale?"

"Yes."

"We were wondering if you could help us with some information about your…" She searched my face for an answer.

"Friend."

"I see. Do you have power of attorney for your friend?"

"No."

"I see. Is there a responsible party? Family?"

"I don't know," I said truthfully. "We just met."

"I see."

"You'll have to get with her about all the insurance business."

"Um…she said she didn't have any insurance or ability to pay, and we were just checking with you before we placed her on our indigent list," she said carefully, fully aware that she might have been overstepping the laws on confidentiality.

"Why?" I asked.

"Well, she said she was working with you."

"Ah." While I felt responsible for Monique, I was not going to pony up a hundred grand to the Asheville trauma center.

"No, we were just working on a mystery together," I told the petite woman, explaining that Monique lived alone and I had no idea what her insurance situation was. I certainly did not give the lady my name or social-security number or any particulars for fear of being held accountable for her bill.

"Thank you," she said as she clattered back out the door.

This was definitely going to be a problem, I thought. Monique might even get placed on the very back burner but maybe not. It would behoove the hospital to get her in and out as soon as possible, since lengthy hospital stays are costly. As an orthopedic surgeon, I was well acquainted with the hospital drill to hurry and get people discharged. They say it's for the good of the patients because the longer they stay, the more likely they are to get an infection, but sometimes hurrying things along is to the patient's detriment.

As the little woman from the business office marched down the hall back to her office, a hospitalist walked into the waiting area with a plan of care in hand for Monique that he wanted to go over with me. The hospitalist was a tall, lean man with a kind face and soft voice. I wanted to tell him that I was familiar with what needed to be done and that I knew Dr. Markola personally but let him continue talking. He worried that Monique might be somewhat malnourished and asked if I knew if she had an eating disorder or if she smoked, to which I shook my head no, saying that I didn't know. Regardless, he was confident that she could be scheduled for fixation as early as tomorrow. As I listened to him speak, I was ever so happy that my role in medicine was orthopedics. His job seemed so...unglamorous.

After my internship I wasn't at all sure what type of doctor I wanted to be. Being a surgeon sounded cool, but my grades weren't high enough to get into a good cardiovascular residency, and neurosurgery didn't interest me. General surgery was the default option, but most specialties have staked out their own terrain, leaving general surgery with very little to do. I had already tentatively accepted a general-surgery residency at the Mayo Clinic when a friend of mine told me about a residency opening in Philadelphia. Because of something unforeseen, Dr. DiAlma needed a resident fairly quickly. Dr. DiAlma had the reputation of being a ruthless maniac but a brilliant orthopedic surgeon. I thought about it and decided there was nothing to lose by just talking to him, so I made an appointment. The interview was short. Dr. DiAlma asked me when I could start, and I told him three months.

"See to it that you start in six weeks" was his answer.

"I'll have to call the Mayo Clinic and turn down their offer."

"Don't worry about the Mayo; I'll call them."

I didn't know what to say. Finally, Dr. DiAlma looked at me impatiently and said, "It seems to me you have two choices, Canale. I'm going to give you twenty-four hours to make your decision. Your first choice is you can flounder around and go to the Mayo Clinic and waste your time. Or you can take my residency." He sat back and sized me up for a few seconds and then continued, his eyes never leaving mine. "The only downside to all this is that you're taking the slot of a resident who hung himself in the call room two weeks ago." He stood up. "This concludes our discussion. Let me know in twenty-four hours what you've decided."

With that I was dismissed. "Yes, sir." I was flabbergasted and fumbled to the door with my files askew under my arm.

A residency under a man like DiAlma would be tough. His resident had hung himself, for crying out loud. But I wasn't depressed and didn't have any psychological problems, so why not go with one of the top orthopedists in the country even if he was an egomaniac and a tyrant? I called Dr. DiAlma's assistant the following morning and told her I would like to accept the position. She said, "Great! Be ready to go to work in six weeks." And that's how I became an orthopedic surgeon.

As is true for most people in medicine, I had good intentions and still do for the most part. It was fortuitous that an orthopedic residency came my way, because it is very lucrative, more so than most other disciplines. But it's easy to lose sight of what's important. Somewhere in there the attraction of making money becomes more incentivized than the art and science of helping people. During my residency, one of the other doctors was showing me around Philadelphia on the Main Line and pointing out all the large homes of physicians who had prospered over the years in suburbia. It wasn't really the wealth that he was showing me but what he said that had such an impact. There are many ways to become successful as a physician, either in patient care, education, or research, but the least measure of how successful you are is how much money you make. That's something I try to remember even though a lot has changed in medicine in the last few years since my residency. There used to be a cooperative relationship between physicians and patients. It was a one-on-one cooperative, if you will. If your patient felt heard and understood, you could rest assured that that patient would adhere to the treatment regimen you provided, which is really fundamental to one's well-being. Patient-centered care used to be what was practiced. A patient was the captain of his or her own ship and destiny, and all patients were invited to enter into the decision-making process about their own care. After all, the patient is probably the most important person on the medical team. That personal relationship between doctors and patients no longer seems to exist. It appears that medicine is no longer a made-to-order menu but has deteriorated and is now as impersonal as a fast-food restaurant. We forget about our patients as individuals and find ourselves just treating a problem. Why this has become so is something I cannot answer. Is it that insurance companies dictate our time with patients? Or is it because of our own accounting and the need to see more patients and do more surgeries to maintain a certain lifestyle? Have we all just become prisoners to ICD codes? I think I work hard to maintain a personal relationship with my patients, but there's always extreme pressure to produce, and I have to admit getting caught up in the lifestyle of the rich and famous all too often. However, I do try to keep in mind that this is a person I'm treating.

Deciding there wasn't much I could do about Monique right now, I searched for a hotel room near the hospital and made a reservation for the night. I was exhausted and hungry, so I grabbed something from the hospital cafeteria before retiring to my room for the night.

24

The following morning I returned to the ICU waiting room before dawn and met Dr. Markola in the hall.

"Did you get Monique's insurance stuff straight? Can she go to surgery?"

"Hell yeah, we're going to surgery. I don't give a rat's ass about her insurance. We'll get her taken care of." He strolled off toward the double doors that had a sign announcing Authorized Personnel Only.

Way to go, I thought as the white coat disappeared behind the double doors.

I returned to the waiting room and sat agonizing again over how I would get Monique to Memphis, running through my options again. No matter which way I turned it, the private plane, the most expensive option, would be the most expedient. Besides the hassle with a commercial flight, it could expose Monique and me to people who wanted her dead. Delmár and Clyde crossed my mind again. Monique had said that Delmár wasn't the one who had shot her. It was possible, though, that he had told someone about us, maybe even just casually. Clyde had never seen Monique, so to whom would he have said something? Then again, maybe the murderer recognized her at the country club. Just because she didn't recognize him didn't mean he didn't recognize her.

Dr. Markola strolled into the waiting room in his scrubs and motioned me out into the hall. His surgical mask hung down around his chin. "She did fine," he assured me. "The gunshot wound to the shoulder was through and through, and we debrided that fully. The humerus was in three parts, so we fixed it with a plate. There was a small amount of metal left behind. For the femoral fracture, we used an IM rod with interlocking screws. Her oxygen stats are slightly decreased—probably some postoperative aspiration. It'll clear."

"How long before I can take her back to Memphis?" I asked.

"Four, maybe five days." He watched my expression of discontent and then said, "Maybe earlier."

"Thanks."

"You bet, buddy." He winked and strolled off down the hall, just as comfortable in his hospital as I was in mine.

Since there wasn't much for me to do but wait around, I made arrangements for a Lear jet to take Monique, MeMoe, and me back to Memphis maybe in four days for a mere six thousand bucks—a small price to pay for all that, I guessed. I took a cab to a rental-car place in Asheville and then took off to Highlands to get MeMoe, square the bill with the hotel, and make sure the other rental cars were returned. I thought about confronting Delmár and maybe even Clyde but decided to nix that idea. Not only was it a bit farfetched that either could be involved, but also if one was involved, he might just put the killer on our trail.

Dr. Markola, understanding that I might be in a sensitive predicament, released Monique for transfer to Memphis two days after surgery, with the understanding that she would be under my care. We rode in silence in the wheelchair-accessible van to the private airstrip where the rented Lear jet and two pilots were waiting. They were happy to accommodate our earlier departure. Monique was loaded with some effort onto the plane in the wheelchair. An ambulance would be waiting in Memphis to take her from Air Metro to my condo in Central Gardens.

Upon arrival, MeMoe and I hustled to the car at the airport parking lot and ended up beating the ambulance to my condo. The minute we touched down, I had called Abigail and gave her a quick rundown of the events of the last few days. Having been gone for so long, I had almost forgotten her name and felt that she may have been on her way to forgetting mine. Being the sweet person she was, however, she volunteered to bring pizza for the three of us that night. Pizza wasn't really MeMoe's favorite, but he knew better than to complain, since beggars can't be choosers. We would see soon enough how this happy family of three—well, four if you counted MeMoe—was going to work out.

Abigail arrived around six, looking as if she had just stepped out of a photo shoot for a tennis magazine. We hugged briefly, and she greeted Monique pleasantly cool. We fell onto the pizza—well, I did. Monique couldn't have cared less, because she was sleepy and in pain. Abigail nibbled on hers, eyeing Monique suspiciously, looking for clues about a possible relationship between us, and MeMoe put his little button nose up over the piece I offered to him. The small talk was strained, and Monique dozed off a couple of times. Abigail, with a practiced hand, helped her get situated in my guest bedroom for the night. When she was sure Monique didn't need anything else, she shut the bedroom door and fixed me with a steely stare.

"So what's this really all about?" she asked, looking at me as if she could see right through the whole affair.

"There's nothing going on between us, if that's what you mean. I've been on ice since you've been gone," I reassured, reaching out to her.

She refused to be drawn in. "Where are you going with all this?"

"I have no idea," I replied earnestly. "But, Abigail, everybody has got to be somewhere, and I guess the three of us are here." Lame words that wouldn't hold this relationship together for sure, but that was all I had at the moment. I reached for her again, but she grabbed her purse and headed for the door.

"She's asleep. I gave her the oxycodone," Abigail said, motioning toward the guest room. She was angry. "Look, I'm pissed that I've been dragged into the middle of this. You know, there isn't room for the three of us in this condo." She opened the door and stopped but didn't turn around to look at me. "I'll be by in the morning to check on her." That was the caregiver in her speaking. Then she walked out, leaving the door and my mouth ajar.

As the sun gleamed in through the slats in the blinds, there was a noise in my kitchen. It was barely six thirty. I jumped out of bed and reached for my pants, worried that someone might have broken in and was after Monique or, God forbid, me. "Some guard dog you are," I scolded MeMoe, who was stretched out across the foot of my bed. He yawned, indicating that he had no intention of looking death in the eye this early in the morning. Abigail came around the corner. She was here to check on Monique, just as she had promised.

"Hey," she said tonelessly.

"Hey," I said back. As she opened the door to my guest room, I saw that Monique was sitting up in bed looking a little more alert, something I was much relieved about but ashamed too, because I hadn't checked on her at all during the night.

I dressed quickly and put on a pot of coffee in the kitchen; then MeMoe and I headed down to get fast food for breakfast for everyone. I had no idea what the ladies would eat, but MeMoe was pretty sure they wanted scrambled eggs, hash browns, and sausage biscuits, although he himself preferred bacon. We returned and set out breakfast on the kitchen counter. Abigail was polite but cool as she nibbled on a hash-brown patty, while an indifferent Monique looked suspiciously at the plate Abigail had placed in front of her. She seemed disoriented, probably still in psychological shock. We had not talked about the shooting since the ambulance ride because she was so fragile. It had to have had something to do with Simone's murder. A simple break-in and theft would have been just too big a coincidence.

Abigail offered to sit with Monique and MeMoe while I went to the Universal Club to work out, a kindness of which I was certainly not worthy. "I'll be back by noon," I promised.

In the car, I put a call in to Big Al. He answered on the third ring. "Hey, Big Al. How's it going?"

"Doin' good. You?"

I told him about Monique having been shot.

"Shit!" was his only response.

"Yeah," I said. "Have you heard anything else about the man from Highlands?"

"Hell no, but it looks like he heard about you, or, at least, that gal." He breathed heavily into the phone. His asthma was always bad this time of year. "I did hear there wasn't enough evidence to indict ole Cooter Amstutz."

"Crap," I said. Even though I didn't think he'd killed Simone, I worried how all this might affect me and whether they could rearrest me.

At the Universal Club, Sunny, the lady whose sole responsibility was to arrange games and matches there, checked to see if she could get a handball game together for me on short notice. Maybe some good old sweat could take care of this fresh anxiety. Sunny could and did find me a partner. It was Malcolm Elias, a longtime handball player. He was older than me and had more hair, but my game was better than his, and I had the really hot girlfriend. He had made his money in natural gas.

"Hey, Malcolm," I greeted him in the locker room.

"Hey, Terry!" he replied, genuinely happy to see me. "So glad you got all that nasty business behind you. I never thought you had anything to do with it."

"Thanks." I didn't want to get into all that with him, so I changed the subject to something he liked to talk about—himself. "So I heard you bought a house recently."

"Sure did. The wife and I bought a house on the Cashiers Country Club grounds."

"Whoa—that must've cost an arm and a leg."

"Yeah, but business is good, so it won't be a problem."

I was happy for them. "That's fantastic. Do you play a lot of golf?" I didn't think he did.

He shook his head. "Oh no, no. The big thing there is croquet and boccie but mostly croquet."

There was the whole croquet thing again. What was it with that sport? I didn't see the allure.

"Two hundred of their three hundred fifty members play croquet," he continued as he tied the laces on his tennis shoes.

"How many play here?" I asked.

"You mean at the Universal Club?"

"Yeah."

"Twenty or twenty-five maybe. It hasn't really caught on here."

I decided to go a step further. "Are there any professional players like in golf?"

"Better believe it. It's a rabid sport. Professionals travel around the country and play for big bucks."

"Really? Wonder why it hasn't caught on here at the U Club."

He explained that the croquet court at the Universal Club was rinky-dink compared to the official croquet courts, like the one in Cashiers. Did I detect a hint of snootiness in his manner?

"Who's the champion there at Cashiers?"

He said a name that meant nothing to me.

"Anyone ever get out of line?"

Malcolm laughed. "We had one guy who had too much to drink and urinated behind some shrubbery but in front of a glass window where at least twenty women spectators sat." He shook his head. "He was immediately disqualified and lost his membership. Other than that, no, everyone's pretty cool. At Cashiers, players have to wear all white, you know."

How hoity-toity, I thought, looking in the mirror at the mismatched ensemble I was wearing for the handball game. Too bad about the guy who pissed on the bushes; I think I might've liked him.

After the match with Malcolm, I avoided the bar but got three meals to go and headed back to the condo. Abigail shrugged off the food and said she had to run. Monique politely picked at hers after Abigail left. It was obvious her appetite was still lacking; then I remembered that I really didn't know Monique all that well, so maybe there never was an appetite.

"I talked to a friend of mine today, and he said that Cooter was being let off," I told her.

Monique shrugged. "I don't think he's capable of killing anyone anyway, Simone least of all." She pushed the food aside and asked if I could help her to the bathroom.

"You can't get up yet," I said, looking around for the bedpan, which Abigail had neatly tucked up under the bed. "Here, I'll help you."

Her brows furrowed. "To hell with that!" She threw back her covers and moved her injured leg with her good arm. "I can't use that thing," she whined, and then she whimpered.

Browbeaten, I did as she asked, helping her into the wheelchair and then onto the commode. It was quite an undertaking and gave me a new appreciation for what nurses do every day. It gave me a new appreciation for Abigail.

When Monique was finally situated back in bed, she leaned back into her pillows, exhausted. "I don't think Cooter killed Simone. But someone did. You have to find him. You know?"

Find him? A tall order for sure. I had less than a week before I had to be back at work. There wouldn't be any time after that.

25

It's not that I'm complaining or anything, because this wasn't Monique's fault but mine and mine alone for having dragged her to Highlands, but none of this was helping my sex life. Having been on ice since Abigail left for the beach, now four by four was totally out of the question, and I was going none for one, or two if you count Monique. In addition to all this, Cooter Amstutz, the prick, was free. The Tylers from Clarksdale, Mississippi, a very prominent defense team, held a press conference at one o'clock, as if the world even cared. His attorney, standing all prim and proper at the podium, was saying, "Shelby County had no cause arresting Mr. Amstutz, as evidence was completely and utterly lacking in this case." I clicked off the television and punched in Mack the Knife's number. His secretary answered but, amazingly, put me right through.

"Hello, Terry," he said enthusiastically, probably because he knew he was soon to be paid.

"Hello, Pat. I guess you heard about Cooter Amstutz? Does any of that affect my being let off?"

"Not at all," he assured me.

Relieved, I thanked him for all his help, wordlessly letting him know that a hefty check for his fee was on its way.

So there I sat, no longer a suspect—and neither was Cooter—but Simone was still dead, Monique was still wounded, and a brutal killer was still at large. Why did any of this matter to me? Hell if I knew, but it did.

I looked in on Monique. She opened her eyes.

"Maybe Cooter will call you now that he's off the hook and want to pick up where you two left off since Simone's..." I wanted to say "out of the way" but instead said, "deceased."

"I can't imagine why," she answered. "With Simone gone he can fish in a great big pond of women, socially acceptable women at that—rich women, not poor strippers like me. Besides, could I ever really trust that he's completely innocent?"

I shrugged.

"Is Abigail back yet?" she asked hopefully.

"I didn't know she was coming back," I said to her.

"Oh yes, she told me we're going to do some physical therapy this evening. What time is it?"

Monique was still out of it due to the pain meds and was asleep before I could tell her the time.

Abigail returned at four as she had promised Monique. The two appeared to have hit it off. I was the odd man out, a spectator in a game, the rules of which were unknown to me. As Abigail expertly followed the physical-therapy regimen for this type of injury, I headed out for Marvell, Arkansas, where the Hebron Angels and the Marvell Eagles were playing a preseason football game. My second cousin, Terry, was on the Hebron team, and I'd promised him some time ago that I would come to one of his games.

I drove down Highway 61 to Tunica, where the casinos are, and crossed the Mississippi River into Arkansas at the Helena-West Helena Bridge on Highway 49, passing the little hamlet of Walnut Corner, and then drove straight into Marvell, the population of which was 1,345 at last count. It seemed everyone in the town and his brother were mobilized for this game and the fair that was in the town. Seven girls were vying for the honor of becoming queen, and it would be announced after the game. They were decked out in beautiful dresses, and all seven convertibles owned within the township were there to showcase these young ladies and block my way into the parking lot. When I finally arrived, the parking space was so far away that it was a five-minute jog to the field. I paid at the gate and stopped at the concession stand, ordering a jumbo knackwurst with grilled onions, mushrooms, and sweet relish topped off with enough mustard to make it worth my while. The atmosphere reminded me so much of my own football days and high-school years. Of course, I never got to enjoy it from a spectator's point of view. I looked for my cousins in the stands.

Haley, my cousin's wife, was waving to me from the stands. "Hey, Terry, we're up here!"

I waved back. None of us knew at the time that we were about to witness the worst football game ever. They were playing eight-man football, which I guess was because there weren't enough players to go around. Marvell had twenty and Hebron had ten. Haley explained that these were private schools; that was why the players ranged from eighth grade to seniors. My little cousin's team was definitely outmanned and outweighed by the Marvell team, and by the end of the first half, Hebron was trailing, 36–0.

Even though this was just a friendly, I knew exactly how badly the players on the Hebron team must have been feeling. Back in college at Virginia, our football team was on a losing streak like you wouldn't believe. In the first game of my varsity year, I intercepted a pass against William and Mary and made about ten yards. That was the highlight of my entire career. We lost that game and that season and the next nine games. By my third year, I finally gave up all together on our football team. So did everyone else. In fact, *Sports Illustrated* wrote an article about us, entitled, "Yes, Virginia, there is no Santa Claus in Football."

I remember one time we were set to play against the University of North Carolina in Chapel Hill. My teammates and I came roaring off the bus and shouted to an older security guard, "Open the gate; we're the University of Virginia, and we've come to kick North Carolina's ass!"

The old man smiled at us. "Son, that may be true," he said. "But today Notre Dame is playing Duke here. You got the wrong stadium."

We were so embarrassed. A lineman sitting next to me said, "Hey, get your ass back on the bus quick, and sit down before we end up playing Notre Dame here today." Our team put so many miles on that old rickety bus, until it finally gave out on us at Scott Stadium, and we ended up having to ride in a Charlottesville city bus. That's how bad things were.

I couldn't just sit by and watch this terrible defeat go down for my cousin, so I made my way to where the Hebron players were taking a break.

"Terry!" I called out.

He jogged over to where I stood. "Hey, Big Terry, glad you could come. I think we stink, though," he said innocently.

"Listen, Terry," I said to my namesake, "football isn't a friendly game. You understand?"

He nodded enthusiastically. "Sure."

"Bear Bryant used to say that 'dancing is a contact sport; football's a collision sport.'"

Terry nodded again. "Who's Bear Bryant?"

"It doesn't matter. What I'm saying is that it's a mean game, and if you decide to play, you gotta play with a sort of controlled rage—not explosive rage, but be consistently mad and defiant. It's OK to be mean during the game. You gotta wanna hurt someone. When this second half starts, I want you to go out there and knock the shit out of the guy who has the ball or whoever gets in your way, you understand? And make it count the first time. Controlled rage," I reminded him, and then I walked off the field.

On the next play, little Terry made the finest tackle in the whole game. He gave me a thumbs-up. It made me think he'd end up being a fine football player. Unfortunately, the game ended 55–0, but the Hebron Angels played their hearts out. My cousin was happy with his spectacular tackle and an awesome pass sometime later and was especially happy when I gave the team enough money for Taco Bell.

I headed back across the river, leaving the Marvell "Friday Night Lights" behind, and decided to stop at the casino and load up on some Paula Deen cooking. I thought about the advice I had given little Terry at the football game. My situation now wasn't so different. Monique wanted me to track down a vicious killer. The question was, could I be mean enough? Was there enough controlled rage left in me for all that? Maybe—then again, maybe not.

When I arrived back in Memphis near midnight, MeMoe had to go out for his final walk. When we returned, there was a commotion coming from Mrs. Habernathy's condo. A young woman was directing an even younger man to remove some art from the condo where MeMoe had previously lived. We stopped and watched. This looked like bad news. MeMoe stepped behind me, a despondent look on his face. He also knew. Well, it didn't really matter, because I was willing to offer a huge sum of money to keep MeMoe, an offer they couldn't possibly refuse. The young woman turned to me, not noticing MeMoe, who was crouched low behind my calves, something he never did.

"Hello," she said. Her bright red hair fanned out around a friendly freckled face; her smile was infectious.

"Hello," I answered, smiling back. "What's happened to Mrs. Habernathy?"

She stuck out her hand. "I'm Cherry Berry, Mrs. Habernathy's granddaughter," she said. We shook hands. "We had to move my grandmother to Golden Farm Manor in Strawberry, Arkansas, where I live, because her memory is just not quite right anymore, you know?"

So this was Cherry Berry from Strawberry, Arkansas. That was almost as good as Penny Nickel from Money, Mississippi. "Oh, I'm sorry to hear that," I replied, jingling my keys and making a move toward my door.

"What a cute dog!" she suddenly exclaimed.

MeMoe cowered and let out a small whimper.

"Thank you," I said, hoping alarm wasn't written all over my face.

"Well, nice meeting you," Cherry Berry from Strawberry said happily as she locked the door behind the man carrying out the expensive artwork and headed to the elevator.

"You too." I opened the door and let MeMoe clandestinely slip into my condo. Evidently, the woman didn't know or didn't care about her grandmother's dog, and perhaps Grandma Habernathy couldn't remember that she even owned a dog.

26

On the morning of the twenty-seventh of May, there was a knock on my door. As usual, I opened without checking to see who might be lurking on the other side. I should have known better, but we had a doorman in the building, so you'd think it'd be pretty safe. Cooter Amstutz turned out to be the lurker, but before that even registered with me, he threw a roundhouse punch at my chin. His aim was off, and I took it full on the Adam's apple and sank to one knee, my vocal cords momentarily paralyzed. It would've been better for him if he had knocked me out cold, because this just pissed me off. Coach Mix had always told us to hit the opponent with the hardest blow you're going to deliver at the beginning of the game. Cooter Amstutz had missed his opportunity, so it was my turn, and he got a knuckle sandwich square on the chin. His jaw popped loudly, and he went down like a sack of potatoes. Before he came to, I jumped on top of him, yanked his hands behind his back, and pulled his arms into a hammerlock. My other arm held him in a choke hold. My first year in college football, I went after a 220-pound guard on the very first play, hitting him hard but missing. He reacted by driving his helmet full into my chest bone, laying me out flat. "Welcome to college football, buddy," he'd said with a grin.

Holding Cooter tight as he squirmed like a wet eel, I croaked, "Welcome to the Canale school of hard knocks, buddy."

"No *mas*! No mas! No mas!" He wiggled around, gasping for air.

MeMoe rushed over to offer his mighty assistance during the struggle, charging and barking loudly, but backed off once he saw that things were pretty much under control.

Monique had been practicing her leg lifts in the bedroom and wheeled herself into the living room. "Cooter, stop that! Stop!" she cried out.

I relaxed my hold just a little.

"You asshole!" he shrieked. "You killed my wife, and now you're putting the moves on my girlfriend! You murderer, I'll see to it you're put away for a long, long time."

I tightened my hold on him again. "Who you calling a murderer? You no-good-for-nothing piece of shit!"

He struggled, but his skinny scarecrow body was easy to subdue.

"You've got two choices, mister," I rasped, sounding a bit like Dirty Harry. "One, we call the police, and I press charges against you for attacking me on my property, or two, I'll help you to your car, and you can leave peacefully."

Cooter gasped for breath. "I'll go. I'll go."

I made the mistake of believing the little liar and let go, and he immediately went for a gun in his right pocket. I kicked him hard in the shin, sending him squealing to the floor, the gun falling from his hand and sliding across the floor to where Monique sat. It was a .38 Midnight Special. Monique reached down and confiscated it with her good arm.

"Your options are running out, mister," I spat. My throat was hurting like nobody's business.

Monique shouted, "Cooter, what in the hell are you doing? Leave! I'm not your girlfriend!"

"And I didn't murder your wife!" I said, placing him back in a hammerlock. I jerked him out the door and down five flights of stairs to his car and slammed him hard against the ostentatious blue Mercedes. I opened the car, literally threw him inside, and slammed the door on his legs, which I guess wasn't nice of me. He was able to get them in before I slammed the door again. Cooter started his Mercedes without looking at me, backed out without looking for traffic, and drove off, tires screeching, without looking left or right. It was a good thing it was a quiet street. Glancing to the parking space where my Explorer sat, I noticed that all four tires were flat—slashed to shreds.

"Well, shit!" I shouted into the wind, but no one cared.

I took the stairs two at a time back up to my condo, threw open the door in a tantrum, and stomped back to my bathroom, yanking open the medicine cabinet. Monique retreated to her room without a word. Only after I had soaked my head under the faucet for a good long while, massaged my throat, and downed four ibuprofens was my anger finally under control. I called Mike at the Universal Club to see if he would get four new tires for my car. He knew I'd make it worth his while and came right away. By nine, we were back in business.

Even though the little weasel had attacked me, his being Simone's killer still seemed unlikely. The man was a spineless wimp. His punch had no pow, and he'd handled the gun like a six-year-old. If he were a cold-blooded killer, he would've just shot me and then Monique as soon as he saw us, instead of making such a spectacle of himself. He knew I could whip his ass in a fistfight any old day. This was a fit—a jealous rage. Maybe that was what had happened with Simone. She had been hit on the head before being stabbed umpteen times, a cowardly act. Was Cooter the coward? Slashed tires flashed through my mind, so I retrieved my Smith & Wesson from the nightstand.

"Hey," I called to Monique from my bedroom, "has anyone contacted you from the police in Highlands yet?"

"No, I haven't heard anything," she called back.

"Me neither." I pushed open the guest-room door to find her sitting practicing her leg lifts. She was doing great. "Monique, you need more protection. I'll give you my handgun, so when I'm not around..." I held out my gun to her, the barrel pointed toward me.

"Are you crazy? I've never shot a gun in my life."

"Well, now's the time to start."

She reached behind her and pulled out Cooter Amstutz's gun, pointing the barrel to the ceiling. "OK, but I've got my own; thank you."

"You feel well enough to go out to the shooting range?"

"Today? In my wheelchair?"

"Yeah."

She hesitated a moment but then agreed. "OK."

When Johnnie found out that I had purchased a gun the year previously, she had gone out and bought me a gift certificate for a gun-use-and-safety course at the shooting range. Since that time, I go every two to three months to practice my marksmanship, which isn't that great, to be honest. You'd think I'd be better at it, since I was in the army a couple of years back. It was after five hard years of internship and residency and a traveling fellowship in pediatric orthopedics that I decided it was a good option and ended up signing on the dotted line for two years. They sent me to the First Cavalry and the Second Armored, the old Patton father-and-son divisions in Fort Sam Houston in San Antonio. They tried hard to make a soldier out of me but to no avail; I barely learned how to shoot a rifle. Although they automatically gave me the rank of major because of my MD, wearing my brass never came easy. The military, thank heavens, seems to give exceptions to their medical corps, but I bet Brooke Army Hospital was happy to ship me over to Darnell Army Hospital in Fort Hood, Texas. If you've never been to Fort Hood in Killeen, a hundred miles or so south of Dallas, for the most part, it's flat, dry, and uninspiring. Lyndon Johnson owned that piece of land at one time and sold it at an exorbitant price to the government. Ever since then, it's been a military post, where at any one time there are between fifty thousand and sixty thousand people stationed. We were being trained for the hell of war, and Killeen was definitely an apt teaching ground. One division would go out on maneuvers, and while they were gone, their wives or husbands would make hay with the other division's spouses and vice versa. Killeen in my memory is just a cloudy haze of motorcycle accidents, helicopter crashes, dead armadillos, and lots of rattlesnakes. Although Lake Belton, where all the brass lived, was nice, after two years I was ready for something different, and that was when the Camp Clinic offered to let me hang out my shingle in Memphis. It was a good thing, too, because I never did get the hang of shooting.

27

I loaded Monique's crutches and wheelchair into the old Explorer and adjusted the seats so she could get in easier, and we headed to the shooting range right off the expressway. The gun instructor met us at the door.

"Hey, Sam," I greeted him as if we were best buds. He smiled noncommittally. "Terry Canale," I reminded him. "Remember me? I bought a gun from you a year ago or so and took your course."

His smiled widened. "Of course I remember you!"

I doubted that but said, "I have a young lady with me who would like to take your course. She's also interested in buying herself a gun."

"Sure, sure. The classes are every Sunday from one to four, two classes minimum, and then to be certified, she has to take a written exam, followed by a lesson on how to actually use the gun and shoot." He also suggested a small .38 caliber subcompact would be the easiest for her to carry. I agreed and signed Monique up for a Sunday class in three weeks.

I asked Sam for some ammo so we could practice. "I'm a terrible shot," I told him.

"Two things," he explained as he retrieved the ammo from under the counter. "Either your target's too far away, or your aim's off."

"Ah." No shit. I modeled my stance for him and showed how I squeezed the trigger, looking down the empty barrel sight. "Maybe it's my sight," I offered.

"Your stance is fine. If you're within ten or fifteen feet of the target, you should be able to hit it whether or not you're sighting," he said.

"Thanks." I went to help Monique out of the Explorer.

When we got back inside, Sam had set up the target and handed me the ammunition. Both of us donned earphones and goggles, and I rolled Monique to the area behind the closed doors. I pushed the button, and the target moved back to about twelve feet. I loaded my Smith & Wesson and fired off six shots in a row, looking straight down the barrel at the target's chest without trying to sight. The bullets hit the target: one in the shoulder, four in the heart, and one in the neck. Then I moved the target back to about fifteen feet, reloaded, and had pretty much the same result: no better but no worse.

"If I shoot six straight shots at a person ten to fifteen feet away, it would land all six shots in his chest, which would probably kill him. Don't you think? Here, you try," I said to Monique. I reloaded and handed the gun to her.

"I'll have to use my left hand," she said, indicating her right arm sling. "I'm right handed, you know."

"Well, try it with your left hand. A bad shot is better than none," I said.

"Sam said not to worry about sighting." Monique grabbed the gun from me and shot pretty much without aiming. The bullet pierced the center of the head, right between the eyes.

"That's impossible!" I shouted. "Here, do it again."

She did it again, three times in a row, each shot overlapping the last.

"That's some damn good shooting for a novice, Monique. You just shot Simone's murderer, whoever shot you, and Cooter Amstutz, all in the same breath. I guess you're a natural."

She gave me a crooked smile.

Leaving the shooting range, I felt a bit better about Monique being able to take care of herself but less so about me being able to take care of me. We drove in silence for a while. I was really beginning to like Monique more than I cared to admit; after all, she was a stripper, and I, a doctor, but there was something about her aside from her looks and her body that intrigued me.

"Have you ever been able to remember anything else about the guy Simone was having an affair with?" I asked after the silence had become too silent for me.

Monique shook her head. "No, all I know is that he was from North Carolina, not from—I don't know where he was actually from, but he would come to Memphis from North Carolina for a couple of days. He was married and probably has kids, but Simone never said that. I'm just assuming he has kids. Sometimes Simone would sneak off on the weekends to the gulf or Miami to be with him."

"How'd she get away with that, being married and all?" I asked.

"She would tell Cooter she was spending the night with me."

"And that was OK with him?"

Monique looked at me curiously. "Sure. Why wouldn't it have been?"

I shrugged. "Just saying."

"Terry, Simone wanted a divorce. She couldn't afford it, though, because Cooter's such a crafty lawyer. So she dragged it out as long as possible, biding her time."

"Biding her time for what?"

Monique was silent for a moment and then said, "Until her mystery lover got his divorce. She told me about a fight they had once. She wanted him to divorce his wife—said that if he loved her, he would. I don't think he ever intended to get a divorce even though he may have promised Simone. They were always hiding and sneaking around. He was always afraid someone would recognize him and tell his wife. Simone told me once that he said he would kill anyone who exposed the affair to his wife."

Incredulously I looked over at Monique. "You never told me that."

Monique waved me off. "I tried to tell her to back off the relation-ship—to stop seeing him and that it was a one-sided affair, but she said he threatened to kill himself if she ever left him. That was how much he loved her."

I stopped at the red light. "So let me get this straight," I said. "He basically emotionally blackmailed her into staying with him and then threatened to kill her if she ever told his wife?"

Monique nodded. "That's messed up, I know. I told her so. But really, Terry, I'm pretty sure that she had quit seeing him. She hadn't seen him in months before she was murdered."

Even so, I still believed that Simone's mystery lover was most likely her killer. It made sense now. Simone could have threatened to ex-pose him to his wife, and he took the next step and eliminated her. And I was now more convinced than ever that he had recognized Monique in Highlands and had come after her or hired someone to eliminate her.

Delmár crossed my mind again. What did I know about the man after all? Nothing, other than he worked at the Mountain Way Country Club, used to work at the Universal Club, and said he knew my dad. I punched in Big Al's number.

"Hey, Big Al. What's happening?"

"Up to no good as usual. You?"

"Wondering if you know a guy named Delmár. Used to work at the U Club. Moved away about ten years ago?"

"Name's familiar."

"Can you tell me about him?"

"Nope, but I can ask around."

"Thanks…again."

"You better be showing your skinny ass around my establishment and spend some money around here, or I won't be feeling all that obligatory to you no more," he said jokingly, and we disconnected.

I glanced back to Monique. I hadn't made a pass at her recent-ly but felt a major "hit" coming on. After all, she should be in my menagerie of four by four. For the time being, though, I was trying to keep my priorities straight and continued to uphold the values taught to me as an orthopedic surgeon, which included, in this order, God, family, patient care, and public service.

Monique asked me to drop her off at her apartment to get some clean things and to check her mail, maybe pay some bills, and take a nap for sure. Reluctantly I agreed and handed her my gun.

"Be careful who you open the door for," I warned, wheeling her and her crutches into the small duplex.

She told me that the apartment next door was empty, because it was being renovated.

As I pulled away from the curb, my cell phone rang. It was Big Al.

"Terry, got some information for you, but it'll cost you."

"OK, what info and how much?"

"It's in person only, and the how much is two Franklins. Dude's here now. Can you come by?"

"Be there in ten."

28

When I entered the Red Eye, Big Al motioned to an older man seated in the same dark corner where Lloyd had sat. The deep forehead wrinkles and gray hair clocked his age at around sixty.

I sat in the chair opposite him and laid two Benjamin Franklins on the table. Big Al stood within earshot, his big arms crossed over his chest.

The man took a sip of his beer and then spoke quietly, his voice a deep baritone, his eyes focused on the door like an old gunslinger. "Your man, Delmár, is well connected there in the Carolinas."

"You mean the mob?"

He shook his head. "No, more like the Muslim brotherhood."

"In Highlands? Give me a break." I glanced at Big Al, but he was wearing his poker face. I contemplated grabbing my two hundred bucks off the table and leaving.

"He hired some guns to go after a gal who knew too much. They're semiprofessional, but they can do some damage."

"What did she know?"

He shrugged.

"Are you sure of this? Hell, there are no Muslims in Highlands. They're all rich and evangelical."

He took another sip of his beer. "Whether you like it or not, there are Muslims everywhere, and there's a cult of Islamic extremists inside Highlands. Not all Muslims are Middle Eastern, you know, and some come from money—a lot of money."

This guy was either a con artist or totally off his rocker, a conspiracy theorist at best.

"Feds have been investigating him for a while," he continued, his eyes never leaving the front door.

"So Delmár, a maître d', is really head of a Muslim cult in the middle of a community of very wealthy, white old farts who play croquet? Is that what you're saying?"

"Naw, he's just the lookout. Law's checked him out and says he's clean, but I know otherwise."

"You know what I think you know?" I rhetorically asked. "Nothing. You know nothing, and you're feeding me a bunch of bullshit! I'm no closer at all to knowing who killed one of my friends and is now going after the other." The urge to snatch my money off the table grew stronger.

The man shook his head, laid his own ten on the table, and, as if he could read my mind, picked up my money. "Aren't you?"

"How do you figure?"

"Know this: Delmár is dirty; I don't care what the cops are saying. The people he works for are dirty and dangerous. The gal he ordered the hit for was a stripper, and now he's got a hit out on some big-time surgeon here in Memphis. That's at least the word on the street. Money's already exchanged hands, so I'd be looking over my shoulder if I was you."

My mouth opened and closed.

The old man pocketed the dough and left. Big Al shook his head but said nothing as the man made off with my money.

"Where the hell did you get this joker?" I asked Big Al.

"He works up there same place as Delmár. Comes to town 'bout once a week on errands and always stops by to have a beer and meet with...*people*."

"A snitch?"

Big Al shrugged. "You know I don't go digging in folks' business."

After my meeting at the Red Eye, I stopped back by Monique's duplex to pick her up. She was dressed in a highly revealing bodysuit. The only things that ruined the effect were the blue arm sling and a crutch with which she ambled about clumsily.

"Would you mind taking me by Pony Tails in Millington?" she asked. By the looks of her sunken eyes and dark circles, I surmised the nap hadn't worked out.

"Pony Tails? Is that a hairdresser?"

"No, silly, that's the club where I work."

"Oh, sure."

It was about one in the afternoon when we pulled into the parking lot of Pony Tails. I drove the Explorer to the curb and let Monique out by the door. She refused the wheelchair and asked for her crutch. Her coworkers greeted her outside the door with hugs and kisses and basically carried her into the establishment. I wasn't quite sure which ones were actual women and which were the fakers. I parked the car and followed them into the dimly lit club. There were only a few patrons seated at the bar, their eyes glued to the stage, and some businessmen in suits at one of the tables. We took a seat in a corner booth. Monique asked for a domestic beer, and I ordered a Diet Coke, not sure that she should be drinking alcohol with the pain meds she was downing like Skittles. In the very dim light of the club, we watched as several buxom dancers with big butts went through their routines, mundanely discarding piece after piece of clothing as they made love to a pole.

A door opened in the back, briefly illuminating the place, and the owner and manager came over and sat at our table. "Hey, Monique. How've you been? Heard that someone shot you," the big fat one said.

Monique nodded and then got right to the point. "Ralph, I need my job back. I can be ready to go to work in two, maybe three weeks."

Ralph smiled a toothy grin. "We'd be happy to have you back. You were the star of Pony Tails, but will you be able to dance like you did?"

Monique said, "I guess. I'll be off my crutches soon, I'm sure."

"Will you still be able to do your more sensuous moves?" Ralph asked, obviously turned on by the recollection.

She pinched his round cheek. "I'll be faithful in doing all my stretches, so I can get it just right for you."

"What about scars?" asked the skinny, slimy one, whose name tag said Pete.

Monique flinched at this and looked my way. "They're not so bad; nothing a little makeup can't hide."

Ralph cleared his throat and his vision of Monique. "Now, Monique, you're still on crutches. Why don't we put your return to Pony Tails back a couple of months? See how you are then."

Monique shouted, "Ralph, damn it, I'm ready to go to work! Otherwise, I'll have to go on disability. I can work behind the bar in the meantime."

"Monique, I get it. I really do, and we'd love to have you back. When you're well, your job'll be waiting here for you. That's a promise. OK?" With that, Ralph stood up, waved off any more argument, and hiked his trousers up onto his jelly belly. A new topless stripper, even less enthusiastic than the last, stepped up onstage, twirling her golden breast tassels to the hoots and howls of the handful of men in business suits.

I touched Monique's arm. "I guess our next stop is the Social Security office."

She wiped a tear off her cheek. "I've got to have some income."

"It'll be fine."

It was pretty late to be going to a government office, but we went anyways to the one in Midtown. I really wanted to tell her about my meeting and about Delmár and how she had been wrong about him, but now didn't seem to be the time or place. I parked not too far away from the Social Security office and this time got out the wheelchair for Monique, which she sat in without argument.

Inside the cold, air-conditioned, overcrowded office, we grabbed a number and waited our turn. We were number 4928, and my guess was that there were around two hundred folks ahead of us even this late in the day. As we waited, I planted a sensual kiss on Monique's neck. She smiled but pushed me away. At least we were making some headway. An hour later, almost at quitting time, Monique's number was called, and I rolled her to the front.

A young woman in a blue suit sitting behind the desk asked how she could be of assistance, and Monique told her she was in need of disability money. The girl briefly looked up at Monique and then shoved some papers in front of her, fanning them out with superlong manicured nails as she spoke. "This one is for you to complete, this one for your doctor, and this one for your employer. Once these are all filled out, call us for an appointment."

"Oh," Monique said despondently, "all this has to be filled out first? When can I get any money?"

The girl's eyes opened wide. "Oh, honey, it'll be a while."

"How long?" Monique asked anxiously.

"Possibly months," the girl said flatly; she then called the next number.

We returned to my condo with an envelope full of forms. Monique avoided any further come-ons by me and announced that she was going to take a nap. I was thinking about taking MeMoe for a walk, when Abigail showed up with a sack full of soft tacos in hand. She looked delicious in her spandex and sports bra, wearing red, high-top tennis shoes, her long blond hair draped over one shoulder. I was so turned on that I forgot all about putting the moves on Monique. Abigail handed me a taco from the bag, but I pulled her to me instead. Surprisingly, she didn't push me away. As we gently kissed, I was convinced that things could go back to the way they had been before Monique. She rubbed her body against mine, pushing me toward the sofa, and soon I was winning this battle of spandex and was under her bra. She pulled my shirt over my head and unfastened my belt, fighting and winning the battle against denim. As I worked my way from her lips to her cheeks, her neck, and her breasts, a third hand began to rub my back and shoulders, and then it gently fondled

Abigail. It was Monique using her one good arm. The ensuing ménage à trois was not exactly what I had fantasized, what with Monique trying to keep her injured leg out of the field of play and me getting my admirable erection caught in her arm sling. Luckily Abigail was extremely limber, and once we had the mechanics figured out and determined who should be doing what to whom, it was pretty damn good. Once we untangled from the sweaty, panting heap, Monique hobbled back to her room, and Abigail wordlessly dressed as I sat totally spent on the sofa, stunned and at a loss for words.

29

The next morning, I wasn't sure how I felt about the ménage à trois the day before—a little like James Bond, I guess. Can something so satisfying leave you feeling empty? Can a man love two women romantically at the very same time? Probably. But can two women love each other and a man? How did I not know this about Abigail? The one thing sure in all this was that my relationship with Abigail had forever changed.

While I pondered this, Monique's phone rang in the other room. "What do you want?" I heard her ask in an unamused tone.

A few moments passed, and then I heard her say, "Cooter, it's over between us. Do you understand?" There was a pause, and then she said, "No, I don't think you killed Simone. I honestly don't, but it's just over between us. There really wasn't ever anything between us, except that. No, I'm not having an affair with the doctor," she lied.

I guess Cooter, the horny bastard, was pleading with her. I doubted that he cared much about her, and Monique probably knew it too. However, this was none of my business, so I stayed out of it. My business was keeping my side of the street clean and not worrying about others keeping theirs clean. My cell phone rang.

It was Big Al. "Hey, I heard Detective Reardon sent someone to snoop around up there in Highlands, checkin' out your man Delmár."

"Really? How would he have known anything about Delmár or what happened in Highlands? I didn't tell him."

"Well, it mighta just been an anonymous call to the MPD. Someone got your best interest at heart."

"Well, well," I said.

"Wanna know what I know?" Big Al asked.

"Sure. How much?"

"Now, don't go making it sound like that," Big Al said, offended.

"Sorry."

"Yo man Delmár is clean as a whistle. He's so slick ain't nothin' sticking to him. He don't gamble, he don't drink, and everybody, including the president of Mountain Way Country Club, thinks he hung the moon. The feds can watch him from now to eternity, but ain't nothin' gonna stick."

"What about all that talk about him being a radical terrorist lookout?"

"He does have two boys. Muslim converts. They go to the mosque there."

I was getting tired of the terrorist narrative. "Well, that doesn't implicate them in a terrorist outfit, does it? And what about the hired guns the old man told me about? And the hit on one well-known surgeon?"

Big Al sucked in a breath. "Don't know. Just talk. No evidence."

We were both silent for a moment; then Big Al said, "You remember Mick McCrory? Used to work at the Universal Club."

"Yeah." I remembered Mick. Not him per se, but I knew of him. He was one of the managers during the time the Universal Club settled a suit with the government for somewhere in the range of seven figures. He went to work for another country club after that.

"He's playing with the big boys now and got big money," Big Al said.

Good for him, I thought but didn't offer any comment.

"He's one of the managers of Mountain Way Country Club. He and his wife live between there and San Miguel. He's putting together a team for an international croquet tournament in Cuba in a couple of days." He put a facetious snort on the word "international."

I waited. Big Al went on. "Some of those uppity folk from Mountain Way Country Club gonna be playin' in it, I hear."

"So what?"

Exasperated, he replied, "You're a doctor! Put some of that schoolin' to work. Simone hung around with those croquet-playing fools."

"OK, OK."

"Lloyd's been putting in some pro bono work for you; must be his Christian upbringing."

I was grateful to Lloyd for his act of charity.

"There'll be four hundred teams of two. Lloyd's saying that eight from Highlands are registered. Three are actually from Atlanta but have second homes in Highlands. Two of 'em's retired—no, three. One's a retired doctor from Hendersonville. Four of 'em live in Highlands full time. Two are Cashiers Country Club members, one Loblolly Pines Country Club, and one Mountain Way Country Club."

"Will Mick be there or Delmár?" I asked.

"Well, they ain't registered to play or anything, but they might be."

"Thanks, Big Al."

"Sure thing."

Monique was still talking on her phone. I stood in the middle of my living room, thinking on Big Al's words. He was right; Simone did hang around those fools. She could've met one of them at a tournament. Simone, looking for a way out of her marriage to Cooter, would have thrown herself on someone who could maintain her lifestyle. The hound dog in me was picking up another scent. I could go to the tournament and try to hook up with Mick or even Delmár, and maybe they would spill the beans about Simone's mystery lover.

"Monique!" I called back to the bedroom.

"Yes?" she answered.

"I think I'm going to Cuba. Will you take care of MeMoe for me?" I punched in my travel agent's number.

Monique limped to the living room. "What's in Cuba?"

"The croquet masters!"

Two days later, as luck would have it, I was bound for Havana. The US government had recently eased travel bans to Cuba. My travel agent had explained that a visa would be required, which might take up to three weeks and would be possible only if I was with a registered tour group. Three weeks would have been way too late. The tournament would have been over by then. Besides, I had to be back to work in a few days. June first landed on a Saturday, and I had to be back in the office Tuesday afternoon to see patients. I pouted and whined my discontent to the travel agent, reminding her that nothing was impossible. She said she would see what she could do, and what she did was get an expedited visa on medical privilege and put me on a flight to the Caymans, where I could catch a flight to Havana.

30

The Cayman Islands were much as I remembered: a sleepy, isolated place at peace with the rest of the world. As the cab drove me along the beach, we slowly passed a cemetery. I noticed the name Boudin marked on all the graves, and as we passed mailboxes, again all of them said Boudin.

"Hey, man," I asked the cabby, "what's with the name Boudin? Everybody has the same name."

"Is that a problem?" the cabby asked.

"No, but are there people with other names here?"

"Well, there's Smith. They're the second-largest family on the islands."

Enough said, I thought, grabbing my duffel bag and paying the man in cash as he pulled to the curb.

My room at the hotel was large and grand, as expected. When I checked with the concierge about my flight to Havana, he had me fill out some paper work and then announced that I was all set for the following day. The rest of the day was spent strolling along the beautiful seven-mile beach. Unfortunately, a visit to Stingray City and sailing, two of my favorite pastimes here, were out of the question. Wolfing down a cheeseburger and a chef's salad helped me get over it and bolstered my confidence in going into Cuba.

The flight from the Caymans to Havana took forty minutes. Seeing that I was from the United States and all, you would have thought customs would be difficult and onerous, but it was no problem for me at all. For the poor Cubans returning home, it was a different story. They had to declare every television, mattress, or sausage they brought back into the country. Outside the terminal, a light-blue '55 Chevy convertible stood at the curb with a cabby in wait. I threw my duffel bag into the back seat and hopped in beside it, thinking, How cool is this!

The cabby looked back at me and smiled a big Cuban welcome and then said, "Amigo, do you mind giving me a push? My starter is broken."

"Sure." Feeling a bit foolish, I hopped back out and went to the rear of the vehicle. "Put it in neutral."

He complied, probably having done this a thousand times before.

As I heaved and pushed, the heavy vehicle began to roll, slowly at first and then faster and faster. Luckily, we were on a downslope. "Pop the clutch!" I called to him just as he thought to do that himself. The engine started, and exhaust enveloped me. He stopped the car a few yards away, and I jogged to where he had pulled to the curb.

"Thank you! Yes!" he said happily. "Where to, amigo?"

"Hotel Internacionale," I replied, jumping into the back seat again.

"Good choice!" he continued, smiling, and turned the radio to something mariachi.

Except for that hiccup, the ride was good, the afternoon fine. My travel agent had made reservations for me at the old Hotel Internacionale, the only five-star accommodation far and wide in Havana. Since that was where the croquet tournament was being held, as expected, the hotel was entirely booked except for one suite, which was only seven hundred bucks a night. The thing about the five-star deal was that their idea of five-star and my idea never did quite agree. The lobby, of course, was magnificent, the architecture a reminder of Havana's glory days, but my suite was small, not four rooms as advertised but two with an extra bathroom and what might have once been a kitchenette. It was light on air conditioning, and the smell of cigar hung heavy on the upholstery. The last occupant must not have known that he could bring cigars back to the United States and smoked the whole box before he left. The tap water was lukewarm and suspect, and there was a sign posted on the wall not to flush toilet paper or feminine products down the commode but rather to place the *waste* into a sack and then into a little basket and place another sack on top. Making a mental note to remember the process of what went where in the john, I opened the window to the let the place air out, checked the bed thoroughly for bedbugs, and then rode down to the lobby in a very noisy elevator.

A sign announced, "World Croquet Tournament Registration," but there was no one at the front desk and no one else from the world in the lobby. It was early evening. Anywhere else, the lobby would have been teeming. My debonair, double-oh-seven alter ego took over at this point and persuaded me to take the opportunity to go around the desk and key Mick McCrory's name into the computer under the field "guest name." Nothing came up. Then I tried Delmár but didn't know his last name. There was no hit on his first name. Before I had a chance to type in Highlands, North Carolina, under place of residence, footsteps from the hall beyond sounded, and I quickly slipped back around to the guest side of the desk and casually walked down the hall toward the bar. The Castro brothers, Putin, some Cuban baseball players, and other international celebrities greeted me from their wall mounts on my journey; a picture of Batista was noticeably missing. There were a few patrons gathered around the bar, but otherwise it was pretty quiet, considering it was the night before the big *international* croquet event.

My moseying took me out of doors, where poles and wickets had been set up on a large field. Whether this was considered a tournament or a match really didn't matter much to me, because my sole purpose here was to track down a croquet-playing fool from Highlands, possibly get him or her drunk, and then question the said person about Simone. Beyond that, my plans were a bit hazy. I wandered back into the hotel and down the long hall past the bar, tipping my baseball cap to Mickey Mantle on the way. A couple of women in ball gowns appeared from one of the rooms. A cocktail party was going on behind closed doors, and I considered mingling but then thought better of it, since I was still in my wrinkled trousers. Feigning interest in the photos on the wall to eavesdrop on the two women's conversation was much more fun anyway. They were checking me out; I could tell.

The ladies were definitely Dixie, but their chatter turned out to be nonsensical stuff about hair and where they had gotten their pedicures done. Bored, I studied the photograph of Brezhnev. He looked positively dead in the picture, especially his eyes. He had dead eyes. Maybe this was a photograph of his wax figure, or maybe he just looked like that. Next to him was a signed picture of an actress from the fifties, who was the spitting image of Mable, my parents' housekeeper when I was growing up. Unlike Brezhnev, her eyes shined with life across the ages. It wasn't Mable in the picture, of course, but the woman in the photo reminded me of her and of the last time I had seen her or thought I had. It was at a funeral home in Orange Mound, a dilapidated, gang-ridden area dead smack in the middle of Memphis. She was all laid out pretty in a pine casket in her Sunday best. Her obituary had been in the paper the day before. As is customary for me, I had ordered a huge spray for Mable and pressed Marvel, a friend of mine from Ernestine and Hazel's Bar, to go with me to her wake. He balked at the idea at first. Marvel was one of the best pool players this side of the Mississippi and an old hustler for the most part; he could sucker anyone into a game and end up taking all his money. But even he wouldn't venture into the Orange Mound neighborhood.

"Terry, you don't wanna be goin' down there," he told me emphatically. "That's a badass area. The Dark Night Disciples patrol there."

But I insisted I had to pay my respects to Mable.

"Uh-uh, no, you don't neither," he argued back.

But I whined, "My Mable died, and I gotta see her!"

He crossed his arms and shook his head, so I held out the contents of my wallet to him, bribing him with the ten dollars I had in there. Marvel knew he was being suckered but grabbed the bill anyway. "I guess for ten bucks I can go to heaven with you, but don't you go making eye contact with nobody," he warned me.

We were both wearing baseball caps when we walked up to the funeral-home door, which was not really fitting for the occasion, and the old usher at the door reminded us of this loudly. Only after we complied with removing them did he allow us into the sanctuary. I signed the guest book. Mine was the only signature. Marvel felt bad about this and signed even though he didn't know Mable. It was just the two of us in the room with her. The casket was open. My spray of yellow and white roses was the only one. We took a seat in the front pew. I wondered where all her mourners were and was so sad as I sat there and stared at the corpse of the woman who had taken such good care of me as a child while my mother was passed out in bed. She was small and slight of stature, not really how I remembered her. Of course, it had been years and years since we had seen each other.

I whispered to Marvel, "I don't remember her being this thin."

He was uninterested and incessantly checking his watch and the door. "Well, death'll do that to a person" was his response.

I went up to her casket to get a closer look. "Marvel?"

"What?"

"This ain't my Mable."

His eyes got big. "Say what?"

"This is some other woman; they got the wrong person in Mable's casket!"

Marvel jumped up, grabbed my arm, and pulled me to the door. "Then why you still be standing there? Let's get the hell outta here."

I took one last look at the imposter and my two-hundred-dollar floral arrangement, and we sprinted down the aisle and out to the parking lot. When we were safe in the car, I lamented, "That wasn't my Mable. I don't know who it was, but it wasn't my Mable."

Marvel waved me off. "I don't wanna hear nothin' 'bout it! Just go. Shoot, get myself beat up or killed for some old woman you didn't even know, and for what? A measly ten bucks! Hope we didn't pick up no haint in that place—be following us 'round there like some kinda polter...ghost." Marvel proceeded to take out his teeth and inspect them before shoving them back into his mouth. His teeth and his boots were his most prized possessions. We both slumped low in the vehicle until we were safe in Midtown again.

As it turned out, I had read the obituary wrong. The woman in the casket was not my Mable. We had gotten out of that neighborhood unscathed, but it occurred to me that I was again putting myself in harm's way, and for what? Simone was just an acquaintance, and except for the one little adventure, Monique was a total stranger. I was just beginning to understand the saying, "The road to hell is paved with good intentions." The two southern belles returned to their party, so I retreated to my hot, humid room with a lukewarm slice of pizza purchased from the hotel restaurant.

31

I awoke to a bright, sunny day, not having slept much because of the heat. I showered in tepid water, which was fine by me, shaved, and dressed casually. Breakfast was included in the price and was being served in a dining room off the lobby. The Cuban coffee was rich and stout, but the only safe thing to eat was Rice Krispies topped with bottled water. Fearful of Montezuma's revenge and with all the toilet-paper regulations, I passed on the milk. If you've never tried Rice Krispies with water, it's not all that bad after the first two bites. There was some meat on the buffet, which looked like pork sausage, though there were no guarantees that was what it was, because a rotund woman ahead of me in the line snatched every last one, stabbing them three at a time onto her fork and placing them on her plate. She absconded with a mountain of food to the elevator. Two sweet rolls remained on the lonely buffet. Evidently, the horde of people in this hotel had come by earlier for breakfast.

Fortified by calories, carbs, and caffeine, I went to the croquet area, which was neatly roped off. There were a lot of people, and everyone was dressed up Gatsby style in white dress shirts, long white pants or Bermuda shorts, and white socks and shoes—everyone except me. Having forgotten about the all-white rule, I was dressed in khaki shorts, a Hawaiian shirt, and sandals—a parrot in a sea of gulls. So as not to stick out, I wandered over to the spectator stands, where a few other patrons who had forgotten about the rule sat. Within the hour, more than a thousand people had gathered around the four croquet courts and were warming up and hitting balls. How on earth could anyone find anyone among all these folks dressed in white?

There is no Internet in Cuba and—guess what?—no cell-phone reception either. All international calls had to be made through the concierge with the help of a little extra cash. We, the concierge and I, placed a call to Big Al, at two dollars a minute billed to my room, not that I was keeping count or anything. Thankfully, Big Al answered.

"Hey, Big Al; it's me, Terry, calling from Cuba. Can you give me those names of the people from Highlands who are here at this croquet tournament?"

"You're in Cuba?"

"Yes, I am, thanks to your information."

"Lloyd's the one who has that information. I'll have him give you a call. So you're really in Cuba, Doc?"

"Yes, but I can't get cell-phone reception here. I'll call Lloyd. I have his number."

"Doc, be careful that someone don't recognize you," Big Al reminded me.

"Right."

The concierge then dialed Lloyd's number, and he picked up on the second ring. I quickly brought him up to speed, but it appeared that Big Al or someone else had already filled him in. I guess I also had Lloyd to thank for the anonymous call to Detective Reardon. He told me that nine, not eight, teams from the Highlands area were going to be there, but the country club would only give up six names. The other three were God knows who. I quickly scribbled the names on a napkin, which didn't include the names Delmár or Mick. Lloyd didn't know much about the players, except that most were traveling with their wives or possibly their mistresses. I thanked him for everything and hung up.

Now all that was left to do was find these people, which was easier said than done. Maybe they would be wearing name tags. At most conventions, people openly exhibit their names. Back on the field, I scrutinized the crowd. Lucky for me they were wearing name tags, but the odds of locating six from these thousand weren't that good. Drifting from court to court, I noticed that the United States had a large contingent of participants.

As balls entered the wickets and winners were declared here and there, indicated by hushed golf claps, it became readily apparent that most players were middle aged or older. Croquet evidently requires some dexterity but no athletic ability, strength, or endurance—no comparison to the game we used to play back in college with croquet mallets and wickets. That took a lot more energy; I'm not sure about the dexterity part, though, because we were fully intoxicated and on bicycles. You can say the game was a cross between croquet and equestrian polo, minus the equine part, of course. Goals were almost impossible, and the first person to get the ball through three wickets was the winner. Mostly we ended up wrecking our bikes and sometimes our bodies, but, hey, it sure beat the hell out of this lame-ass game.

Eventually the referees called a break, and groups began to assemble, thankfully by nationality. As unobtrusively as possible, I meandered from group to group until I heard American being spoken. There were about two to three hundred in this particular congregation. Casually I strolled through the crowd, narrowing down the field according to accent. Pinpointing the southerners was quite easy. All in all, there were about sixty. Finding six from Highlands wouldn't be that hard, one would think, but the many names I checked before the crowd dispersed didn't match any of the names on my napkin. The greatest knowledge gained from my spying was that the heavy favorite in this tournament was an Italian team from Lecce.

For the afternoon, my strategy changed. I decided to stand by the scorekeepers for the American team and peek over their shoulders at the names on the scorecards. There were so many teams, and the scorekeepers, those ornery bastards, caught on to me quickly and covered the names quite efficiently after that. By the end of the afternoon, it was apparent that this had been an enormous waste of time and money. Discouraged, I went back up to my too-hot room to sulk and watch reality television à la Cuba, which was an even greater waste of time, because I couldn't understand one word.

As evening set in, music from outside drew me downstairs. Festivities were underway on the patio with a reggae band and a magician, so I joined them, adamant about salvaging some of my time in Cuba. The black beans and rice, bread, and pork went a long way in helping me get out of my afternoon funk. Someone told me they were celebrating the anniversary of the Cuban revolution, but if my memory of history served me correctly, that was a lie. Raoul Castro said otherwise, however, and gave a two-hour speech on television. Who was I to disagree? Thank heavens Fidel was now a no-show. Someone told me that he used to give ten- and eleven-hour speeches on Revolution Day.

There were some Americans floating around in the crowd, but they weren't wearing name tags. One couple sounded as if they might be from the South, and a guy from Des Moines was droning on and on about going out to Ernest Hemingway's place in the morning. He adored Hemingway and the six-toed cats he'd kept. When I suggested joining him and exploiting his cab ride, he backed off and wandered away to obsess about Hemingway with someone else.

Since I do not drink and was afraid to eat the ice cream, I was off to bed early, locking the door to my suite behind me and securely fastening the chain. Sleep came without effort, probably because of the night before, but a full night's rest was not in the stars. Sometime after midnight the door to my suite burst wide open, the chain not putting up much of a fight. Two strong men grabbed me and threw me out of bed and onto the floor, and before I even had a chance to react, my feet were bound together. Stunned, I flailed and punched into the air, until one of them grabbed both my hands and held them against something hard.

Pow pow—two quick shots rang out, and I felt sharp pains in both hands that coursed up my arms. I shrieked, which resulted in the smaller of the two men stuffing one of my dirty socks into my mouth.

In the dim light of the room, I could see that my attackers were wearing masks. "Go home, gringo. This is the day of our revolution!" the larger of the two said in a heavy Spanish accent. With that they left without so much as touching my wallet.

I looked down at my hands. They were nailed to a board! I don't remember ever having experienced so much pain in my entire life. When they were out of earshot, I struggled to my feet, levering my body against the bedpost. Shuffling inch by inch, I made it to the broken door and out to the elevator. No one was in the hall. They probably heard the commotion but decided it was too dangerous to get involved. I punched the elevator button with my elbow. The door slid open. A middle-aged woman studying her shoes screamed when she looked up. I toddled into the elevator, and the door shut before she could run out. Too bad for her, I was wearing my boxers—some nights it's commando. The woman asked me something in Spanish. I answered by spitting out my dirty sock.

When the elevator doors opened to the lobby, she ran out, screaming, "*Ayuda! Ayuda!*"

I shuffled on out and fell to the floor just as a security officer arrived, frantically hollering to the front-desk clerk. "*Policia! Ambulancia—ahora!*"

He untied the ropes that tethered my ankles, and the front-desk clerk wrapped a blanket around me as I sat on the floor, stunned and bleeding. The woman from the elevator was gone.

An old, beat-up white van with large red letters painted on one side that I assumed was the ambulance took me to a medical facility not far away. With my hands still stuck to the board, they carted my stunned self on a pre–World War II gurney into a sparse examination room. I felt a bit like a sow on a spit, and worry about the damage this may have done to my hands and whether I would ever be able to do surgery again plowed through my brain. A pleasant-looking older gentleman arrived and explained in broken English that he was a doctor but, unfortunately, not a surgeon, whatever the hell that was supposed to mean. Whether the good man held a degree in medicine, philosophy, or shamanism was neither here nor there for me at the moment.

"Well, can you at least pull this board off?" I asked him, holding out my boarded hands.

Just then, an English-speaking nurse entered the room.

"Oh my!" she exclaimed, her brown eyes the size of half dollars.

"Can someone help me, please?"

"How did this happen?" she asked, looking at the doctor.

He shrugged.

"Please, will someone just take the board off? I'm an orthopedic surgeon in the United States, and the longer I remain nailed to this board, the more damage can be done to my hands!"

The heads of the nails were dorsally up against my carpal bones, third on the left hand and the fourth on the right hand. In thinking it through, I could see that these were finishing nails with no heads to speak of, and they could probably be pulled all the way through the hand. The not-surgeon said that *el hospital* didn't have any X-ray equipment, so he couldn't determine whether the nails had gone through bone. I didn't think they had, but it couldn't have smarted any worse. The *doctoro* then ordered the nurse to draw up some bupivacaine. She returned with a bottle of disinfectant and a really large needle and syringe that looked as if it might have seen better days. She disinfected my hands, and Dr. Carlos, as his name tag indicated, injected the anesthetic on the right side. Slowly the pain in that hand abated. It was fairly numb in that area but not deep, so I asked him to inject through the nail hole into my hand on the dorsum of my third and fourth fingers. Stingily he obeyed, probably realizing that my degree outranked his. My hand swelled but was totally dead.

Suddenly the curtain was swiped to the side, and a suit walked in, saying something feverishly to the doctor in Spanish.

Dr. Carlos turned to me and said apologetically, "I'm sorry. I have to leave you. My nurse will take good care of you." Then the two men were gone, and I was left with the young, totally inexperienced nurse.

I asked, "What's your name, sweetheart?"

"Yolanda," she replied, her big brown eyes large with worry about the heavy responsibility that had been foisted on her.

"Orlando or Yolanda?"

She smiled shyly. "Yolanda."

"Yolanda, you're going to have to buck up and bite the bullet and do as I say, OK?"

She looked confused.

"I want you to help get my hands off this board."

She shook her head. "No, no, no, Dr. Carlos will be back soon."

"Not soon enough! I'm a doctor, so it's OK. Just hold the board. I'll pull."

I can only describe her expression as one of sheer dread, but she held both ends of the two-by-four steady as I pulled my right hand back. There was no pain because of the local, but it was strange seeing the nail disappear under my metacarpal. Yolanda paled as the nail passed through and my hand parted from the board. The suit walked back into the examination room without Dr. Carlos just as my hand pulled free, and he fainted flat out. Someone in the hall ran to his aid. Even though I'm an orthopedic surgeon, former army officer, and former college football player, I did not feel so well either—something about seeing your own blood and all. Yolanda placed a big wad of gauze on the open wound and taped it in place for the time being.

"One down and one to go, Yolanda," I said to the bewildered nurse. "Here, inject right here, over the fourth metacarpal—now under, all around. Now inject down into the hole just like Dr. Carlos did."

Reluctantly, she complied.

"Hold that board, just like before."

I pulled my left hand back evenly but with force, and the nail slid out from my palm, a slight ripping noise filling the air. Totally flustered, Yolanda upset the instrumentation tray with the freed two-by-four, and medical utensils went flying all over the floor. Ignoring the mess, she reached for the gauze and tightly wrapped my left hand.

Fortunately, I had brought antibiotics with me in case Montezuma decided to seek his revenge on me, and they would work fine for this situation as well. But all I had for pain was acetaminophen, and I knew once the feeling came back, this was going to hurt like hell. Sweet Yolanda left for a couple of minutes and came back with some little white pills in hand.

"For pain," she said in her precious Spanish accent, "when the injection wears off. Here, let me wrap these for you." She pulled up the gauze and poured what looked like mercurochrome onto the wounds. It poured out through the little holes in my palms. She then redressed my hands with rolls and rolls of new gauze.

When I got back to my hotel room, I popped a gram and a half of cephalexin and five hundred milligrams of ampicillin and a couple of the little white pills from Nurse Yolanda, which was no easy feat with my hands bandaged to the size of footballs, but I was too exhausted to care and fell into bed.

At daybreak there was a knock on my door. My hands throbbed underneath the dressing, and I considered taking more of Yolanda's drugs, although it had only been a couple of hours since my last dose. I made my way out of bed and looked through the peephole, expecting more of the same trouble as the night before, but it was the hotel manager. I opened the door just a slit.

"Sir, it has been recommended by the *hospitale* and *policiá* here that you immediately return to your country for medical care."

I squinted against the light. "Immediately" wasn't soon enough for me.

"There is an Air Aruba flight at nine a.m. to Cayman. From there you can fly to Miami. I will drive you to the *aeroporto* myself. Hotel Internacionale is very sorry for this incident. We have never had this kind of brutality happen before."

I doubted that but said, "I can be ready in about fifteen minutes."

"Very good, sir. Just come to the lobby. I will be waiting at the front desk."

I count myself among the lucky souls that the night manager was just who he said he was and didn't try to murder me en route to the *aeroporto*. Security was no problem, and at 9:05 a.m. Air Aruba with my lucky soul onboard lifted off. My sleuthing days in Cuba ended as I watched the country disappear beneath the wing.

Back on American soil, my bandaged, boxer-sized hands made quite a stir at the Miami airport, and on the plane to Atlanta and then to Memphis, there were a lot of annoying questions, to which my answer was "A construction accident." In Miami, I called Nurse Johnnie at home and told her to get me in ASAP to see one of my partners, a hand specialist, and to meet me at the airport if she would be so kind. As always, she was, and she didn't ask questions. Johnnie knew that in my own time, the whole story would be revealed. Once I was back safe in my condo, I redressed my hands and downed some more pain meds.

32

J immy Camaloni, the hand specialist and my partner at the Camp Clinic, greeted me in the patient area early Monday morning.

"What happened to you?" he asked.

"I had a run-in with a nail gun."

"Really?" He raised his eyebrows and smiled.

"Really."

He had never known me to be a nail-gun toting, hammer-swinging, tool-belt sort of guy, so this had to be some kind of joke. His smiled widened, his face primed for the punch line. When he realized none was forthcoming, he led me into the examination room and unwrapped the gauze, never pursuing the when, where, and why of the matter. Instead he picked up the phone and called our radiology department. "We're gonna need an X-ray and an MRI to see what's damaged," he said while he was waiting for someone to pick up the line. As I am a partner, radiology had no problem working me right in, and after studying the images and testing my hand function, Jimmy confirmed that there were no broken bones, but it looked as if two extensor tendons were injured, one to the third finger on the left hand and one to the fourth on the right hand. In addition, it was possible I'd lost the ring-finger sublimis tendon on the right hand, which is one of the two tendons that flexes the fourth finger. Since the injury was from a nail gun, he worried most about infection but thought that there wouldn't be major hand disability. My hands were splinted in neutral, and Nurse Johnnie gave me a tetanus shot. It didn't need saying that antibiotics had to be continued for a long time.

Back in my own office, I assessed my Cuban crisis. To say I was frightened would be putting it mildly. Why hadn't they just killed me? I refused to accept it as coincidence that someone would nail my hands to a board without a motive. There was no doubt in my mind that somebody had recognized me and noticed my snooping. Maybe they thought murder would create an international incident. My phone rang. I fumbled with it and used the thumb of my right hand to hit speaker. Lloyd was on the other end. He now knew the identities of the other three croquet players from Highlands, two of whom were on up there in age, as were their teammate wives, and one who was from San Miguel. How any of this information would help me now was anybody's guess. Since I was back from Cuba and it was too late for all that, I told him not to bother with giving me the names. After we disconnected, I walked over to the CEO's office and stuck my head in the door.

"Hey, Hap," I said.

Startled, he looked up from his phone. When he saw me, he waved me in.

I held up my bandaged hands.

"What on earth happened to you?"

"Nail gun," I answered without elaborating. "I don't think I can get back to work this week. Jimmy Camaloni said about a month."

"I see." He sat back in his leather chair. "Will this affect your surgical dexterity?"

"I don't think so. I can probably see patients, just not do surgery right now."

He shook his head. "I think you should give this time to heal and then come back full duty. That's my recommendation, Terry."

I thanked him and headed back to my office, where a stack of paper work waited. The remainder of my day was spent dictating what my assistant needed to do with each piece of paper.

The rest of the days came and went as I whiled away the time watching mind-numbing television. Monique and Abigail worked on physical therapy and seemed to be getting closer by the minute while I was being shoved to the outside of our threesome. Trying to play the sympathy card on Abigail only brought on an exaggerated eye roll from her. In light of the injuries Monique had sustained, my two little nail holes didn't garner much attention. Other than that, my days consisted of me explaining to MeMoe, the only other living being on the planet who seemed to give a damn, my reasons for not wanting to go out of doors. When nature couldn't wait and we had to venture outside, we kept close to the condo. Don't think for a minute that I was complacent and wasn't looking over my shoulder constantly. According to my imagination, shadows and enemies lurked in every corner. Being attacked when you sleep will do that to a person. My hands were mending fine, but my psyche was a mess. I obsessed about being targeted and lived with the expectation of a silver bullet tearing my guts out.

The only solace I found during that time was in my painting, the provisions for which were the only things that coaxed me from the safety of my condo. I contemplated doing a nude of Abigail or Monique or both, but they never seemed to have time for me, always coming up with some kind of flimsy excuse or somewhere else to be. It was just as well, I guess, because with my hand injuries, only my first fingers and thumbs worked and only for a little at a time before the cramping would start.

Art was something I got into well after my residency time, but I'd always doodled around before then. My desk calendar is full of fanciful art. Johnnie always keeps these, telling me that I'll be famous one day and she'll be rich. I doubt that, but one can always dream. Winston Churchill, who took up painting after he retired, pointed out that even when you lose the ability to physically move about, you can always paint. I agree. Even with my hands splinted, it was still possible for me to paint, although only in short intervals. I also read that Mr. Churchill was nervous when he first started to paint, and so was I.

Maybe it's because we tend to overthink things, but he said that if you wait to take lessons and become good at it before taking it seriously, you would surely die before producing a beautiful work of art. So that was what I did—I picked up a brush and started painting. Basically, I'm a self-taught folk artist with no talent, really, but I've managed to show and sell some of my art. Confidentially, though, I believe the people who buy my paintings are really just being kind. It doesn't matter. I love to paint just for the sake of it. When I first started out, I used watercolors exclusively, but they're notoriously unforgiving, so I switched to acrylics. The great southern painter Walter Anderson painted exclusively with watercolors. I've read that he was quite the character. He died of mental illness and alcohol abuse in the sixties, but legend has it that he would load his rowboat up in Ocean Springs, Mississippi, full of quarts of bourbon and row for miles out into the gulf to Horn Island, a small, eight-mile-long, one-mile-wide island, where he would paint anything he could find. He would also drink. When his bourbon supply ran out, he would head back to Ocean Springs for a refill and then return to his art. A mural he painted for Ocean Springs, I've been told, is worth $30 million. It's about half the size of a football field.

Since I had oodles of time on my hands, I considered following in Walter Anderson's footsteps—not the drinking part but going and painting wildlife on Horn Island. At least there I could concentrate on my art undisturbed by dark thoughts of death. MeMoe seemed excited about the prospect, so we packed a duffel with my art supplies, MeMoe's toys, and bug spray, and off we went. I told the girls where I was going. They didn't seem to mind. Abigail even thought it was a wonderful idea and helped me carry my bags to the Explorer. Was it my imagination, or were they trying to get rid of me?

Exactly 438 miles later, MeMoe and I arrived in Biloxi and spent the night in one the few dog-friendly hotels, although MeMoe's stay cost more than mine. We ate at Doe's Steakhouse—filet mignon, MeMoe's favorite. He didn't get any gumbo for fear of gastrointestinal issues that might make the rest of the trip unpleasant for the both of us.

The following morning gale-force winds greeted us, so we had to hang around Biloxi for the day, visiting all they had to offer. Since it was the middle of the week, tourists, especially at the old lighthouse, were sparse. In fact, MeMoe and I pretty much made up their afternoon crowd. At the lighthouse pier, a souped-up dark-blue speedboat sat idling near the shore. A young, strong black man sat at the helm, apparently waiting on someone. He darkly eyed MeMoe and me as we made our way to the end of the pier, where a gentleman wearing a light-colored linen suit stood overlooking the gulf. At first I didn't think much about the man in the speedboat, but then something began to tickle my amygdala. Hadn't Monique described her attacker as a young, strong African American man? I realized then that we might be in danger but decided to continue to the end of the pier toward the gentleman, a witness, in case the man in the boat was an assassin. I looked over my shoulder to make sure he wasn't pursuing us, because if he was, my plan was to scream for help at the top of my lungs and put some of my running skills to use. Not much of a plan, I know; that was why sweat broke out under my armpits and across the back of my neck. MeMoe, brave and undeterred, marched on with purpose, pulling me behind. When we reached the end of the dock, the man standing there turned to look our way. He was a white man, a little shorter than me, wearing a fashionable straw hat to match his suit and dark reflective sunglasses that hid the upper half of his face. His age was undeterminable, but from the lower half of his face, I would have thought him to be around thirty.

"Nice day, but windy," he said in a friendly tone, smiling and chewing gum at the same time.

I looked back at the boat, which hadn't moved an iota. Starting to feel a little better, I returned the man's smile and answered, "Sure is."

MeMoe whimpered and hid behind my legs.

The man ignored him. "We were out for a ride," he said, pointing to the boat, "but I think we're gonna call it a day. Just too dangerous." The swells were slamming hard against the wooden posts of the dock.

"I don't blame you."

He peered down at MeMoe and grinned, looking every bit the part of the Cheshire cat. "Cute dog."

MeMoe hunkered low, half growling, half whimpering, letting me know of his prejudice.

Fully respecting his opinion about the man, I didn't tell MeMoe to behave. "Thanks," I said blandly, drawing myself up to my full six-foot-two-inch height.

"Well, I guess I'll be moseying. You have a great day. Life's too short, you know?" said the Cheshire cat.

"Yeah, you too," I replied as he walked back toward the shore and hopped down into the boat. The engine roared to life, and within seconds they were speeding eastward.

MeMoe didn't like the man one bit, and neither did I, but then again we were both on high alert since finding out there was a price on my head.

Luckily the wind subsided that evening, and we left for Horn Island the following morning. We were on a twenty-eight-foot Boston whaler, seaworthy no doubt, but I wore a life preserver, and so did MeMoe. Once out of the lagoon and the Mississippi Sound into the gulf, the waves were still over four feet high, and the wind picked up dramatically again. MeMoe did not dig this. Horn Island is twelve miles out into the gulf, and Captain John was heading straight into waves that were crashing unmercifully into the boat and splashing up onto the deck. It was probably good thinking on my part not to give MeMoe any of my gumbo, because it would've most likely made a reappearance.

When we arrived at Horn Island, we were totally alone there, except for the Coast Guard. It's a desolate place that's been heavily scarred by hurricanes. There were no signs of artists here, as I'd imagined—no signs of anyone. Maybe some animals, but they weren't immediately apparent either. Captain John was able to pull up to the pier, but despite this fantasy I had about staying there overnight and producing this wonderful painting, seeing it all up close, I felt oddly ambivalent and uninspired about the whole thing, and MeMoe was scared to death, especially since our encounter with the man in the speedboat. Being all alone and unprotected on an island in the middle of the ocean didn't sound like such a hot idea anymore. Instead of getting out, I had Captain John cruise up and down Horn Island so at least I could get my money's worth of scenery and wildlife before we headed back to Biloxi. Walter Anderson had written that he navigated these waters with his small boat and did so by sailing or rowing. After seeing the swells, one has to wonder how much Anderson's bourbon played into his story, but we'll never know. I thanked Captain John, and we headed back to Memphis, glad to be able to cross that off our bucket list. Since that time, I've had no desire to see Horn Island again, and neither has MeMoe. The whole boat thing traumatized him, and he wasn't the same until we got back to the condo and had a good night's sleep.

33

We had been gone a little over three days, MeMoe and I, but we were both restless. With nothing to do, my mind was blowing things out of proportion, and I spent many hours the following day anxiously pacing. By this point, I wasn't as concerned about who had killed Simone or even who had attacked Monique but was extremely concerned about my own safety and was ticked off because there was someone out there who was forcing me to live in fear. I really couldn't stand for that, you know?

"MeMoe, you wanna go for a walk out at Shelby Farms?" I asked in the early afternoon after having watched four episodes of Dr. Phil, back to back, an exhausting marathon to nowhere.

MeMoe jumped off my recliner and bounced around on his hind legs, glad that I was finally graduating from my pity party. Without telling the girls where we were going or when we would be back, sincerely doubting they cared, the two of us headed out, purposely not looking left or right or behind us as we got into the Explorer. I do have to admit to flinching when the door slammed and once when the car started, momentarily convinced that someone had rigged a bomb. I also checked to make sure the brakes were working OK as we drove north to Poplar. They were, and the car didn't explode, and so far no one had taken a shot at me, which was a good thing; otherwise, my story may have gone untold. Once in heavy traffic out on Poplar, my tensions eased, and I tuned the radio to easy listening, jamming to the beat all the way to the Walnut Grove exit and straight out until we hit Shelby Farms. For those of you who are unfamiliar with the Memphis area, Shelby Farms is a huge, almost five-thousand-square-acre park with miles of walking and biking trails. One of the big attractions there is the bison herd. We weren't going to see the bison; we were headed to the dog park, where MeMoe could run and play without a leash, which I felt was befitting of any self-respecting, intelligent, charismatic, four-legged best friend.

We parked in the lot closest to the dog park, where a couple of other vehicles sat baking in the afternoon sun. MeMoe, in a leaping bound, jumped from the passenger seat onto my lap and was out the door before my foot had a chance to touch the asphalt. Fortunately, he couldn't go far, since he was still wearing his leash. A large, handsome Dalmatian was utilizing the field in front of the pond, catching high-flying Frisbees that his muscled, shirtless owner was tossing to him. We jogged to the other side to avoid any inferiority complex MeMoe might develop because of his small size. Winded from the short run, I unleashed him and sat near the pond, my back against a large oak. He ran to the pond's edge and sniffed at the water but didn't jump in. It was a hot and muggy day, and the piss-warm water was unlikely to bring him any relief anyhow. Watching MeMoe bark and show a knot of polliwogs swimming near the edge of the pond who was boss, I settled into a cesspool of ugly thoughts. Not having worked out or jogged since before Cuba, I was pitifully out of shape, probably getting fat too from eating all day and watching the tube. And, for all intents and purposes, I was unemployed. Technically it was considered sick leave, but it all added up to one thing—not making money. And to top it all off, guess who hadn't had any nooky since the infamous ménage à trois incident? Me. And whose fault was that anyway? Well, ultimately Simone's, the careless Jezebel, for getting herself killed.

My right-hand wound twinged, reminding me of the bastard who'd nailed my hands to a board. Who does that? A monster, I guessed.

It had to be someone who wanted me maimed and in pain—but not dead. For what purpose? To scare me? Well, he'd certainly accomplished that. He'd also accomplished something else—getting me out of Cuba in a hurry. He definitely didn't like my snooping around, but in the end I evidently wasn't important enough to kill. Perhaps he knew that I would never be able to figure out his identity. Monique, on the other hand, he wanted dead—not just maimed or frightened but dead. The reason? Simone's killer knew that sooner or later, Monique would figure it all out; maybe she already had and just didn't know it. It was unfortunate for him that his hired gun was a bad shot, because that meant he would have to revisit her murder. What it boiled down to was that Monique would never be safe again with him out there. I thought about her being alone at my condo. Abigail had been there when I left, but what could she do? They were both in danger. Monique did have a gun and knew how to use it, which made me feel a little better. There were really no two ways about this—the son of a bitch had to be tracked down. But how? Slowly a plan began to take shape in my mind.

I stood and wiped off the seat of my shorts. "Come on, MeMoe. Let's go fishing."

His snout came up out of the water, his muzzle dripping but his paws dry. He looked at me quizzically.

"What bait, you ask? Well…Monique."

MeMoe cocked his head to the right, quite alarmed at my good idea.

"She wasn't my first choice, buddy, believe me," I said.

His nose twitched.

"We really don't have any options," I argued. "We have to flush him out. She's never gonna be safe until we take him out." I made a gun of my fingers and mock tested my shot.

MeMoe whimpered nervously. He had never seen me quite like this. With one paw up, he stood panting, his eyes avoiding mine.

I sighed. "I didn't mean actually kill him, buddy. Just get him off the streets and behind bars."

MeMoe sneezed twice at that. He doubted that was what I meant.

"I do too take my Hippocratic oath seriously," I assured him as he reluctantly allowed me to reattach his leash.

34

With a certain degree of trepidation, something I was feeling all the time now, I let myself into the condo, afraid of what might be hiding behind the closed door. All was quiet—too quiet. MeMoe shook himself, his collar jingling, but stiffened when I shushed him.

"Monique?" I called out.

There was no answer.

"Abigail?"

No answer.

MeMoe, not understanding why I could make noise but he wasn't allowed to, began to yip loudly at me.

"Quiet, buddy," I whispered.

He snorted and walked in a little circle. If there was something amiss inside my condo, he sure wasn't picking up on it. I released his leash, and he went straight for his water bowl and then to his recliner. Shutting the front door behind me quietly, I stood listening for sounds of life, remembering that my gun was in my room. Too scared to blindly race to the guest room and play the knight-in-shining-armor bit, I grabbed my signed Cubs baseball bat from the wall and darted across into the kitchen. My plan was to lie in wait until someone emerged from the bedroom to come find me, and then I'd go on offense. Maybe "scared" is too strong a word here. You see, it was because of my nose, which, as I have mentioned, has been broken twice. It happened during a football game against Clemson my sophomore year when I accidently insulted their head coach. All I said was "Hey, Mack! Throw me that ball, will ya?" He gave me a dirty look and kicked it other way, and then I said, "Thanks a lot," realizing too late who he was. Anyway, in the second quarter, their all-American player delivered a blow through my helmet mask, breaking my nose in several places. Then he did it again. My honker hasn't been straight since, which is why I'm a bit overprotective of it and which is why I continued to stand motionless in my kitchen, waiting for something to happen. But nothing did, and no one came out of the bedroom. Seconds and then minutes passed, and by this time, MeMoe was snoring softly in the chair. In my mind this meant that either the girls weren't home, or they were both dead in the guest room. Slowly, my heart racing, I made my move out into the hall, the baseball bat ready to swing. Suddenly the front door flew open behind me! Startled, I yelped, dropping the bat onto the tile floor with a loud clang. A surprised Abigail jumped back two feet into Monique and screamed.

"Terry, you scared the shit out of me! What the hell? Where've you been? Monique and I have been looking all over for you."

"Huh?"

"When you didn't come right back from walking the dog, we thought someone kidnapped you. Your car was gone; you didn't even take your phone or anything. What the hell were you thinking?"

I retrieved the bat and mounted it back on its rack. "Nothing, I guess."

Monique came into the condo wordlessly and headed to the guest room. Her limp had improved by leaps and bounds and was no longer even noticeable.

"I'm so glad you care about where I am," I said sarcastically. "I didn't think you'd notice."

"Really? I can't believe you just said that—to me! You, you of all people, judging me?"

I was silent.

"Look," she said, breathing in deeply to keep her anger in check, "there's a killer out there who killed your friend Simone, tried very hard to kill poor Mona Bell here, and now he's after your ass and maybe mine. We should all try to stay in touch is all I'm saying."

"You're right," I said plainly. Her cozy name for Monique had not escaped my notice, nor had the fact that she'd never bothered to come up with one for me. "Along those lines, I have to talk to you guys about something. Monique?" I called out to the back of the condo.

She stuck her head out the guest-room doorway. "Yes?"

"We have to talk."

She came into the living room, picked up MeMoe, and sat in his recliner, placing him on her lap and gently stroking his soft white fur. He was soaking it all up, he and everyone else in the world—except me. Abigail sat on the far end of the couch, while I paced.

"Look, I can't go on living like this."

Neither spoke.

"I can't live in fear. I refuse to live in fear."

Monique shrugged one shoulder.

"Something has to be done," I said flatly, staring her down. "Simone's killer, your attacker, whoever he is, is lying in wait; I can feel it. I feel it all the way to the marrow in my bones. He's out there, watching, waiting for the right time, the right place…when we think we're safe."

"So what're you saying?"

"We need to find him before he gets to us. It's plain and simple. We gotta flush him out."

"Like how?"

My gaze dropped to the floor.

"Oh" was Monique's response.

Abigail shook her head vehemently when she figured out what I was getting at. "Uh-uh, no way! No way, Terry!"

MeMoe rolled over onto his back, allowing Monique to scratch his belly.

Glancing at Abigail and then zeroing in on Monique, I continued, "The way I see it, we have no choice. None of us—and I mean none of us—will ever be safe again. Sooner or later we'll end up dead, and you, Monique—you'll be the first. You know something, or at least this guy thinks you do. He'll come for you—if not today, then tomorrow or the next day. You'll never be safe until he's off the streets."

Monique was silent as she stroked MeMoe's belly. "I have to admit I've thought the same thing myself," she confessed, looking into Abigail's eyes.

Abigail shook her head again.

Without dropping her gaze, Monique said, "I think Terry is right." Her eyes shifted to me. "Do you have a plan?"

"Not a full plan...yet. I have to make a couple of phone calls and, of course, get the police involved."

Monique nodded. Abigail, holding back tears, got up to leave. "I don't know what to think. This scares the hell out of me."

"Where're you going?" Monique asked, alarmed.

"I've got to go to that PT meeting at the Holiday Inn at six. There'll be a lot of people there. I'll be safe," she promised Monique, with a light kiss on the forehead. She threw a cold glance my way, hiked her purse up onto her shoulder, and left.

When she was gone, Monique and I discussed my nebulous plan. Drawing this guy into a trap wasn't going to be easy. It wasn't as if Monique could just go down on Union and strut her stuff and say, "Here I am; come get me." He was clever. He'd know a trap. We had to do it right. I phoned Lloyd.

"Hey, Terry, what's up?"

"Hey, do you have a few minutes to swing by my place? I need to run something important by you—get your opinion on something."

"Sure. I don't go on duty till eight."

"You got your old job back?"

"Yeah, DA said I didn't use excessive force in restraining the twerp. Only thing now is his mama has a civil suit against me, saying I caused her son to have PTSD because of the violent arrest."

"What about his girlfriend, the one he was beating up on?"

"Yeah, well, they're back together."

"That sucks."

"It doesn't matter. Even if they win in court, I have nothing to lose. I got no money to speak of, no property. What're they gonna take, the clothes off my back? It's a hassle, though. If they only knew how shallow and empty my pockets are, they wouldn't bother."

I felt bad for Lloyd and considered just asking him over for a beer without burdening him with all my stuff.

"So, I'll be there around six?"

"Great! Thanks."

35

As promised, Lloyd rang my doorbell promptly at six o'clock, all showered and shaved. MeMoe ran to greet him as if he were his long-lost friend. Lloyd petted him for a second.

"Come in," I invited, holding the door wide open. His body filled my doorframe. I'm by no measure a small guy, but Lloyd towered over me and was twice as broad. In my younger days, I might have had a larger neck than Lloyd. The size of my neck was the only thing Dallas and Cleveland were interested in when they asked if I wanted to play football for them, that and how fast I could run the hundred-yard dash.

Lloyd followed me into my kitchen.

"Can I get you a beer?"

"No, thanks. I'll be on duty in a couple of hours."

"A Diet Coke?"

"Sure."

I grabbed two from the fridge and handed him one, popping the tab on mine.

"Whoa!" he said. "What the hell happened to your hands?"

I glanced at my now-yellow-and-green hands with two perfectly round holes in each. One was still looking a little angry.

"Some Cuban fuckers nail gunned my hands to a two-by-four."

"Say what?"

"Yeah, they broke down my hotel-room door, tied me up, and nailed my hands to a freaking board!" I reiterated. "They look much better now. A couple of weeks ago, I couldn't hardly hold my paintbrush." I'd been going to physical therapy, and the tendons were scarring over. "I think I'll get full extension back, and I'm working hard on my flexion," I said, trying to sound upbeat.

"Did you talk to the police? What'd they say?"

"Yeah, right. The *policiá* there in Cuba couldn't send me packing fast enough. Had me on a flight outta there faster than a New York minute."

"Did you get a good look at the attackers? Can you describe them?"

"Yeah, one was a big guy, looked like the Lone Ranger, and the other was shorter and looked like Tonto."

Lloyd gave me a baffled look. "Whoa! What?"

"Masks. They were wearing masks."

"Oh. What all did they take?" Lloyd assumed they were robbers.

"That's the strange part. They left my wallet and passport. They took nothing. It was like they just wanted to scare me off."

"That's interesting—I mean, in light of all the other stuff you guys have had going on."

"Here, have a seat," I said to Lloyd, removing some of my clothes from the couch to make room for him. "Sorry about the mess. I thought it was interesting too. It couldn't have just been a coincidence."

"Yeah, you're right." Lloyd took a sip of his Coke.

Just then Monique's bedroom door opened, and she strolled into the living room stark naked except for a large, green-feathered boa wrapped around her body, hiding her most private parts. She was raining feathers. MeMoe thought it was a game and jumped after the stray floaters. Lloyd turned fifty-one shades of red.

"Monique," I said evenly, "this is an old friend of mine, Lloyd. Lloyd, this is Monique."

She held out a hand to Lloyd, which caused a nipple to pop out. He took her hand briefly and then undertook a close study of the top of his soda can. God love her, modesty was not a strong suit.

"What's with all the feathers?" I asked, gently tugging on the boa so that it would hide the nipple again.

"Well," she said matter-of-factly, "I was practicing my new routine for Pony Tails, and when I was checking myself out in the mirror, I saw that the scars are still real noticeable." She turned a full 360 degrees so we could also see.

Lloyd smiled sympathetically, his large fingers working the little tab on his Coke can.

"What do you think about the boa? Does it hide the scars pretty well? 'Cause I can work the boa into my routine."

MeMoe jumped around in circles.

"Works great!" I told her. Lloyd nodded vigorously, taking another long sip.

"Oh, good, thanks!" She turned and swayed back to her room, her gait almost normal. Before then, I had never noticed the python tattooed on her derriere.

"Sorry, where were we?" I asked, turning my attention back to Lloyd.

He cleared his throat. "You were telling me about...um...the Lone Ranger...and...um, the...the...robbers."

"Right, right. Lloyd, I'm just going to come right out and say this—someone is out to kill Monique and me, and we want to set a trap for him before he gets to us."

Lloyd sucked in his breath, put his Coke can on the coffee table, sat back into the cushions, and crossed his arms.

"Well, what do you think?"

"I think it's dangerous."

"Tell me something I don't know."

"How would you go about doing it?" he asked.

"Somehow we would have to get the word out that Monique can identify Simone's killer and that the police are looking for him already. That'll get his ass in gear. Then when he makes a move on her, the cops can take him down."

"That's very, very risky business."

"Think the cops will go for a sting like that?" I asked him.

"Reardon might, but you guys are gonna need round-the-clock protection, and it'll have to be literally invisible; otherwise, the guy'll know it's a trap."

"Can that be done?"

"Sure, as long as it doesn't take forever. You know, funding for the department isn't that great and sure doesn't cover chasing ghosts. If he doesn't surface in a couple of days, you guys'll be on your own again. As I said, risky business."

I nodded.

"I'll get in touch with Reardon. He now knows we're old friends. I'll have him give you a holler." Lloyd checked his watch. "Well, I better get going."

We stood up. "Thanks for coming," I said.

At the door he turned to me and said, "Terry, if this guy's gunning for you or Monique, the two of you aren't that safe here in your condo. Your doorman downstairs was asleep."

Henry, our doorman, was ninety if he was a day. "He's really old," I said, wanting to defend Henry's right to work...or not.

"Well, I waltzed right on up here, nothing stopping me. If I were you, I'd stay somewhere else for the time being."

"You have to have a code to get in," I continued, trying to argue the point.

He punched the elevator button. "I came in right behind some woman who was walking out."

That explained how Cooter Amstutz had arrived unannounced and everyone else evidently.

"OK, OK," I conceded. "I'll think about it."

36

Reardon did Lloyd one better and showed up at my door the same evening. Evidently Henry was still asleep on the job downstairs.

"Detective!" I greeted, opening the door wide.

"Dr. Canale."

"Come in. Come in. Thanks for coming so soon."

Reardon reached for his little notebook, which he kept in the pocket of his dress shirt along with an array of writing pens. He looked uncomfortable in his button-down shirt and tie, over which his ample neck folded.

"Here, have a seat in the living room. Can I get you something to drink?"

"I'd kill for a beer right about now. Oh, I forgot you don't drink."

"No problem. I keep beer and wine on hand for guests."

Reardon appraised my living room. "Doesn't that present a problem for you?"

MeMoe woofed a couple of times from his recliner but didn't see the round guy as any big threat.

"No. I can have alcohol in the fridge all day long, and it doesn't bother me. It's when I go to a bar and people are laughing and drinking; then I want to join in. Problem is, it always goes too far for me."

Reardon nodded, satisfied with my answer.

I went to the kitchen and brought back a bottle of beer for him and a bottle of water for me. "Do you need a glass?"

"No, bottle's fine, thanks. Did you happen to catch the Cubs game last night?" he asked, pointing to my bat on the wall.

"No, but I heard they won."

"Yeah. Milwaukee's on some kind of losing streak."

"Seems that way. Shoot, I know what that's like too. Back when I played football for Virginia, we lost so many games it wasn't even funny; our morale was in the basement." I shook my head. "The coaches tried pumping us up by getting us some new jerseys to wear. They were orange-and-blue tearaways. We were so excited about them, and then one of our halfbacks noticed that the numbers on the front of the jerseys didn't match the numbers on the back. Sure enough, every jersey was off by four numbers. I was number fifty-three, but on that day I was wearing fifty-three on the front and fifty-seven on the back."

Reardon laughed heartedly. "I didn't know you played football."

"Sure did. Longest losing streak in history, but I guess for me it was a saving grace. I didn't venture further into football, or coaching, for that matter and became a doctor instead. They demoted me to the third team in my senior year, but I always dressed out, and I did get to play in a game we actually won, which after twenty-eight straight losses was pretty sweet, as you can imagine."

Reardon nodded and took a long swig of his beer. "So Lloyd told me about this little scheme you have in mind," he said, changing the subject.

"'Little' is an understatement."

He smiled. "Why don't we start by you telling me how you came to the conclusion that you needed to play cop?"

I shrugged. "Simone's dead; my name's sullied. I started snooping around and came up with Cooter having an affair with Monique. We met up, and she told me about Simone having a mystery lover."

As if on cue, Monique walked into the living room, this time fully dressed.

The detective and I both rose. "Detective, this is Monique Glazer. Monique, this is Detective Reardon."

"We've met," Reardon said.

Monique nodded and sat on the edge of the couch. She had removed all of her show makeup, which made her look small and vulnerable. I scooted one of the dining-room chairs over and sat rodeo style, facing them on the couch.

Reardon sat back down and consulted his notebook. "So, tell me about this mystery lover." He glanced at me and then Monique.

Monique chewed on the inside of her cheek for a moment. "She was dating a married man. As I told Terry, I never got to see him up close. From a distance, my guess was that he was in his forties, maybe younger. I'd never be able to pick him out in a lineup." She studied her hands and then continued, "Simone told me that he threatened to kill anyone who exposed their affair to his wife, including her, but, as I told Terry, she'd stopped seeing him months before she was murdered."

"So why did you go to Highlands?" Reardon asked her.

"Terry went there to look for the mystery man."

"Why Highlands? What made him want to look there?"

"She—they—played croquet up in Cashews."

"Cashiers," I corrected.

"The mystery lover and Simone?" Reardon clarified.

"Yes."

"Then what transpired?"

"Terry asked me to come help him see if anyone looked familiar, because he didn't know who he was looking for. So I went."

I said, "I thought we should check out some of the high-end country clubs there, the ones where croquet is the big thing. Monique didn't recognize anyone, though. We got to meet Delmár, the maître d' who used to work at the Universal Club. He seemed like a nice guy and all—said he remembered my dad. Then that night someone broke into Monique's room and shot her."

Monique rolled up her sleeve so he could see the wound.

"Yeah, I heard about that."

"It's my theory that even though Monique didn't recognize any-one, someone recognized her, and that's why she was shot," I told him.

Reardon scribbled something into his little notebook.

"Since then, she's been here recuperating."

The detective looked up from his notebook at me. "Tell me what happened in Cuba." Lloyd had evidently informed him of my run-in with the Lone Ranger and Tonto.

"Well, I found out that there was going to be a world croquet tournament there, and several folks from Highlands were going to be playing in it." I purposely left out Big Al's name as my informant. "I got on a plane and went to Cuba to see if I could corner someone into spilling the beans about Simone."

Reardon winced.

"I know, I know. It sounds lame. My game plan could've been better."

Reardon snorted. "You think? Did you find out anything?"

"Not a damn thing. There were hundreds of folks there. But someone must've thought I did because they broke into my room, tied me up, and nail gunned my hands to a board. They didn't steal anything."

"Lloyd told me about that."

"That brings us to right now," I said. "We want to flush the killer out."

We were all silent for a few moments. Then Reardon said, "I checked around up there in Highlands when I heard about what hap-pened to Ms. Glazer." He nodded to Monique. "Checked on your guy Delmár, even."

I said nothing.

"He's been on a Homeland Security watch list. The feds don't share much, but from what I gather, they thought he might be a look-out for a terrorist cell in that area."

I didn't tell Reardon that this wasn't news to me. "A terrorist cell? In Highlands?"

"Yeah, that's what I thought too at first. But there's a lot of money up there, so why not? Anyway, Delmár has led them to nobody so far, and they been watching him for better than six months."

"Maybe he's not the guy," Monique offered.

"Maybe," Reardon said. "And then again, maybe he is. Maybe he's just that good."

My stomach lurched. Suddenly feeling dehydrated, I chugalugged my water. Reardon watched me with interest.

"Do you think this is about more than just a mystery lover?" I asked nervously, my mind beginning to connect the dots. "Are you thinking that Simone may have been involved in something bigger, like a terrorist cell?" My throat went dry again.

"Maybe," he said noncommittally. "However, just looking at Simone's murder, I'd have to say no. Being stabbed however many times shows that this was personal. Someone was really angry with her. An execution would look entirely different, but I'm not discounting that there might be something bigger at stake. I just don't know what at this point. In fact, these could be two separate things." He pointed at my hands. "You could have just stumbled upon something that has absolutely nothing to do with Simone."

None of us spoke for a full minute. Then Reardon said, "Do I dare ask what this new plan of yours is? Hope to hell it's better than your last two harebrained schemes."

Ouch—that was insulting. True, but still painful. I chose to ignore his comment and remain on point. "Monique and I believe that the killer would figure out pretty quickly that we're trying to trap him, so we think it's best if we just go about our routines as usual. We can spread the word that Monique knows something and is getting ready to spill the beans. That'll flush him out. Then, when he makes his move, you guys nab him, hopefully without getting any of us killed."

Reardon took a long swig of his beer before speaking. "It's dangerous," he finally said.

"I agree, but sooner or later he's gonna try anyway—better now than later, when we aren't expecting it."

"True."

Monique cut in. "I've already called Ralph, the owner at Pony Tails, and he's letting me start back Saturday, day after tomorrow."

"And I'm planning to go back to seeing patients on Monday," I added.

"I can get a team together by Saturday," Reardon said.

"I do three routines," Monique told him, "at eight, ten, and the last one at midnight. Also, I'm going back to my duplex. The place next door is empty. You can put someone in there if you want. I have a key to the place." She went to get her purse so she could give Reardon the key.

"What about you, Doc?" Reardon asked.

"I'm going to stay here and start back at the clinic on Monday."

"We'll give your doorman downstairs a little vacation starting Friday." He got up to leave, handing me his bottle. At the front door, he turned and said, "Until then, you guys keep your eyes open, and don't venture out unless you absolutely have to."

What the hell did he think we had been doing this whole time?

"Also, your other gal, the blonde…"

How did he know about Abigail? Had he been watching me?

"Abigail?"

"Yeah, her. We'll keep an eye on her too. Y'all just do what you normally do, and we'll keep a watch. We're gonna keep this on the down-low, radio silence—got that?"

I nodded.

"Thanks for the beer," he said, and with that he was gone.

37

Saturday rolled around with Monique in a tizzy about her upcoming performance. First she wasn't sure about her hair and screamed because she had the wrong hair straightener; then she wasn't all that sure about her boa hiding all the scars, for which she blamed Dr. Markola; and then she couldn't find the keys to her apartment, the blame for which fell squarely in my lap. We were all out of sorts, to say the least. Even MeMoe wasn't in his usual playful mood and remained all business during his business of doing business in the yard. The four of us were playing with fire, and we all knew it too. Earlier in the day, I had given Big Al instructions to put out the word about Monique knowing the killer. Although not fully comprehending how Big Al's grapevine worked, I was still confident that the gossip would meet up with the right ears eventually.

After Monique's final rant on how bad she looked, I wondered if a bouquet of flowers might be in order for her opening show; after all, Ralph, the owner of the club, was touting her as the First Lady of Pony Tails. But I wasn't real sure about the protocol in this type of show biz and gave it a pass. Around seven we finally loaded up the Explorer and headed out to Millington. For a nude dancer, she sure needed a lot of stuff. Her makeup alone required a small suitcase. A young woman manning Henry the doorman's place in the lobby nodded a greeting to us on our way out.

Around seven thirty we pulled up to Pony Tails, and Monique ordered me to drive around to a side door.

"Okeydoke," I said, feigning lightheartedness, as I pulled up to a gray metal door. Monique grabbed her makeup case and boa from the back seat and got out, leaving me to retrieve her mountain of stuff from the trunk, which I dutifully did and followed her into the building, down a long, dark passageway to her dressing room—a disappointing, dingy, eight-by-eight-foot cell with no window. That it was windowless was a good thing, because at least we didn't have to worry about her being targeted through that.

"You get ready," I told her. "I'll go out front and check to see if the cops are in place. Lock the door behind me."

"OK," she replied absent-mindedly as she carefully laid out her makeup on a dark-red handkerchief in front of her vanity mirror.

The dimly lit club reeked of fried food, booze, and sweaty bodies. It was jam-packed that night, the crowd eager to see their First Lady. I looked around to see if I could spot the surveillance team, but no such luck. They were either not there, or they were that good. Hoping the woodwork was made up of cops, I took a seat in a booth and ordered a club soda. Onstage a couple of drag queens were playing out a macabre parody that the crowd thought was hilarious. The joke was lost on me, however, as I kept searching the place for some indication that Reardon hadn't dropped the ball on us.

Promptly at eight o'clock, the two gender benders left the stage, the lights in the club dimmed some more, and the crowd quieted. A couple of heartbeats later, three spotlights sprang to life and lit the center stage as the DJ introduced the "lovely First Lady of Pony Tails." The crowd went wild when Monique sauntered out onstage, fully dressed in a silver-sequined, body-hugging, to-the-floor gown with slits on either side. The green boa was loosely draped around her neck and shoulders. She had a figure like Cher in her heyday, except Monique had bigger boobs. Some men in the crowd were whistling, some were hooting, and some were actually crying, "We love you!" as her hips began to move to Def Leppard's "Pour Some Sugar on Me."

She made her move on the pole haltingly, playfully, as if it were a person, a dance partner, her tongue licking it lightly. The pole seemed to quiver under her touch. I know I did. As Def Leppard started in on the drums, she let go of the pole and strutted across the stage in her stilettos. With slow deliberation she began to discard pieces of her gown and then her garter, which she jettisoned into the crowd, and then the stockings, bit by bit, and the teddy, until she was down to just a thong and her boa, of course, which hid the scars just fine. With her back to the audience and on a full forward bend, I could see now that the python tattoo had been strategically placed to point out her forbidden fruit. Why she was considered the First Lady was quite clear to me now. She was phenomenal. When she began working the pole, the intensity of my visceral reaction came as a total surprise, and I had to force myself to look away and concentrate on the task at hand—namely, searching the room to see if there was anyone out in the crowd gunning for her, but all I could see was a wave of swooning men. All flags were flying at full mast that night.

I stayed for her next showing but decided to call it a night after that and head back to the condo. Monique said she would catch a ride with a friend to her duplex, but I begged her to spend at least one more night at the condo, assuring her that, no, I wasn't going to hit on her. Reluctantly she agreed but only because I told her Abigail was coming by. Their relationship, which in the beginning had amused me, was now becoming seriously irksome.

Saturday night had gone off without anybody getting shot up and without me getting laid. Abigail politely put me off with the "I've got a headache" bit, and I'd given Monique my word not to try any funny business. There is really nothing worse than getting aroused at one of those shows and then having no closure. I tossed and turned, sweating in my sheets throughout the night, deciding it wasn't a good idea for me to watch her perform again. Besides getting all hot and bothered, I didn't like all those other guys ogling her. The troglodyte in me wanted to jump up onstage with a large club, beat my chest, and shout, "She's mine. I seen her first!"

The crowd on Sunday night was a little less boisterous than Saturday. Probably all those husbands who had been in the crowd the night before were at church functions. Unlike me, they had probably gotten some follow-up when they returned home, so they were good to go for a few days. I still didn't see any cops around or anyone who looked like a cop, but that's probably the way it should be for undercover workers. While Monique was in her dressing room, I sat at the bar and studied the menu. Hot legs onstage and hot wings on the table—what could possibly be better? I'd hoped for a Cobb salad but had to settle for some nachos and refried beans, wondering if I would ever get back to my organic eating habits. This time, instead of watching Monique's performance and getting irritated each time some jerk-off in the crowd slid a ten into her thong, my eyes searched the audience. Still nothing. I started to worry, first that Big Al hadn't put out the word and then that the cops might not be there and finally that the killer would take his merry time until the cops became lax or nonexistent before he made his move. The best thing for me to do was go back to work Monday morning and quit worrying, which was exactly what I did.

Monday turned out to be an extremely busy day at the clinic. The parking lot was full to the brim, and Chad, our parking-lot attendant, was double- and triple-parking people. The wiry, hundred-pound-soaking-wet twenty-one-year-old wore a camo jacket whether it was summer or winter, which might or might not have been hiding a gun. Someone should have approached him about the dress code, but no one did since he was doing such a good job keeping unruly patients from parking in the doctors' spaces. As usual, Nurse Johnnie overbooked me, and there were forty-five patients on the schedule, ten of whom were already waiting for me when I walked in at seven. Getting back into the groove of working after such a long time off was a bit of a challenge. By noon, my strength and resolve not to eat lunch were waning, so when Nurse Johnnie wasn't looking, I sneaked some peanut-butter crackers and a Diet Coke from the machine and scarfed them down in the dictation booth. She gave me a dirty look when she found the wrapper and complained loudly that she had not had a lunch break and then confronted me head on about our policy of "lunch is for sissies" and whether it was still in effect. I had no answer for her other than to say that I still wasn't myself. Would I ever be? Well, that was a question for the ages.

Finally, the clock struck five, and my last patient, Mrs. Goldstein, was called back. Goldstein isn't her real name, by the way, because by law I'm not allowed to tell you who my patients are, but I can tell you that she's the widow of a very important fat cat in DC and a nosy member of the Universal Club. She knew my parents way back when and seemed to enjoy always bringing up the fact that they were dead, clucking regretfully as she spoke. She had come in to see me about her bunion but mostly to get the scoop about my having been in jail. Her gossip tank must have been running low.

She looked at me conspiratorially. "Terry, now I heard about all that awful business and you bein' in the big house over that Simone killin'. You know, just between you and me and the wall, I never liked her. Bless her heart, she was not a nice girl, and I never thought you had anything to do with all that."

"Well, that means a lot to me, Mrs. Goldstein. It was pretty awful, but now enough about me. Tell me what's going on with your toe here." I gently stroked her tiny wrinkled foot, the one with a giant burl protruding from the side. "You've been wearing tight shoes again, I see."

She flirtatiously batted her long, fake eyelashes. "Now, Terry, hon, you know I can't wear those ugly orthopedic numbers. I've got to keep up with the fashion."

She was doing a good job of that too, because looking at this seventy-something woman from behind, you'd have thought she was sixteen. My cell phone dinged a message, and solely out of habit, I glanced at the first line.

"WTF!" I shouted out—except I didn't use the abbreviation. The whole enchilada came out right in front of nosy Mrs. Goldstein.

Shocked, she put a hand to her chest. "Oh my!"

Equally shocked, I stared at her and apologized profusely. "I am so sorry, Mrs. Goldstein; this is an emergency call. I've got to go. I'll find someone who can finish you up. Will you please excuse me?"

"Why, certainly," she replied with a sly smile. "You must be a very bad boy, after all."

I closed the door behind me and stood outside the treatment room, reading the entire message from Lloyd.

> *911! Shots fired at ponytails. Dancer down, shooter down.*
> *Meet me at trauma center. Coming by wings.*

My forehead broke out in a cold sweat. Freddie Esser was just passing by in the hall in his new, crisp white lab coat, when I grabbed him by his lapel and pulled him toward the examination room.

"Freddie, will you go in there and help Mrs. Goldstein with her bunion? I have to run across the street and don't know when I'll be back." I swiped at the dribble of sweat trailing down my cheek.

Freddie's eyeballs nearly fell out of their orbits. "Bunion, sir?" He looked confused.

"Yeah, bunion!" I yelled at him, forgetting that he was only a first-year medical student and probably didn't have a clue on what part of the body a bunion could be found. "Her feet, son, her feet!" I clarified.

"Feet? Oh…oh…her feet." His look of confusion suddenly changed to one of enthusiasm as he pulled a stethoscope and percussion hammer from the pocket of his lab coat.

"That's right. Just go in there and rub her feet for a while and say nice things to her…and…and tell her she looks lovely in big shoes."

With those instructions, I tore off down the hall at warp speed.

"Don't worry. I've got it covered, sir!" I heard him call out just as I was rounding the corner to the door. That boy was going to go far in this business.

38

Within five minutes I was across the street and in the heart of the Memphis Trauma Center. It was the usual hustle and bustle, the waiting room stuck full of indigent folks with runny noses, careless folks with broken bones, tripped-out druggies with oozing pustules, and criminals with stab wounds. Ignoring all that, I raced past and into the treatment quarry. One of the trauma docs recognized me.

"Terry, what brings you to the lion's den?" he asked, surprised. It'd been many moons since the likes of me had been seen in the trauma center.

"You got some gunshot wounds coming in?"

"Yeah, the copter's a couple of minutes out. Another's coming by ambulance. Someone you know?"

"Maybe. A friend or two." Lloyd hadn't said it was Monique, but my gut knew it was.

A few minutes later, the double doors in the back hall swung open as two gurneys arrived, one carrying Monique and the other carrying Lloyd. Blue scrubs surrounded them. As Monique was rolled by, she recognized me and smiled weakly behind her oxygen mask. Even so, the look on the nurses' faces told me this was bad. A medic was holding the IV bag and didn't stop for us to exchange pleasantries, wheeling her hurriedly into a room, a flurry of white coats following.

Lloyd called to me from his gurney. A medic had parked his behind out in the hall.

"Lloyd, what the hell happened out there?" I asked. Thank heavens he didn't look very injured.

"I got him, Terry. I got him! I got the son of a bitch!" he told me excitedly.

"Where did he get you?" I asked, looking for his bullet hole.

"He didn't get me. I stumbled and blew my knee out chasing his ass down. I don't know why they're insisting on me being brought in like this. I told 'em I was fine."

"Is he dead?"

"I dunno. I dunno." He was still all hyped up.

One of the ED docs stepped over, but I told him I would take care of Lloyd, yanking back the sheet they had placed over his legs. His knee was a little swollen, and according to him it hurt, but he had a full range of motion.

"So tell me what went down."

He carefully re-covered his bare leg. "Monique came in early 'cause she wanted to work out a new routine on the pole. Me and Darrell, my partner, were on duty and watching her practice, when a pickup truck drove by outside and sprayed the damn front of the building with bullets. I ran out the front door and shot him through the truck window. Hit him the first time, and he went down—pow—just like that," Lloyd said, admirably replaying the scene for me. "The truck went outta control and ran over the top of a Mercedes in the parking lot. Lucky there wasn't anyone in it. Bar doesn't open up shop till six on Mondays."

I didn't mention to Lloyd that he should've been watching the outside instead of watching Monique practice, but what was the use? "Who is he?" I asked wearily, rubbing my eyes.

Lloyd shrugged. "No friggin' idea. He was packing a military-grade machine gun."

"An Islamic terrorist?"

"Could be Islamic, could be mafioso, could be the one Marx brother, for all I know."

I told Lloyd to get off the gurney and try to bear weight on his knee. He could but said it was painful. An orderly arrived to take him down to X-ray. I gave the orthopedic resident instructions on what to do with Lloyd and said he was to come see me at the clinic in the morning; then I went over to check on Monique.

The doc said her vital signs were stable, but she was having trouble breathing, and he was pretty sure bullets had punctured her lung and perhaps some other organs. She had been sent for a CT and MRI, and the results would be known in a few minutes. He was sure enough about his diagnosis that he was headed to the surgery suite to scrub out. It couldn't have been more than ten minutes when Monique was returned, and they wheeled her straight from there to surgery. The scans showed that a bullet had penetrated the base of the right lung, fracturing a rib on the way in, and one went through the liver. The pericardium and heart appeared to be normal, and there was luckily no bowel perforation, which would have been a bloody mess. A thoracic fellow was on his way down to help with her surgery.

It was right around this time they wheeled the assailant into an adjoining examination room. He was Middle Eastern, of that much I was sure, and he was gravely injured, paralyzed from the waist down, one of the nurses said. Evidently Lloyd was a good shot. Teddy Rodriquez, our orthopedic trauma doc, assessed the man's condition and deemed that early stabilization was necessary, although it was doubtful he would ever regain his ability to walk, as they were pretty sure the man's cord was severed. Good, I thought. He got his comeuppance. I want to say that I felt guilty about thinking this because of my Hippocratic oath and all, but that would just be a lie. The best I could do at that point was to keep my extreme personal resentments to myself so that he would be afforded equal billing.

The thoracic fellow finally showed up in the ED, and I walked with him to the OR area, asking if his attending was planning to come in also.

"Yeah, I don't think so." He laughed out loud.

That ticked me off. "That's not good enough," I scolded. "You get his ass on the phone and tell him to get in here right now! The city of Memphis is paying him to be here. If anyone needs his help at this moment, it's that young lady on the stretcher. Tell him Dr. Canale said so!"

Shocked at my outburst, the young man called his attending, the head of the Thoracic Surgery Department. Even though he probably didn't give two hoots what a Dr. Canale had to say, the old man did make an appearance but was already two sheets to the wind.

Not knowing what else to do with myself, I decided to drive over to Pony Tails and see the damage firsthand. Still angry about the whole shit and shebang, I stomped toward the elevator and was hit by an oversized bed with a tiny-looking man perched in its center. It was my good friend Marvel.

"Terry, my man!" he said groggily, giving me a big snaggletoothed grin.

"What the hell, Marvel? Why're you in bed?"

He snorted. "Got myself the big C, Doc."

"When did this happen?"

"Aw, a couple months ago. There's this pain I got, right here." He pointed to a place on his abdomen, suspiciously close to the liver area. "They gives me the radiator cells through a little cut here today, and tomorrow they says I can go home again. I guess so's I can kiss my ass good-bye. You all right, Doc? You don't look so good; your hair's standin' all up?"

"I'm fine," I said, looking back over my shoulder toward the operating suites, worried about Monique. "Are they treating you well?"

"Oh yeah, got me a fine-lookin' nurse and a free ride. What more could a man want for? 'Cept..." He looked away for a second, embarrassed.

"Except what?" I asked.

He grinned big at me.

I shook my head.

He smiled again and pointed to his mouth. "My teeth—they lost my teeth. Man, I can't be smiling at these pretty young things without my mouthpiece," he complained.

Well, that was just the final straw for me. "They lost your teeth?" I asked, exasperated.

He nodded but seemed to be drifting off.

"Don't you worry, Marvel. I'll get your teeth," I said with conviction and stormed up to the head nurse's station.

She looked at me over the rim of her glasses. "Yes?"

"We need to find Marvel Jenkin's teeth."

"We're looking into that," she replied snappishly, her piglet eyes never leaving mine.

"Now!" I growled, glowering down at her.

Another nurse, younger than the one at the desk, walked up, a surgical mask pulled down around her neck. "We've looked all over, Dr. Canale, and we can't find them."

I turned back to the head nurse and said in a flat, even tone, "We're not going to do another goddamn orthopedic operation in this hospital until we find Marvel's teeth. Do you understand me?" With that, I turned to the chief orthopedic resident and two others. "As of this moment, all orthopedic cases are canceled in this hospital until Marvel's teeth show up!"

I assured Marvel about finding his teeth and then left the building. It wasn't forty-five minutes later when they called, saying his teeth had been located and that orthopedic cases had resumed. Sadly, Marvel died a week later, but he left this world with his teeth in and his boots on. What more could a man want?

39

When I arrived at Pony Tails a little before seven, cops were swarming like angry bees. One of the men in blue wouldn't allow me to drive into the parking lot, telling me, "Move along; nothing to see here." I asked the man if Detective Reardon was there, because I needed to speak with him about the shooting. The cop waved me into the parking lot but wouldn't let me near the building.

"Wait here," he commanded and walked off toward the club. I lost sight of him among all his fellow officers. A short while later, he resurfaced and ordered me to drive to the side entrance. As I pulled alongside the building, Reardon was waiting, a look of disdain on his face. Feeling deeply guilty, I placed the Explorer in park and got out, ready to face the music about my harebrained scheme.

All he said, though, was "How is she?"

"Not that good." He grunted some reply. "The bullets went through her lung and liver and broke a rib. They're working on her now."

"She gonna live?"

"Barring anything unforeseen."

"What about the shooter?"

"He'll live; he just won't be able to walk anymore."

"He'll be in jail, so he won't have anywhere go. Can he talk yet?"

"Probably'll be a day or two before they let you interrogate him."

He slapped me on the back. "Don't worry; we'll figure out who he's working for."

Reardon used his key to unlock the door, and we went inside, walking the long, dark hall to the front, where the stage was located. Broken glass was everywhere, and bullet holes riddled the walls, floors, tables, and bar. The wall-to-wall mirror lay in shards onstage. The only object left standing was the shiny chrome pole with a pool of blood around it—Monique's blood. The forensic team was measuring and digging out bullets and marking the places of impact. Four or five employees were standing around in their slinky outfits with blankets thrown over their shoulders, still being questioned by the police. By the looks of the place, it was amazing no one else had been injured; a couple of hours later, this would have been a bloodbath.

"I guess this wasn't a good idea after all." I laid it all out there for Reardon.

To my surprise, he shrugged. "We got him, didn't we?"

"Yeah, but the cost...the cost." I shook my head.

"She'll be fine," Reardon said confidently. "She's young and beautiful. Maybe she'll get out of this awful business here."

"Maybe."

We left it at that. I walked over to the front window. The blacked-out pane was busted into millions of pieces. You couldn't avoid stepping on the shards. The pickup truck the shooter had been driving was a souped-up, four-wheel-drive black Lexus with dark tinted windows and a North Carolina plate. It was still sitting in the place it had landed after Lloyd shot the driver. From the looks of it, Lloyd was one hell of a shot. Glancing back at the busted window front, it occurred to me that this must have been the work of an amateur. The guy could no more see at whom he was shooting than the man in the moon, and it was only serendipitous that Monique had been hit.

"Are you thinking what I am?" Reardon had come up behind me and was looking at the gaping opening.

"Depends on what you're thinking."

"How did he know he would hit Monique?"

We pondered that question. "I'll have forensics make sure the bullets that hit Monique were actually from that shooter's gun." He scribbled notes to himself in his little black book.

"Maybe he didn't care who he shot. Maybe he's a terrorist and any old body would do," I offered.

"Now wouldn't that just be the biggest coincidence this side of the universe?"

I had to agree. From the corner of my eye, I could see a woman in a white suit and a microphone hurrying our way. It was Christine Hulsaker from *Channel 6 News*. I ducked out of sight, hoping she hadn't seen me. Wouldn't that just beat all to have my face plastered on the ten o'clock news? I could see it now: "Renowned Memphis Surgeon Involved in Shooting at Millington Strip Club." Wouldn't that look good on my curriculum vitae?

"Shit!" I whispered to Reardon.

He threw his thumb toward the back of the club as he intercepted the news lady. I took off to the back and slipped out the side entrance to my vehicle, hoping I hadn't been spotted, and returned to the medical district.

Back at the trauma center, Abigail and I collided in the hall near the emergency department.

"Why didn't you call me?" she shouted in front of everyone.

I just looked at her and stammered, "I...I...I don't know." It was the truth. I hadn't even thought to call her.

"I had to hear about it on television," she said accusingly.

"Huh," I replied absently and went for a chair in the waiting area, not feeling so hot all of a sudden.

"You OK?" she asked, concerned. "Your hair's all standing up."

"I'm OK." I rubbed my head vigorously, which I do sometimes when I get nervous, which was also probably why my hair was standing on end.

She sat in the chair next to me. "I hate to say this to you, but I'm gonna say it anyway. I told you guys so, you and Monique, but y'all did it anyway."

"I know, I know. Shit…I know."

I started scrubbing my head again, but she gently took my hands in hers. "How is she?"

"It was a machine gun," I told her somberly.

The thoracic fellow saw Abigail and me in the waiting area and came over to give us the low-down on Monique. The surgery had taken much longer than anticipated, because they had to open her up to take out the lower right lobe of her lung and about a third of her liver and the gallbladder. Luckily they got the bleeding stopped quickly, so she remained pretty stable throughout. Her stem-to-stern thoracotomy wound was closed over drains. So much for hiding scars, I thought bitterly; now she'd be forced to look for another line of work.

Abigail stood and took me by the hand. "Come on, let's go home. Have you eaten anything today?"

"I dunno. I ate breakfast and some peanut-butter crackers." I allowed her to pull me along the corridor.

"Let's stop at Three Little Pigs and get some takeout."

"OK," I said, but my tiredness was bone deep, and I didn't have a clue if I could choke it down.

She must have realized my fragile state of mind, because she took full responsibility for me—driving my car, buying my food, and getting me up to my condo. She even started the shower for me and then went to take MeMoe for his walk. I remained in the shower until the water ran cold, wrapped the bottom half of myself in a towel, and went into the living room, where Abigail was setting out the food. Amazingly, I was able to eat and was even hungry. Under the circumstances the barbecue was delicious. Finally, my hands and feet came back to life, but Abigail insisted it was time to turn in, helping me unwrap my towel and get under the covers. She too undressed and came to bed, wrapping her body around my shaking one. We stayed that way for some time, before she began caressing me in places that pulled my brain back to the present and away from all the horrors of the day. It occurred to me that this was probably pity sex on her part, but, hey, I was a starving man and would take whatever was up for grabs. We fell asleep naked in each other's arms, and it felt as if things might be as they'd been before the shooting, before Monique, before Simone even. But, unfortunately, MeMoe's low growl told me something different. Sitting next to me on the bed, he had obviously heard a noise outside of my auditory range. Then, two short blasts, like firecrackers in the distance, pierced the silence. What the hell? It wasn't the Fourth of July. Sensing that something wasn't right, I listened for another shot. MeMoe tensed and began to frantically lick my ear. I shook Abigail awake, holding her mouth, so she wouldn't scream out.

"We gotta get outta here," I whispered.

"What?" she answered sleepily.

"They're coming for us."

She snapped awake and jumped out of bed, fumbling for her underwear and a T-shirt. I worked my way into some dirty gym shorts that were on the floor and grabbed MeMoe. As we headed for the door, I could hear the *click, click, click* of the elevator outside.

"The balcony," I told her.

We ran through the dark living room to the balcony, but idling in the lot below was a black Lexus SUV. I pulled Abigail back into the condo and to the bedroom, locked the door behind us, and opened the window.

"Climb out," I ordered.

"Climb out? We're on the fifth floor."

The elevator door squeaked open.

"There's a ledge—hurry up!"

She climbed out onto the ledge. MeMoe and I followed. Squeezing him between my chest and the wall for a moment, I quietly slid the window closed just seconds before my condo door came crashing down.

"Move!" I ordered in a loud whisper. The ledge was narrower than the one at the Roosevelt Hotel, requiring that we hug the wall and walk sideways.

"Go faster!" I pleaded.

"Where are we going?"

"Mrs. Habernathy's balcony around the corner. Hurry!" I heard the crunch of my bedroom door being smashed to pieces.

Just as I made it around the corner, gunshots erupted from my window. MeMoe yelped. Abigail climbed onto Mrs. Habernathy's balcony and took him from my arms so I could get over the railing.

"It won't take them long to figure out where we are," I said to her.

"Let's climb up," she suggested.

"To the roof?" My instinct would have been to go down.

"Well, yeah." She grabbed hold of a metal gutter that went all the way to the ninth-floor balcony. We would have to figure out how to get onto the roof once we made it that far.

As I think I may have previously mentioned, Abigail's in much better shape than I am, and she climbed up without a problem, making it to the top balcony in less than a minute or two. I was holding MeMoe, and that presented a big problem for me. The shooters were now outside Mrs. Habernathy's condo, knocking politely and saying they were the police. No way was he going to face down these killers on his own.

"Hey!" Abigail said from above. "Here's a bucket—catch." She lowered a construction bucket down to me. It clanged noisily against the railing. I placed MeMoe inside and told her to pull; then I grabbed hold of the metal gutter, said a short prayer that it would hold me, and started climbing. As I reached the next floor up, I heard Mrs. Habernathy's door explode.

"Shit!" I shimmied up faster, and just as her balcony door was ripped open, I hiked my last appendage over the ninth-floor railing.

40

We lay in total silence, listening to the killers discussing where we had gone. One of them said, "We must have hit him, 'cause here's some blood." I checked myself. There was blood on my arm but no bullet hole. What the heck? Then it dawned on me—MeMoe! He had been totally silent in the bucket. It was too dark to see him fully, but his eyes were open, and he was sniffing the air, so he was alive. In the distance we could hear sirens. Someone had alerted the police. The killers decided it was time to scram, and moments later we heard the four-by-four peel rubber out of the parking lot. The three of us sat in silence on the ninth-floor balcony until the police drove up and surrounded the building.

"This apartment is empty," Abigail said as she cupped her hands on the windowpane and peered inside. She tried the door. It was unlocked. Evidently this condo was being renovated. We stepped into the bare room, made our way to the front door, unbolted it, and let ourselves out into the hall. Police were charging up the stairwell, and when they saw us, they pointed their guns.

"Hands where we can see them!" one of them demanded. As if half-naked people have any pockets.

I gently placed the bucket on the floor and put my hands on my head. "My dog's been shot," I pleaded with the young cop. "He's bleeding." He glanced at MeMoe. "What's your name?"

"Canale, Terry Canale, Dr. Terry Canale," I told him.

"Stay right there," he replied and then spoke into his walkie-talkie. "Detective Reardon, we have the good doctor here on the ninth floor."

Reardon's voice boomed through the mike, "Is he alive?"

"Yes, sir. He's fine, but his dog's been shot."

"I'm in his apartment now. Send him down."

"Yes, sir." He pressed the elevator button for me and handed me the bucket of MeMoe, who still had not barked a word.

Reardon was waiting for us in my living room.

"Some police protection! My dog's been shot!" I shouted at him angrily.

He held up a hand. "They neutralized our officer downstairs."

Abigail put a hand to her mouth. "They killed her?"

"No, thank heavens. When she saw there was about to be trouble, she drew her weapon on a black SUV, but someone from behind tased her. She got off two shots before she went down but missed, unfortunately."

"Like I said, some police protection! I've got to get my dog to a vet! Where are my keys?" I snatched them off the top of Abigail's purse and headed for the door.

"Doc, shouldn't you get dressed first?" Reardon suggested.

Being that I was naked from the waist up and had on no shoes, he probably had a point. I put the bucket down and went to my bedroom to grab something to wear. Abigail did the same. We were out the door in a hurry and on our way to the animal emergency center out on Summer Avenue. While I drove, Abigail consoled MeMoe, instructing him to stay calm and that everything would be OK. At the emergency center, a vet tech unlocked the door for us, and we rushed MeMoe, in the bucket, up to the desk. There were no other pet emergencies at the moment.

"My dog's been shot!"

"Oh no! Poor thing," the young blond tech said. "Bring him on back into a treatment room. I'll get the doctor."

I was expecting more hustling on their part and a gurney and maybe some oxygen or intravenous fluids, but she led us into the tiny room, left, and shut the door behind her. Abigail sat on the only chair, and I paced next to the bucket. A door on the other side of the room opened, and a young kid in blue scrubs walked in and held out a strong hand to me. "Hi, I'm Dr. Johnson. We have a gunshot wound?"

Worried that someone so young would be handling my best friend in his time of great need, I looked at his hand for a moment before accepting the help he was offering. "Yes, my dog's been shot." Tears shot into my eyes.

"OK, let's see how bad it is." He picked MeMoe up out of the bucket. MeMoe didn't make a sound. His white fur was pink with blood. He didn't cry or flinch or anything. I took this as a very bad sign. My knees began to buckle as Dr. Johnson placed MeMoe on the examination table.

"Would you like to step outside for a minute?" the vet asked me, concerned.

Nodding, I left the room and stood outside, my back against the wall.

"He'll be OK," the vet tech offered when she saw me hyperventilating. "How did it happen?"

"He was shot. They broke into my place, and he was shot."

"Oh, I'm so sorry. Was anyone else hurt?"

Why was this person asking me all these intrusive questions? How would I know who else was hurt, and why would I care? MeMoe was the only thing I cared about. The door to the treatment room opened, and the doctor and Abigail walked out. MeMoe and the bucket were gone. My breath caught in my throat.

"He was shot…lost…blood but…blah…blah…blah," the vet was saying. There was a pounding in my ears, and only pieces of information were reaching my brain. "It'll all be over very quickly…and… can pick…say tomorrow…" The vet stopped talking and looked at me expectantly.

I looked at him and then Abigail. "What?"

"What would you like to do?" Dr. Johnson asked.

"About what?"

"Sew it back on or amputate? Dogs do quite well without tails."

"They shot his tail off?" I asked, horrified.

Dr. Johnson looked at me suspiciously. "Well, not off, off—it could've been a lot worse."

Well, I couldn't see how. MeMoe would be a freak with no tail. How would he greet me without a tail? How would I know if he was happy or sad? How could he possibly win best in show at the Universal Club Westminster dog show with nothing but a stump? As far as I knew, there were no prosthetic tails. "Well, can you sew it back on?"

"Sure. As I said, there're no guarantees it'll be the same, but I've seen a lot worse," Dr. Johnson assured me.

"OK, so sew it back together."

"Good, I'll do that. You can pick him up tomorrow sometime. Just leave your information at the front desk."

"OK," I said hopefully, shaking his hand longer than necessary. We stopped at the desk and gave the vet tech my contact information. As we turned to leave, I thought of something and asked if they would be willing to board MeMoe for a few days for his own safety, since being associated with the likes of me seemed to be detrimental to one's good health these days. The tech said it was no problem.

At Abigail's suggestion, we checked into a hotel for the rest of the night, and our plan was to use a different hotel every day, since the killers probably had a tail on me and possibly on her. I had no idea what to do, and at two in the morning, my brain refused to solve any more problems as sleep poured over me like manna from heaven.

41

The pleasant smell of freshly brewed coffee brought me back to consciousness. Sunlight, streaming through a slit in the curtains, reached all the way to the bathroom door of the hotel room. I checked my phone. It was almost eight o'clock. Abigail must've made coffee, but now she was gone. There was a note on her pillow.

> *Gone to check on Monique, parked your car out of sight be-*
> *hind the Dumpster downstairs, probably wise to take Uber or*
> *a cab so they can't track you. See ya.*

Not "Love, Abigail" or "Love you" or "Take care" but "See ya." So much for last night and us getting closer, I thought resentfully. But I had to admit that her idea about calling a cab was probably wise. I sat on the edge of my bed, thinking about my schedule for the day and scrolling through my many missed calls and messages, which I chose to ignore, all except the two from Nurse Johnnie saying that newspaper people were after me and one from Lloyd about his knee. The shooting at my condo was breaking news that morning. I texted Nurse Johnnie and told her to decline all interviews and texted Lloyd, letting him know to meet me at the clinic around ten. Realizing I didn't have anything fresh to wear and too afraid to return to my condo, I decided to go by the Universal Club, where I always keep a change of clothes in my locker. Even if Uber were to drive me, the killers and certainly the media would be watching the front door, so I called Mike at the U Club and asked if he could pick me up...quietly. As usual, he could be counted on, arriving at the hotel in fifteen minutes in an old white Ford Taurus, and as usual he didn't ask superfluous questions even as I slid way down in the seat so as not to be seen. Sure enough, the media people were at the U Club gate. He drove us through without them noticing and around back to the service entrance. We slipped quietly into the least-used door. I hit the showers and shaved, but before I could get away from the athletic building, a half-dozen members besieged me with questions about the shooting, which I dodged as well as possible, shrugging and playing dumb. Mike was waiting in the back to whisk me away through yet another door and drove me all the way up to the private entrance of the clinic. He thought this was all about keeping the newspeople away from me, but it was more about keeping the killers away from everyone associated with me. I thanked him with money, for which he was ever appreciative, took the back stairs to my office, and locked the door securely behind me. I texted Nurse Johnnie to send Lloyd up whenever he arrived and told her not to let anyone else know I was there, especially the CEO. It was lucky that there were no patients for me to see that day in the clinic, and my surgery had been canceled. I could stay on the move evading the killers, but the next day I had a meniscectomy in the morning over at the new surgery center and a half-day clinic scheduled in the afternoon. Basically, I'd be a sitting duck with patients all over the place. My cell phone rang. It was Big Al.

"Hey," I said.

"Just heard the news, my man. You get into all kinds of fixes, don't you?"

"Which news?"

"The girl got all shot up and you too."

"Yeah, I guess you putting the word out hit the right ears."

"I guess," he said. "With a little luck, they can waterboard the SOB till he squeals about who he's been working for."

"If we're not all dead by then."

"I'll keep my ears open," Big Al said.

"You better keep your eyes open too. That piece of shit didn't care anything about collateral damage when he started shooting."

"I hear ya."

Just as we disconnected, there was a knock on my office door, which sent me into a nosedive under my desk. "Who is it?" I squeaked in inquiry.

"It's me, Lloyd."

"Oh, OK, hold on." I unlocked the door.

Lloyd, his knee in a brace, limped into my office. "Jeez, Terry, I heard about them coming after you last night. How's MeMoe?"

"They shot his tail off!"

"Damn! Is he OK?"

"Yeah, the vet's sewing it back on. I'm not sure how all that's going to work out, though. Just makes my blood boil, Lloyd! We've got to stop this madman."

"Well, we're getting closer to Mr. Big, who's causing all your problems. They already started squeezing the little shit who shot Monique. He's Muslim, has a North Carolina address, and knows—guess who?—Delmár."

Hell, I could've told him that. "How's your knee?"

"It isn't bad. Here, I was supposed to give you this." He handed me an envelope with his medical information, X-rays, CT, and MRI results. Basically, he had some stretched ligaments but no tears and no fractures. I had him remove his brace to check his range of motion for myself. His knee would be fine in a couple of days. He wanted to go back to work, but I told him no, not until Monday, and wrote a note to that effect.

When he left, I called about MeMoe. The vet on the phone was not Dr. Johnson. He'd already gone off duty, but this one assured me the surgery had gone great, and there wasn't as much damage as one would think after a gunshot. Once all the fur on his tail grew back, he probably wouldn't be disfigured at all. That was great news! With renewed optimism, I decided to walk over and see about Monique, picking my route to the hospital with great care. She was recovering satisfactorily. The chest tubes were still in place, of course, and she still had considerable rib pain, which I told her could be expected for at least six or seven weeks. We didn't talk about the nasty gash across her torso that her green boa would never be able to hide. Unless she got very expensive plastic surgery, her pole-dancing days were over, which in my opinion wouldn't be all bad, but seeing it from her perspective, it was pretty devastating. How else could she make that kind of money? How was she going to live until she could find other work? Did she have any other skills? There were no easy answers to these questions.

As I was leaving the ICU, I ran into a cousin of mine, Cohen Canale. He was there visiting a nephew on his wife's side of the family. Cohen was one of the gifted, famous Canale boys who'd grown up in Mama's house at 620 South Belvedere. We hadn't seen each other in ages, just lost touch, and I don't even know why that was. He'd matured into a man with big, strong arms, which probably benefited him in his grocery business. He invited me down to the coffee shop, but with the worry about the bull's-eye on my back, I led him down into the bowels of the trauma center to an underground tunnel that crossed the street and exited near the children's hospital. We slipped out that door and into the other hospital, making damn sure no one was following. In the cafeteria, we purchased two cups of coffee and found a quiet corner to sit and reminisce about the old times. This time, I sat facing the door, my back to the wall.

"You remember our softball-playing days?" Cohen asked me, blowing steam across the top of his paper cup.

It made me smile. I had not thought about in years. One of my uncles, who'd made his money buying and selling jukeboxes, which was why we kids had referred to him as Uncle Nickels, donated a bunch of equipment for a slow-pitch softball team for all of us Canales. There were fifteen of us on the team, including the Taggett boys, and most could hit the ball way over the fence at the fairgrounds, no problem—everyone except me, that is.

"Yeah, I played right field," I said.

Cohen laughed. "You remember the last play-off game when we were so far ahead? The other team had a man on first and one on third, and the ground ball went to Bob, who threw it to Barry."

I did remember that game. My cousins, Walter and Dustin, had already hit the ball over the center-field fence for home runs. "Yeah, the runner was coming in to home plate, and Barry kept blocking him until he got hold of the ball and tagged the guy. The ump called interference, and ole Barry went ballistic, didn't he?"

Cohen howled with laughter. "He did, and then Barry tagged the runner again, but on the head, and then stabbed him with his cleats."

"You're outta here!" I said, adding what I remembered the umpire hollering.

"Yeah, yeah, and then Barry dropped the ball, hit the umpire on the head, yanked off his mask, and knocked his glasses off his hat and then stepped on 'em for good measure. Everybody came running out on the field, and the fists were flying."

"Shoot, Cohen, I didn't stay to the end of all that. I was in right field and took off running when I saw what was coming, got my shoes from the dugout, and left."

"Yeah, well, they banned the Canales from playing slow-pitch ball ever again," Cohen said, still chuckling.

"We were pretty bad, weren't we?" I said to my cousin.

"We weren't anything compared to the Tilner brothers. They were the bad boys. The Canales kept them in line, though."

Sitting there talking to Cohen, I realized something. As children and teenagers, we Canales were the keepers of the peace in our neighborhood. No one crossed us—no one dared, not even the really bad boys. Maybe that was why I couldn't let this evildoer now get away with what he was doing. He had pissed in my yard and crapped in my neighborhood. He was going down.

When we got up to leave, I told Cohen, "Well, you tell your brothers I said hi. I saw those trophies they got. They're headed for the hall of fame. Made me proud." I sincerely meant that. My cousins were all fantastic high-school, college, and pro football players. The six brothers were probably the best high-school football players to ever come out of Memphis. They'll ultimately be placed in the Tennessee Sports Hall of Fame, I'm sure of it. My football career was good but nothing when compared to theirs.

He smiled. "I will."

"And," I added, "your grocery store out there on the Tipton County line has the best ham sandwiches ever."

He beamed with pride. "You take care of yourself, Doc. I saw the news today. If you need the rest of us Canale boys, you just call us."

"I will, but it's probably best for me to just tuck my ol' turtle head back into my shell."

We laughed and headed back to the ICU.

That night I made the decision to sleep on the futon in the library at the clinic. That futon had been there ever since I could remember and had served as a napping ground for countless exhausted residents. It was purchased by one of our old retired doctors and placed in an out-of-the-way nook just for that purpose. The librarian named the nook "the Dr. Richards Reading Corner" in his honor. Tonight it was mine, because Abigail was spending the night with a friend down in Mississippi. She told me she was taking some time off from work because she was afraid and had plenty of PTO hours saved. I didn't blame her. Nurse Johnnie agreed to drive me to Target so I could buy a change of clothes and some toiletries for the next day. Only she knew where I would be staying for the night. Soon I'd have to venture back to my condo, though. At my instruction, workers had already replaced the damaged door with a new break-in-resistant metal one that looked like old wood to match the others in the hall and installed a super-reinforced doorjamb. I'd be pretty safe there—tomorrow.

For the time being, I was going to surf the web; have a bag of fried pork rinds, a cinnamon roll, two bags of M&Ms, and a Diet Coke from the snack machine; maybe watch a movie online; and then hit the futon when my eyes wouldn't stay open any longer. As I worked my way through one bad snack after the other, I started thinking about the killer again. Who the hell was he? My hands doodled on the desk calendar while my mind studied angles again. Simone had been married to Cooter. Simone and Monique had been friends. Monique had had an affair with Cooter. Simone had had an affair with a forty-something-year-old man who was married and didn't want to divorce his wife. They played croquet in Highlands, or at least Simone did. Mountain Way Country Club had a large contingent of croquet players. Delmár was the maître d' there. Delmár had two sons who were Muslim. Delmár was possibly hiding a terrorist cell. Delmár was being watched by the feds. The feds said Delmár was clean. Delmár was an efficient maître d'. Delmár's boss was Mick McCrory, the manager of the Mountain Way Country Club. Mick McCrory was in big money and lived part-time in San Miguel.

Suddenly a little light went off, and I reached for my wallet and searched the contents for the information Lloyd had given me of Highlands members who had gone to Cuba to play croquet, pretty sure he'd said one of them was from San Miguel. Shit, the list wasn't there. Maybe it was in my desk drawer. I rummaged around and then checked under my desk calendar. Only a receipt fell out; then I remembered I hadn't bothered writing down any names. Regardless, I was sure that Lloyd had said San Miguel.

I punched in Big Al's number. He picked up on the second ring. "Hey," I said. There was bar noise in the background, and it sounded as if he had a full house.

"Hey, what's going on, man?" he said. "Hang on a minute, so I can get somewhere quiet."

I waited. The background noise quieted.

"OK, I'm back in my office. What's going on?"

"Oh, not much, just running for my life is all."

"Dude," Big Al replied sympathetically.

"Can I ask you a question?"

"Sure."

"I know you always say not to ask you where you get your gossip from, but just this once, I'm gonna ask. How did you find out that Mick McCrory was manager at Mountain Way Country Club?"

"Son, that wasn't gossip. He told me."

"Really?"

"Yeah, he comes in here a couple a times a month."

"Really?"

"Yes," he replied slowly as if I were not on my game.

"So he told you about the Cuba tournament too?"

"Uh-huh."

How interesting. "You said he was big money now."

"That's right. He and the wife travel all over. They have a house in Highlands, one here, one in San Miguel, and I don't know where else. The man brags a lot about hisself, but he's a pretty good fella."

"Big Al, do country-club managers make big money?"

"Aw, hell no. He married his money. His old lady's family is in the import-export business. They have a warehouse here in Memphis; that's why they come every so often."

"When you say 'import-export,' like imports from where?"

"Egypt," Big Al said without hesitation.

"The Middle East?"

"Yeah, Cairo, to be exact."

"Well, how 'bout that." My brain processed this information at light speed.

"Terry, what're you thinking?"

"Dunno, Big Al. Dunno yet."

42

When the sun finally announced dawn, I moved from my fetal position on the futon and hoisted myself up to a sitting position. There was a crick in my neck, and both my hands and feet were asleep. It was six in the morning. The nurses and front-desk staff would be arriving in about thirty minutes. I hurried to the restroom with my bag of new clothes, dunked my head under the faucet, sponge-bathed, shaved, and brushed my teeth, all within ten minutes. It is at times like this that it is good to be a man. We don't have to fool with all the hot iron or makeup stuff. I got to my office just as Nurse Johnnie walked in.

"Hey, how was sleeping on the futon last night?" she asked as she started a pot of coffee.

"Slept like an embryo," I told her truthfully.

"Here are a couple of bagels and cream cheese for breakfast." She tossed a little brown bag my way.

"Oh, thanks. You didn't have to do that."

"Really?" She rolled her eyes and headed to the nurses' station but returned and poked her head back into my office. "Don't forget you have a case at ten and patients promptly at one." She emphasized the word "promptly."

"OK," I said absently. My mind was not on the knee that was on my schedule to scope but on Mick McCrory. We had never met, so to speak. I knew of him because of the rumors at the Universal Club and the million-dollar government lawsuit but had never actually seen him and had no idea what he looked like. All that had gone down at the U Club a good ten years earlier. I thought about calling Big Al to see if he could give me a description but then thought of Sunny, the front-desk lady at the Universal Club. She'd been working there for most of her adult life. If anyone could give me a description, it would be her. Fortunately, the two of us were pretty tight, so I rang her up, and not only could she describe Mick, but she also had a photo of him—an old one but one nonetheless. She scanned and e-mailed it to me. It was an old, grainy résumé photo, but at least it was something. I printed it out. Next I Googled "Mick McCrory" and "Mountain Way Country Club" and eventually hit on the name of his import-export business. It appeared he was in Egyptian cotton bedding, the expensive stuff. There was also a wedding announcement in the *Highlands Daily Gazette* from five years ago. He and a Bazi Rajeesh married first in the Mosque there and then at Saint Timothy's. Neither of them had a Facebook page. I sat back and studied Mick's picture. There was something naïve and innocent about him, but looks often can be deceiving, and the picture was old. Regardless, it was time for me to meet Mick and have a little chat with him. But how to go about making that happen was the question.

My cell phone dinged a text message and a picture. It was from Abigail, who was with Monique at the hospital. They had taken a selfie just for me. Evidently Monique was being discharged from ICU. They had pulled her chest tube, and her oxygen was above 95 percent. That was good news. I made a mental note to send a contribution to the Camp Foundation for all the hard work the orthopedic and trauma residents do. Sometimes we tend to forget just how difficult their job is and how hard the residents have to work to become top-notch surgeons. I vowed to be more sympathetic toward the residents and medical students in the future.

At ten, I headed over to the surgery center for the scheduled meniscectomy, taking a roundabout route through the hospital, across the bridge, and through the covered parking garage before crossing the street, so as not to be followed. At noon, I went a different way back to the office, where I hid out in the john for thirty minutes before going to the annex to see my patients.

At the end of clinic that day, I had Andy, our patient transporter, paged. I wanted to ask if he would drive me over to where my Explorer was parked, but when he showed up at my office door with rabbit-red eyes and a cloud of cannabis scent surrounding him, it was obvious he had been toking up behind the water heaters in the basement again. The last time Autrie took me anywhere, we ended up doing a full 360-degree slide on busy Madison Avenue, and I ended up walking home in an ice storm. Sooner or later there had to be a conversation with human resources about him.

"Never mind," I told Autrie and then begged Nurse Johnnie to lend me her wheels.

She didn't want to but held out her keys anyway. "Remember, you break it, you bought it," she warned.

"Thanks, Johnnie. I'll take care of her just like she's my own."

"That's what worries me."

"Here, let me drive you home first."

"No, thanks," she answered curtly. "You got some bad juju going on around you. I'll walk. It's only a couple of blocks."

"Well, be careful," I said to her.

"You just remember to bring my car back in one piece." She shoved the heavy door open, repositioned her little red purse, and marched off in the direction of her apartment.

Donning Ray-Bans and a beige baseball cap pulled way low, I snuck out the side door and jogged to Johnnie's blue Toyota, stealing glances in all directions to make sure no one was watching. I typed the address of Mick's warehouse into my GPS, and soon a little red dot that was me flashed to life on the screen, ready to lead the way.

Mick's warehouse was located in a desolate area off Jackson Avenue, not too far from the clinic. Within minutes I was coasting by his so-called business. A high chain link fence with barbed wire on top surrounded the entire property. It seemed deserted, with grass growing out through the asphalt in the parking lot. There were no trucks or cars or any other signs of life. I hung a left down a narrow dead-end road with crater-like potholes and drove around to the back of the property. It was even more overgrown than the front. Outside the fence at the rear of the building, a Dumpster sat full to the top with empty boxes that didn't look all that old. Not really sure what I'd hoped to accomplish and not wanting to Dumpster dive or climb over a fence with barbed wire, I decided to bring the car back to Johnnie and call it a night. Tomorrow my plan was to call the Mountain Way Country Club and find out where Mick McCrory was.

A sudden jolt threw me forward in my seat belt, and my head hit the headrest with a bang. A sickening, crunching noise accompanied that. Surprised and dazed, I checked the rearview mirror, which confirmed my suspicions that something big had hit me. A huge, dark-blue garbage truck was glued to the back of Johnnie's Toyota. Who picks up trash after hours? I wondered. It wasn't the city of Memphis; that was for sure. A big man with a wife-beater shirt climbed out of the cab. Shit! I thought and ducked low, expecting a hail of bullets, a swift execution Mafia style, but the man banged on my window instead, his face bright red and frightened. Realizing he wasn't about to shoot me, I let the window down a few inches.

"Buddy, are you all right?" he asked, all upset. "I didn't see you. I swear! The lifters were already up, and I totally didn't see you parked here!"

"I'm fine," I assured him, not wanting to get out of the car.

The man dug through his pockets and pulled out a cell phone. "I gotta call this in," he told me.

"No!" I shouted.

He looked at me, dumbfounded. The last thing I wanted was for him to alert the police and me have to explain what I was doing there. Reardon would be furious.

"I gotta at least call my boss," he argued. "You got some serious damage back here."

I didn't want that happening either because his boss might well be Mick. "It's fine," I said resolutely, putting the car in gear and giving it some gas. The man stood back, his mouth agape. The wheels spun, so I put the juice to it, sending up clouds of dust until the bumper finally broke loose, and we were separated. The bumper clanged loudly on the concrete. Working feverishly to get the car turned around, I could see he was punching a number into his cell phone. Once the vehicle was in a favorable position for a quick getaway, I jumped out, picked up Nurse Johnnie's bumper, and threw it into the back seat.

"Have a good day," I called out to the man and got the hell out of there before the cops showed up—or his boss.

Fifteen minutes later I was backing the car into a parking space at Johnnie's apartment building. I rang her doorbell. When she answered, I held out the key to her Toyota and my credit card.

She rolled her eyes. "I knew it! I knew it! What happened?" She put both hands on her hips.

"Some asshole rear-ended me."

"Where? Did he have insurance?"

"Out off Jackson. You're gonna need a new bumper. I didn't ask about insurance, sorry."

She snatched her key and my credit card and slammed the door in my face.

Without wheels I was forced to call a cab to take me back to my condo. I had the cabby pull over a few blocks from my building so I could walk the rest of the way through backyard alleys. After hiding in a bush and scoping out the parking lot to make sure there weren't any black Lexuses parked in front, I slid into the building through a side utility door using my code and took the stairs two at a time up to my place.

It was good to be back in my element except for the fact that it was empty. MeMoe wasn't there to greet me, and neither was Monique or Abigail. As a precautionary measure, the next five minutes were spent throwing open closets and checking behind doors and under beds, although it was unlikely the killers would strike in the same place twice, especially since they didn't know where I was. My car was still parked behind the Dumpster at the Holiday Inn on Union, or so I hoped. Also, Reardon had stationed two new cops at Henry the door-man's desk, and besides, my new front door would require a rocket launcher to get through. To be on the safe side, though, I retrieved my gun from the nightstand and stuck it in the back of my pants before checking out the fridge. The bagel Johnnie had brought for breakfast had long since been digested, and I was starving. Normally pizza or Chinese delivery would have been an option, but that was probably not a wise thing to do. There was a tub of hummus sitting in the back of the fridge that passed my sniff test, some celery with just a few slimy parts, and a box of Ritz crackers from last year's Christmas party up in the cupboard. It'd have to do. I couldn't really remember when I had last been to the grocery store and bought the hummus, but what was the worst that could happen? With all the cards stacked against me lately, what's a little salmonella poisoning, I thought.

Well, of all the poor judgment calls I had made in the last few months, that one was by far the worst. Dying of salmonella is a hundred times worse than being shot to death. By midnight my stomach had started talking crazy; by two I was intimately acquainted with the rim of my toilet bowl; and by five I was sprawled supine on the bathroom tile, begging the good Lord to deliver my raunchy, undeserving soul out of purgatory. Fortunately, our God is ever loving and decided to shed his grace on me around seven in the morning, when I finally collapsed into bed.

Sometime in the afternoon, I regained consciousness, the inside of my mouth feeling as if I'd been chewing on cotton and my body so dehydrated that my eyelids peeled off parts of the cornea when they opened. Groaning, I stumbled to the bathroom, which still reeked of vomitus, and threw open the window. After rinsing my mouth copiously with cold water, my heavy head resting on the sink basin beneath the faucet, and then with mouthwash, I went to town scrubbing the grit from between my teeth with a brand-new electric toothbrush. Only then did I feel well enough to venture into the kitchen for a bottle of water. The hummus tub still sat on the counter, mocking me, along with the crackers, which caused another wave of nausea. I swallowed hard, breathed through my nostrils, and concentrated on looking out the window. One thing was for certain: if I lived to be a thousand years old, never, ever would that gritty-tasting shit find a place on my plate again.

My phone dinged a message. It was from Nurse Johnnie. *I'm putting $4,500 on your credit card for a new bumper.*

Forty-five hundred dollars? That sounded like a hell of a lot, but what did I know about bumpers? *OK,* I meekly texted back.

The phone dinged again. *Just kidding. My cousin said he'd get me a used bumper for $250, and I'll live with the dent if you promise never to borrow anything from me again.*

Deal. Use the credit card, I replied.

Almost immediately she replied to my message. *I'll collect when I see you again. You can run, but you can't hide. Just don't go dying on me.*

If she only knew how close I had come to death these last few days, she'd have used the card.

43

Even with the ruckus going on in my bowels, I stayed on track with my plans to call the Mountain Way Country Club and find out the whereabouts of Mr. McCrory. His assistant told me he wasn't in the office.

"I'm an old friend of his," I lied. "Is there somewhere I can get ahold of him?"

"He has a cell phone, but what did you say your name is?" She was hesitant about giving me his number, and that wasn't really what I wanted anyway. I wanted to know where he was—exactly.

"Oh, that's OK; you don't have to give out his number. I'll just show up and surprise him."

"Well, he's in Florida this week," she said, leaking a smidgen of information.

"That's right; he's playing croquet this week in…uh…ah…" I was fishing. I had no idea if he was playing croquet.

"The Florida Keys," she provided helpfully.

"That's right. He's down in South Florida; shoot, he did tell me about that. I forgot. He usually stays at that really nice place down there with the little umbrellas on the beach…uh…oh…what's that place called again? My mind always quits working when I get such a lovely voice on the other end of the line." I played with her a bit more.

"Mangrove Island Resort, down in Little Torch." She was eager to help.

"There you go," I said. "Mangrove Resort. Nice place, isn't it?"

"I guess. I've never been there. He's playing golf, though, not croquet," she flirted back.

"Really? I thought he was all into croquet these days."

"No, he plays some, but I think he really prefers golf. If he calls, I could give him a message," she offered. "He can call you back. I've already stored your number. What's your name?"

Crap. "No, that's OK. Thanks. I'll catch him some other time. Bye now." Boy, was that a dumb mistake. Now they had my number. I could only hope she'd forget to tell him about the dubious call she'd received. This hadn't accomplished a thing but open up the possibility of me becoming the "spud." That was a game we'd played in college where you take a tennis ball and throw it up in the air and call a person's name. If that person catches it without dropping it, he can throw the ball up and call another name, but if he doesn't catch it, he has to try to hit someone else with it. If he misses, he becomes the spud and has to bend over and grab his ankles while the others throw the ball as hard as they can at his rear end. If this woman told on me before I could get to Mick, I'd be the spud. Only now the stakes were higher than just having tennis balls lobbed at my ass.

The next call I made was to Nurse Johnnie. "Get me on a plane down to Miami like today. I gotta get down to Little Torch Key."

"Little Torch Key? You've got patients on Monday afternoon. You'll be back by then, right?" she asked fussily.

"Of course. Get me outta there by Sunday."

"OK, I'll call you back in a minute."

She was able to make reservations for a flight from Memphis to Miami through Atlanta, but I'd have to do the rest by car. The other bad news was that she couldn't get any aisle seats for me, just a window and a middle seat. Usually that's a deal killer for me, but I went ahead and took it. She also made a reservation for me at the Palm Tree Hotel in Key Largo, which I wasn't happy about, but after her car fiasco, I wasn't about to complain. She was still trying to get me in at the Mangrove Island Resort. I packed my bag in a hurry and called a cab to take me to the airport.

From Memphis to Atlanta, the window seat was no problem. A small, five-foot-two, ninety-eight-pound woman was in the seat next to mine; she didn't talk at all, and she smelled nice. But on the flight from Atlanta to Miami, I knew it was trouble when a husband-and-wife team with matching Humpty Dumpty T-shirts waddled down the aisle to my row, studying the alphabet above my head. I offered them my middle seat so they could sit together, but Dumpty was a window-seat-only flyer, and Humpty was an aisle-seat-only, which left me sandwiched between the two for an hour and forty minutes in addition to the usual thirty-minute tarmac delay. Not only had aisle-seat Humpty brought an enormous carry-on with her but also a huge purse, a laptop, and a grocery bag full of snacks that she intermittently fed to Dumpty on the other side of me. If my bowels started acting up again, there'd be no way the woman could get up in time. At one handoff of chocolate-pudding packs, Humpty upset the Styrofoam cup on my tray.

When the stewardess saw, she asked, "Sir, would you like some more coffee?"

No, bitch, I want some more seat with a side of legroom, I thought. I couldn't see how the airline's policy of giving people twelve more inches of seat belt was of any benefit to me. That wasn't even enough to hang myself. I didn't say any of that, though.

We landed, and the pilot's voice came over the intercom: "Thank you for flying with us. Again, we apologize for the delay."

Well, screw you too! I thought angrily and told aisle-seat Humpty I was a surgeon and had a patient waiting for me on the table.

At the Miami airport, I went in search of a bathroom and then the car-rental place. This time a compact Nissan Versa would have to do. Annoyingly, my bank-account balance was showing that my bottom line had taken a serious hit in the last couple of months with all the extra expenses, but I tried not to think about that on the drive to the Florida Keys and instead focused on the warm breeze and the smell of the open sea. The landscape had disappeared with twilight, leaving only dark silhouettes of palms and live oaks lining the road.

I arrived at the hotel well after room service closed, which really didn't make a bit of difference to me since my stomach was still in cleansing mode. The room was a far cry from what I'm used to, which prompted another thorough bedbug search on my part. It's only for one night, I told myself, and in the morning it would be off to Mangrove Island Resort.

I put in a call to the resort and asked for Mick McCrory. They put me right through, and after two rings a sleepy voice answered, "Hello?"

"I'm sorry. I must have the wrong number," I said and hung up. OK, so he was there. Now my plans could go forward. I dumped the contents of my bag onto the bed and surveyed my clothes piled in a wrinkled heap. To get into a place like that, I'd need something nicer to wear, which meant stopping at the overpriced gift shop. This was just the kind of thing that was breaking the bank.

Sifting through the clothes, I dialed the Mangrove number again.

Little Torch Key, which is seventy-five miles from Key Largo, is pretty well known in my neck of the woods. Some prominent Memphians bought one of the small islands, the only one with freshwater. They ran power to it and opened a swanky resort. It used to be one of the president's summer retreats way back when. Their website boasts decked-out bungalows, the only white beach in the keys, and a chef from New York City.

A female voice answered, "Mangrove Island Resort. How may I help you?"

I could have called Johnnie about the reservation but was pretty sure that disturbing her at this late hour would result in her pinching my head off Monday morning.

"This is Dr. Terry Canale. I'm just calling to confirm my bungalow for tomorrow night."

"Certainly," the female voice said to me. "We have you scheduled in one with a queen-size bed."

"Great."

"Is that for one night?"

I wanted to ask how much the room cost but didn't want her to catch wind of my economic downturn. "One night."

"Certainly. The cost of the room is six hundred and...thirty-five dollars plus tax for tomorrow night, with check-in tomorrow at two."

"Great," I said without enthusiasm. Having to be frugal really sucks, by the way. The new duds would have to wait.

It occurred to me that no one except Johnnie knew where I was, and I briefly considered calling Big Al to let him know, just in case something went down. Even though we had been friends for a lot years and I trusted him for the most part, how he came about his information was an enigmatic process, and I wasn't all that sure it was a one-way street. It probably was better for me if he didn't know anything. Abigail and Monique also didn't know my whereabouts, and that was better for them.

My room overlooked the ocean and the private beach below. A full moon was mirrored in the water just beyond the breaks. Although the traffic wasn't visible from my balcony, I could hear it along the causeway that spans the coral islands for over a hundred miles, almost to Cuba. Abigail would sure enjoy this, I thought, picturing her golden hair and deep blue eyes, her perfect mouth, the elegant curve of her neck, the place right above her cleavage where the little golden cross from her necklace always found a home. I missed her. What in the world was I doing in Key Largo alone without my leading lady? I was Bogie without Bacall. Low-lying clouds passed over the moon, and the night darkened, and so did my mood. My thoughts were not about my plan for tomorrow and not about Mick McCrory but about Abigail and me, about us. Just a few months ago, she and I really did have it all—money, sex, freedom, and, if not love, then certainly friendship. Did we still have it? As the wind picked up and the first drops of rain fell, I crawled into bed with a sinking heart, pretty much knowing the answer to that one.

44

It was drizzling the next morning, and all I wanted to do was throw the covers over my head and sleep the rest of the day or maybe the rest of my life. But there was this business of running down a murderer hanging over my head, so I got up and picked through the clothes pile. None of it was ritzy, but with a few tweaks, it could pass for grungy chic. I showered but didn't shave, tore some holes in the knees of my Levis with an envelope knife, rolled up the sleeves of my pinstripe shirt to midarm, left the top three buttons open, and slipped into my sandals. After eating a bowl of complimentary Rice Krispies for breakfast, with milk this time, I stopped at the gift shop and purchased a straw hat and a shell necklace to complete my look. It was the compromise my budget conscience and ego had reached. By ten, I was on the road and, unbeknown to me at the time, southwest bound to big trouble.

The rain stopped somewhere near Marathon, and by the time Big Pine Key was in sight, it was hot and humid. By Little Torch Key, the sun was back out in all its glory. I hung a left on Pirates Road, pulled into the parking lot of the check-in center, got out my bag, and strolled into the white building. I gave the woman at the desk my name and credit card. She let me know politely that it wasn't quite check-in time yet but invited me to wait inside, where it was cool. I asked if it would be all right if I sat out on the wharf to just enjoy the scenery until it was time.

"Why, of course," she said pleasantly.

Outside the building a young Latino man dressed in white handed me a beverage that looked like a hurricane, but I, ever polite, declined and walked to the end of the pier, where I took a seat on a wooden bench overlooking the ocean. Seagulls soared overhead, taking a keen interest in me and my bag. The actual resort where the bungalows are could only be reached by boat, so a yacht served as the ferry from morning until night. One was just docking. I took the photo of Mick out of my bag, and as the guests disembarked, I closely scrutinized the faces of the men. None of them looked like Mick. Of course, the man would now be ten or fifteen years older than in the picture, which meant he could be gray by now or not have any more hair at all; he could be heavier; he could have jowls—jeez, for all I knew, he could have had a sex-change operation. Shit, the picture was no help at all.

A white gull circled low above my head, landed on the bench next to my bag, and turned its head this way and that, obviously begging for food. Another landed on the railing in front of me, and a few others quickly followed suit. Opening the bag was evidently some kind of signal to them that it was feeding time. I stuffed the photo back into place and zipped the bag shut. In the time it took me to do this, just mere seconds, this bird situation had become a scene out of Hitchcock's movie. They were perched everywhere, at least a hundred of them, their beady little eyes watching me with intense curiosity. I sat perfectly still, as did they for the most part. A couple of bullies in the mob hurled bird obscenities my way, to which I could've responded, but something inside told me the better part of valor in this circumstance was to keep calm. Cautiously, I reached for the handle of my duffel and slowly got up, trying not to cause a full-blown riot and bring unnecessary attention to myself. As I moved with deliberate care through the white throng, a few took wing, complaining loudly at my blatant stinginess, and the more they were ignored, the more belligerent they became, diving and taking potshots at me. Then, without warning, one of the bastards swooped down and plucked my new straw hat right off my head. I swatted at the bird, but it was too late. It flew straight up in the air and hovered, the hat dangling from its beak, and then it let go. I watched as my sixty-dollar hat fluttered into the ocean. The other birds hooted and cawed insults in their ugly avian language and took off in a swarm to harass someone else on shore.

Son of a bitch! I watched as my hat floated away from the dock. "Damn it, damn it, damn it!" I ranted, tearing out of my shirt and sandals. I threw my phone and wallet on top of my bag and jumped into the water. No way was my new straw hat getting away.

The water was cold and invigorating and smelled scantly of seaweed and fish—dead fish, that is. I captured my wayward hat and swam to the ladder at the end of the pier. As I accomplished the last rung, the young Latino waiter came running toward me with a starched bar mop in hand.

"Sir! Sir! Are you all right, sir?"

A small group of Good Samaritans was also standing by to make sure their assistance wasn't needed in my rescue.

"Sure, I'm fine. Just went in after my hat," I said nonchalantly, as if it were the most normal thing in the world. And it was, for me. Whenever I encounter a problem, I just jump right on in and take care of it—don't need anyone or anything, just taking care of business. It was a bold and confident move, an exhilarating experience, really. My mind and body felt effervescent, bubbly. There was a downright tingling sensation all over my skin. A glob of pink slime dripped from my ear and hit the wooden pier.

The waiter handed me his bar towel. "Red algae," he confirmed. "It's toxic. We've been under red-algae warnings all month. You should wash that off right away." He got on his walkie-talkie to find out about my room.

Red algae—nice. And the day had started out so promising.

45

There is an upside to swimming around in toxic sludge if you're a guest at a fancy resort. Thanks to our litigious society, the resort was very sorry that their sign wasn't posted more prominently, and in an effort to make amends, they had my room ready in no time flat—and all drinks were on the house. Too bad drinking wasn't my thing anymore, but I was happy for the early check-in and boarded the next yacht out.

The word "yacht" conjures an image of a cabin cruiser for millionaires, but this was more like a riverboat modified to hold people instead of cargo. From Little Torch Key, it was a fifteen-minute jaunt south to the resort. Looking to my right, the dot that was Key West was barely visible in the distance, and to my left was the Atlantic. The day was ruled by a high-pressure system with high cotton-candy clouds floating in a sea of blue above and below, but I wasn't enjoying the view. A young Middle Eastern man had my full attention. The man had jumped on board just as the boat undocked and had taken a seat across from me. His attention, though, was on the Atlantic side of the ferry and not me. Maybe he appreciated the vista. Not packing heat was worrisome, although it probably wouldn't matter that much, since I'm a terrible shot. Hopefully it wouldn't come to needing guns.

When we arrived at the resort, the man jumped off and jogged toward the main pavilion. I watched him disappear into the building as a young woman handed me a map, giving me a quick rundown of all the island had to offer and pointing out that bungalow four on the Newfound Harbor side was mine. According to the map, in addition to the white beach and pool, the island housed a store, a dive shop, a lounge, a fitness center, an outdoor massage area, a dining room, and a library. It was strictly pedestrian, however, with no cars, golf carts, or bicycles allowed. You either walked to wherever you wanted to go, or you didn't go.

I followed the map to my bungalow. As promised, it had a queen-size bed draped with mosquito netting, a wet bar, Jacuzzi tub, and air conditioning. The French door opened to a private patio overlooking a paradise garden.

"Terry, boy, oh boy, you could get used to this," I said to myself as I peeled off my wet jeans and called the concierge to have someone come launder them. I jumped into the shower, still didn't shave, donned my swim shorts, and headed out to explore this little piece of heaven. My first stop was the pool. Except for a bored, well-tanned lifeguard, no one else was there. I dove right in and swam some laps to get rid of nervous energy and then set off to do some real snooping. It would have been futile to call the front desk and ask which bungalow was Mick's, so I went for an island stroll instead, ultimately ending up in the gift shop. After perusing the shelves and racks there for better than an hour while checking out everyone who walked through the door, I decided to grab a canoe and try my luck snooping by water.

It took a while to get used to paddling again, but once I got the hang of it, the canoe glided smoothly through the water. It's like riding a bicycle; you never really forget once you know how. I'd earned my canoeing badge of courage on the Greenbrier River in Alderson, West Virginia, back in middle school. It's one of the best white-water rivers in the eastern part of the country. My canoe mate was Draden Neighbors, a wild child from Birmingham whose parents just sent him to camp to get a break from him. Our canoeing party started with seven canoes, but I'm not sure how many were left in the end. The first rapid, Little Rattler, wasn't too difficult—a lot of white water, but the challenge was in dodging the boulders. After that we had to portage a ways, and when we stopped to catch our breath, we were informed that Sunshine was our next rapid. It's called Sunshine not because it's a happy place but because the glare off the water and rocks totally blinds you. Early in Sunshine, one of the other canoes hit a boulder and capsized, but luckily we were able to get their canoe turned back over, and they could still use it. All in all, there were probably nine or ten rapid sequences, but by far the worst was Big Rattle Snake, which flushes through a narrow gorge. It's considered a class 3 technical rapid because you have to maneuver an insane obstacle course while being pummeled by white water. Our canoe took a brutal beating. I may have peed my pants, but who's to say, because we were drenched from head to toe, and the canoe was half filled with water when we came out of that gulch. Some of the other canoes didn't make it. Everyone had on a life vest, and no one was bludgeoned to death by the rocks, but I made a mental note that white-water canoeing wasn't my sport. Big-talk Draden Neighbors, by the way, also didn't have much to say after Big Rattle Snake.

By comparison, paddling around Mangrove Island was a leisurely activity. Unfortunately, the bungalows were all hidden behind vegetation, so spying from the water was out of the question. Although I discovered a deserted body of land so overgrown with bushes and fauna that there was no place to land a boat and some unique sea turtles that floated by my canoe, I was drawing a big fat zero regarding Mick McCrory.

With the canoe returned to its place, I reclined on the beach and did some people watching and then hung around the cabana to see if Mick or Delmár or anyone else suspicious might materialize. No one did, so I ran surveillance on the pier, watching guests come and go on the ferry. Except for a few small speedboats racing in and out of the harbor, nothing of interest seemed to be happening at all. The Honeymoon Cottage, a large houseboat parked in the marina, caught my attention, and because it was empty, I ventured a look inside. The interior was fascinating, but again none of this had anything to do with my mission of finding Mr. McCrory. By early evening I gave up on just sitting and watching and hit the Jacuzzi to reassess my strategy. The island wasn't that big; surely the two of us would run into each other sooner or later. The trouble was that my stay was going to be over sooner rather than later. I checked my cell phone. It hadn't made a peep all afternoon because the island had no service—no Internet either, which was a good thing, I reasoned, because it meant that Mick might not have been in touch with his office to find out about my call yesterday.

For dinner I dressed in my best khaki shorts, a white long-sleeve shirt, a blue blazer, and Weejuns without socks. Quirky enough, I thought. At the bar, the bartender asked for my choice of poison and frowned ever so slightly when I said Perrier. He handed me the water and busied himself polishing wineglasses. With my elbows on the counter and my water in hand, I tried some small talk with him, asking about the Honeymoon Cottage, the weather, and the small island I had discovered, which, it turned out, was owned by the Boy Scouts. When the conversation ran dry, I asked casually, "Do you know Mick McCrory?"

"Yes, sir. He always comes by before dinner. I'm surprised he isn't here yet. Would you like for me to tell him you're waiting?"

"No, that's OK. I'll catch him later. I'm gonna go check out your library."

I took the water with me to the library and continued to wait. The library was full of historical books and some best sellers, the titles of which I pretended to study, all the while keeping a watch out for Mick. By seven he was still a no-show, so it was off to the dining room, where they were serving crab legs and a salad. I sat facing the door, my usual arrangement these days. The entire establishment was in view, and the ocean beyond as well. All the island's comings and goings were now known to me, but still there was no Mick. I stopped back by the bar after dinner and asked if he had come by, but the bartender said he had not and suggested he might have gone to the mainland or Key West for dinner.

I waited on the pier until way after the last ferry left before deciding to return to my hut. This had been another disappointing endeav-
or, another blown chance to catch the man off guard. My hamstrings
were aching from the canoe trip, and on the way back to my bungalow, my right leg actually cramped up. I stumbled into my room and
went straight for the whirlpool tub, where I sat soaking for more than
an hour. Not knowing what else to do with myself, I decided to go to
bed and dropped almost immediately into a sound sleep.

Bang, bang, bang.

I shifted under my netting, dreaming about duck hunting, another sport I don't appreciate.

Bang, bang, bang.

There it was again. I opened an eye. Someone was rapping on my
door.

I sat up straight. "Who is it?" I demanded.

"Security. I'm sorry to bother you, but you have an emergency call
from Memphis at the front desk."

Who would be calling me from Memphis? Johnnie? Big Al?
Abigail? Had Monique died? Was it Reardon? Did they want to lock
my ass up after all? I looked at the phone on my nightstand.

"Why don't they put it through to my room?" I asked suspiciously.

"They've been trying, sir, but your phone is out of order."

"It wasn't earlier." I distinctly remembered calling the concierge
upon my arrival.

"I'm sorry, but apparently it's not working now."

I picked up the phone. No dial tone.

"Sir?" the man outside said.

I felt like one of the three little pigs. I stalled. "I'll be right there.
Just let me get some clothes on."

"I'll wait right here for you, sir."

Damn it. "You don't have to," I told him through the door, dressing quickly in whatever was piled closest to the bed, a T-shirt and
shorts and my Weejuns. I grabbed the lamp off the nightstand, pulled
the cord out of the plug, and tested its weight.

"I don't mind, sir, really."

Peering through the peephole, I said, "I'm a bit nervous because I've had several things happen to me over the past couple of months. Do you mind showing me some identification?"

"Of course not."

"Can you hold it up, please?"

He complied. It looked authentic. He looked authentic, a short Latino man with a moustache. His badge said Frank something or the other. He looked like security. He had on a uniform. Convincing myself that this was paranoid behavior, I put the lamp back in its place, deciding to open the door.

"Sorry about that," I apologized, stepping outside, looking left and right.

"Not at all," he replied politely and led the way briskly down the lighted walkway toward the office building.

As Frank and I rounded the library, something hard pressed into my left side.

"Don't say a word or you're dead," a man's heavily accented voice said.

Ahead, Frank kept walking, disappearing into the night. I looked down and saw a .38 with a silencer pointed upward to my heart. Attached to the pistol grip was a large, bald man. A smaller guy moved to my right side. It did cross my mind that these might have been the same men who'd attacked me in Cuba.

The big guy nudged me with his piece. "Walk this way."

Alone in the darkness with these killers, my options seemed limited, so I didn't scream or try to get away. In retrospect this is not the thing to do. I've since decided that if someone tries to kidnap you, you should fight and kick and scream as loud as you can. If they kill you, so be it. If you do whatever they say, they'll kill you anyway and no telling what else. It's the "what else" that's extremely unpleasant; I'll tell you that much. I lived to talk about it, but it could have just as easily gone the other way.

We took a shortcut through some bushes to the Atlantic-side dock, where a midnight-blue, thirty-foot speedboat waited, just like the one MeMoe and I had seen in Biloxi. It didn't take a genius to see that this vessel was a smuggler's tool. With a narrow body, a hull built for planing, and multiple motors, a boat like this could easily do seventy knots an hour and probably couldn't be detected by radar. I guess that's why they're called go-fast boats. The small man waved an arm, inviting me to jump on board, and as soon as we were in our seats, a third gentleman, Frank, the so-called security guard, started a small trolling motor and quietly floated past the marina without lights, out past the Honeymoon Cottage, and away from shore. At fifty yards out, he fired up one of three engines but continued to quietly putter out to sea until the lights from the island were mere speckles in the distance. It wasn't the best night for smuggling or human trafficking, because there was a full moon and the ocean was relatively calm, but the three kidnappers didn't seem concerned. I expected once we were far enough out, we would race to wherever they were destined, but that never happened. Frank cruised out of the main channel and headed southwest, doing about fifteen knots.

46

As the lights of Key West came closer, we slowed and pulled up alongside a Chris-Craft cruiser, also painted a stealthy dark color. Frank cut the engine and grabbed his Beretta, pointing it at me and then at the ladder, making it clear I was to board the other boat. Three other men were waiting up on deck, one at the helm, one with a gun, and one was Mick McCrory, an older and heavier version of his résumé picture. He was slightly shorter than me and possibly better looking, with graying hair but otherwise boyish features. He was wearing a dinner jacket with his blue jeans and black T-shirt. The other two men looked alike—Delmár's sons, no doubt.

"Hello!" Mick greeted me jovially as the go-fast boat pulled away from the cruiser and motored away.

"Hello," I replied evenly. He nodded to his man, who proceeded to search me for weapons or bugs, I supposed.

"I'm Mick McCrory." He pointed to himself. "And this is my boat." He waved his arm around in an arc. "I hear you've been looking for me, Dr. Canale."

With nothing dramatic to say, I remained silent.

"Am I sick or something, Doctor? No communicable disease, I hope."

His voice sounded oddly familiar.

"No," I answered carefully.

"Then what do you want?"

"I wanted to ask if you could show me how to play a deadly game of croquet," I answered, looking for an escape route.

"Is that all? For me to show you how to play croquet?" He smiled wryly. "Well, it would be my honor." He put a hand to his chest and bowed slightly. "Why didn't you just say so?"

"I didn't want to just come right out and ask. That would be rude." I continued the charade.

"Really? I don't think so, but who told you I teach croquet? I don't give lessons to just anyone."

"A mutual friend sent me here," I said, suggesting that someone else knew I was there. It was a lie, of course.

"Does this mutual friend have a name?"

I weighed my options on this question and decided to deflect. "What's with the guys and them whisking me away from my bed like that? Do you always greet potential students this way?"

He crossed his arms. "We have to be careful."

"Why is that?"

"Why not. I own a very successful import-export business. People can't be trusted."

"Egyptian cotton," I said and could've bitten my tongue off for having done so. From the corner of my eyes, I could see an open crate of automatic weapons near the cabin door. I resisted the urge to look over at it. Reardon had been right. None of this really had anything to do with Simone. I had stumbled upon a hornet's nest.

Mick smiled. "That's right, Egyptian cotton."

"Obviously lucrative." I motioned toward his cruiser, casting a glance at the open crate.

"I could do worse."

I smiled pleasantly, looking him dead in the eye. He didn't look away.

"So, who was this person who recommended me so highly?" he asked.

"One of the staff at the Mountain Way Country Club," I replied.

"Ah. So this person told you where I could be found?"

"I wouldn't want to get *her* into trouble," I said.

His tone grew frosty and his eyes mean. Clasping his hands behind his back, Mick studied me for a long moment. "Who knows you're here, Doc?"

"Well…let's see…A few friends, the hospital administrator, the mayor, most of my colleagues, your secretary, the lady who does my pedicures…why? Do you require references before you give lessons? Or are you worried someone else might know about your little set up here?" I nodded my head toward the weapons.

He snorted but began pacing. "You know, you should've left well enough alone after Cuba."

The game was quite over. "You were the one who nailed my hands to that board!"

"No, of course not; I would never do a thing like that. You have my men to thank for that."

I stood perfectly still.

He stopped pacing and came so close I could smell his peppermint breath. "You're interfering with our operations, Doctor, you know that? Now, who knows you're here?" he demanded.

"I stepped back not because I was afraid but because face talkers have always bothered me. "Well, to be honest, I can't really remember…I told so many." I shrugged. "I think I may have told that cop who put me in jail. I'm not sure. Will that be a problem for you?"

"No, not really."

"They'll come looking for me."

He smiled blandly. "Won't matter, since I won't be here when they come looking. My business has made me a rich man, Doc. A very rich man—so rich, I plan to give it up and start going to church after this run."

"They say God forgives everyone." I couldn't stop myself, but at least I didn't say God only forgives the penitent man.

He smiled wide. "See, now that's what I think too." His tone became disturbingly conversational. "I'll do this one last run, close down the warehouse in Memphis, and move to San Miguel for good. And I'll join a church."

"Is that why you didn't have me killed in Cuba or tonight? Because you're basically a good man?" Some more buttering up couldn't hurt.

He shook his head. "No, no, that's not it. I just wanted to see how much you know and to whom you might have blabbed, although... seeing you squirm the past month or so has been very gratifying, I must say." He moved his eyebrows up and down and began to theatrically chew his gum.

It hit me like a blow to the head—the Cheshire cat! This was the man I had seen on the pier in Biloxi! I swallowed hard and hoped he hadn't noticed.

"Yes, that's right, Doctor; I've been watching you." He chewed while he smiled, motioning to the young man with the gun. "Why don't you have a seat? You'll be more comfortable while we get on with business."

His hired gun tried to push me into a seat, but I resisted.

Mick reached for a nearby harpoon, removed it from its rack, and tested the sharpness with his thumb. "A bit dull," he concluded, shaking his head. He pointed the harpoon at my belly. "I really don't wanna have to mess up my boat, Doc. So please, have a seat."

Stall, stall, stall was all I could think of as I sat and allowed his goon to bind my ankles together with neat sailor knots. "I guess you were the one who had my friend Monique shot?" I came right out and asked.

"Yes," he answered plainly, putting the harpoon carefully back in its place. "Made sure myself that we didn't miss the second time around." He threw a dirty look to the man at the wheel. "I took her out right after my boy sprayed that building with bullets and then just walked away. No one ever saw. Cops are so dumb."

"Why? She didn't know anything about your operation. This was always about her friend Simone, not guns." I didn't tell him that Monique had survived.

For a split second, his back straightened. "Simone," he repeated flatly, turning away from me and silently looking out over the black ocean. He didn't speak for a long moment. "She was..." His voice faltered. "Simone was the best time I ever had," he finished wistfully. When he turned back to face me, his eyes were devoid of humanity. "Before she..." He paused. "Passed."

Holy moly, what have we here?

"We had the world's greatest love affair, she and I."

Hell, with a love like that, who needs hate in the world? "So then why'd you kill her?" I challenged, looking frantically around the boat for options. Should I jump?

"She got to be a lot of trouble," he said, not even trying to deny this deed either. He was obviously pretty confident that I wouldn't live to tell about it. "Just like you and your girlfriend Monique and that little blonde you hang with."

I began to sweat. After he killed me, he would go after Abigail and then Monique when he found out she wasn't dead.

"That gal Monique—she's like a cat, isn't she?" He laughed. "I got her dead in the chest, and she lived!"

Damn, he already knew she'd survived. "Monique knows nothing about any of this, I promise, and certainly not the blonde." I wasn't about to give him Abigail's name. "Monique has no idea it was you."

"Whoops, my bad, then," he said, rubbing his beardless face. "But she'll figure out who I am sooner or later, so...it's bye, bye, baby, time."

"How'd you get away with it?" I asked, just to buy myself more time. "I mean, did you kill her at the U Club? They have security cameras there."

He watched me for a full ten seconds. "You know what I think?" he finally said.

I shook my head.

He grinned, evidently having reached a decision on what he was thinking. "I believe that nobody knows you're here. You came here all by yourself."

"You're wrong."

"Am I? I don't think so. But I'll tell you what. Since we have a little time, and you went to all this trouble to come find me, I'll tell you the whole story."

I didn't think I really needed to hear the whole story, because last I checked I wasn't wearing clergy black, but he seemed to disagree with me and kept talking, obviously enjoying his captive audience. "Simone wanted me to get a divorce, and I promised her I would; you know how it is with women. But she just kept on and on about it." He leaned against the side of the boat, casually resting one elbow on the railing. "The night it all came to a head between us, she'd had one too many martinis at the U Club and got downright mean and ugly— a nasty woman, actually. I told her that I would call my wife in the morning and tell her about us, but she didn't believe me."

Smart girl, I thought.

"Instead of doing me out there on the croquet court like she was supposed to that night, she just kept arguing with me. I ripped off her dress, you know, to move things along. Usually she liked that, but that night she started screaming and wouldn't stop. That's when I had to bonk her pretty little head with her own croquet mallet. She made me do it."

I watched Mick's benign face, realizing that this was the countenance of true evil: a bankrupt soul that feels nothing.

"Here's the thing, Doc. I really didn't mean it. I mean, don't get me wrong; sooner or later she was gonna have to go. I have people who take care of such unpleasantness for me, but at that moment it was a reflex because she wouldn't stop squealing. I had to shut her up."

"So then you proceeded to stab an already dying woman to death with a croquet wicket?" I couldn't comprehend how someone could do something like that. He hadn't loved Simone. She was no more than a cheap lay with an expiration date that he had clearly marked on his calendar.

"What else was I supposed to use? We were on the croquet court. We were fighting right there next to that...wicked wicket. She was suffering, so I pulled it out of the ground and put her out of my... her...misery." To my disgust he demonstrated his benevolence with a quick stabbing motion in the air. "Didn't know she'd had a boob job—not until they started leaking."

I gasped! The image of beautiful Simone in that violated state, lying there bleeding with deflated breasts, stabbed me deeper than his harpoon ever could. He guffawed at my reaction, allowing me a glimpse of the demon within him.

"It was tragic and heartbreaking for me," he continued with a frown, but his eyes were still shining. "In the end, there was this gurgling, sucking sound. So horrible. I wonder what that was. Do you know?"

I could see the lights of Key West in the distance. How far were we out? A couple of miles? Could I swim that?

"Doc?"

Red-hot rage began to simmer in my core, so intense and dark that it made bile rise in my throat. Slowly it replaced my fear.

"Pneumothorax," I answered coldly.

"Which means what?"

"It means that not only did you smash her skull in, but also you stabbed her twenty-five friggin' times. The noise you heard was air coming of out of her lungs and not going back in! You can't live very long with no air in your lungs; that's a medical fact." My voice had gone up a couple of octaves as I fought to control my fury. "Tragic, my ass. I guess it surprised even a hardened asshole like you, Mick. The fact that you punctured her silicone breast implants probably even excited you, gave you something to fantasize over—empty breast implants of your dead trophy girlfriend!" I spat the last three words at him.

Mick's face was astounded. "Twenty-five times. Is that so?" was all he had to say for himself. As my stomach churned with anger, the monster's confession just kept on coming. "It sure made a mess too. There was blood everywhere. I got Kublai here"—he pointed to the young man who'd tied my feet—"and Amman to get it all cleaned up."

Amman was the boy at the helm. "They rolled her up in a tarp and threw her under the pool cover. They had to haul a shitload of water over to the croquet court to wash all the blood into the ground. We were fortunate the security guard was asleep. It was perfect, really; no one would know until summer what had become of the beautiful Simone...Oh, and the cameras around the U Club property, they're out of commission, except the one at the front gate."

"Lucky you," I said sarcastically.

"Yeah, it all turned out perfect—all except for them finding her body only two weeks later. That was a bummer. I had one of the boys put the croquet mallet in a locker—your locker, as it turned out."

"What about the croquet set found with Cooter Amstutz?"

"What about it? The set belonged to Simone. We just put it back in the locker room. Someone else must have given it back to Cooter." He suddenly checked his watch and ordered, "Finish tying him up."

His goon, Kublai, obeyed, tying my hands tightly behind my back.

"You're a sicko, you know that?" I sputtered.

"And you're dead," Mick said coolly and then leaned in close until we were eye to eye.

I think he was looking for fear, but I wasn't about to give him that and glared back without blinking, without feeling, ready for the last scrimmage, the final Hail Mary, before they pushed me into the drink. With controlled rage just like in football, I lowered my voice and said calmly, "When you kill me, you better make damn sure I'm good and dead, because if you don't, I'm coming back for you, Mick McCrory. I'll be there the day they do your colonoscopy, you murderous scumbag, and I'll make sure you know what having a wicket shoved up your ass feels like while you're still on this side of hell."

He blinked, my icy promise seemingly disturbing to him, because he straightened, brushed off his jacket, and stepped back. Throwing up his hands, he covered his unease with an impudent laugh. "Thanks for the warning. I'll make damn sure you're dead." He waved for Amman to start the cruiser. The engines came to life, and Amman throttled up. If death was to be my only option, I was prepared to die well, and one of those bastards, preferably Mick, was coming with me straight to hell. Kublai grabbed my arm and forced me to stand, but he shouldn't have looked away for the split second he did, because before he even knew what hit him, I head butted his cranium into delirium, and in full-tackle mode bulldozed him up and over my shoulder and over the side of the boat. His head hit the railing with a loud crunch. Amman, realizing his brother was overboard, turned the wheel so forcefully the cruiser banked at an impossible angle, sending Mick stumbling to the starboard side. With my hands and feet tied, there was no place to go, so I flopped back into the seat, frantically wriggling my hands back and forth to loosen the knots. Mick recovered quickly, shouting to Amman to forget about his brother and come help with me. Flustered, the inexperienced man let go of the controls entirely and pulled his gun, but with no one manning the rudder, the boat veered to port, and he lost his grip. The gun slid across the deck and came to rest under a seat. The unbridled boat sped out of control, its course all over the chart.

"Forget the damn gun; grab his ankles!" Mick shouted at him.

The two men closed in on me. I kicked at them with my tied feet, aiming high for their testicles. One blow landed damn near Mick's, hitting his thigh instead. The next kick connected with Amman's kneecap, and he went down with an agonized shriek. The boat swerved violently to port side again, propelling me up and out of the seat and facedown onto the deck. Before I could roll myself over, Mick kicked me hard on the side of the head and then for good measure kicked his thug, who was wailing and holding his knee. He yanked the harpoon from its rack again and aimed it at my gluteus maximus, but the boat turned starboard just in time, and his shot went wide. In a rage, he threw the harpoon barrel at me, grabbed the rope between my feet, and dragged me in a circle toward the back of the boat. Desperately I thrashed about, struggling to free my feet from his grip or at least turn myself over. He shouted to his thug to get the hell up and help, and then suddenly something hard hit my skull, and my vision went dark. Vaguely I felt my body being dragged, turned, and thrown overboard, the rudder of the boat slicing my buttock as I sank into the cold depths of the sea.

47

Plunging, down, down, down into the dark, salty water of the Gulf of Mexico, my unconscious brain must have maintained its sense of self and switched the controls to automatic pilot, because water didn't make it into my lungs, and somehow my descent to the ocean floor slowed. Bit by bit my mind rebooted itself as one by one my senses came back online. My lungs were bursting, my head throbbed, my eyes burned, and my butt hurt like hell. Gently I began to move my tethered feet back and forth and soon managed to stop sinking and finally gained enough momentum to actually surface.

I breathed in the tepid air, resisting the urge to cough, which would certainly have sent me back under the swell. My hands were useless, tied behind my back, so I just quietly floated on my side, using my feet like a merman fin, trying to empty my mind of everything but getting my hands untied. Each time I tried, though, my head would go under. If I wiggled my hands, my feet would stop moving. It was as if trying to rub your head and pat your stomach at the same time.

A coppery taste filled my mouth—blood, I decided, my blood. In the moonlight I could see the red tint on the water surrounding me. It was probably from the gash on my hind end, I reckoned. Sharks came to mind, but I forced those thoughts away, knowing that panic would call in death surer than cyanide and certainly quicker than sharks, which then reminded me of Mick and his goons. I shifted position to look around, until I spotted his boat a couple hundred yards out, its spotlight on, searching. This was definitely some kind of movie gone bad, and it was all being played out in slow motion. I wondered if the bastard was coming back to finish me off or just to watch me die. Maybe he was coming back for Delmár's son.

The sound of another boat motor pierced the night. It was coming from the direction of Key West. The spotlight on Mick's cruiser went dark, and quickly the boat turned tail as a fully lit Coast Guard cutter topped with an American flag motored past me and picked up speed when it caught sight of the cabin cruiser. The enormous swell the vessel left in its wake sucked me under. Fighting the rising panic in my chest, I let the sea take me, thinking, Where is MeMoe when you need him? I longed for his comfort in my final moments and wondered what would become of him if I didn't make it. Coming up out of the water for a second time, I saw that Mick's cruiser was headed out to open sea along with the small go-fast boat that had kidnapped me. The cutter, in hot pursuit, was closing in, and gunfire erupted from one of the boats, a string of firecrackers lighting the night sky from my vantage point.

Suddenly the *slap-slap-slap* of helicopter blades passed overhead. It was a fully gunned, yellow Jayhawk flying so low that it was creating its own waterspout and an onslaught of new waves. Its searchlights moved over the water until Mick's boat was fully illuminated.

"This is the Coast Guard! Put down your weapons and surrender!" a voice blared.

Mick's boat answered with a hail of bullets. The chopper tilted dangerously to the left to avoid being hit, its skid almost touching water; then it let loose on Mick with full firepower. Another smaller military boat coming in from the east veered off to intercept the smuggler boat, which without warning made a U-turn in my direction. I had no idea what to do. They were coming straight for me at an amazing speed. With a rush of adrenaline that only the threat of sure death can incite, I kicked my makeshift tail fin hard and launched myself out of the water like a marlin on a hook and dove out of the path of the speeding boat. The military craft must have caught sight of me, because it veered, missing my feet by inches. It slowed for a mere second and then continued its pursuit, obviously deciding that my life wasn't worth saving. Wave after wave from all the agitation swept over me, and it soon became clear that I wasn't going to make it. Death had already taken both my hands and arms, which were numb to the point they didn't belong to me anymore, and the Grim Reaper was slowly creeping up my legs, the only things still keeping me afloat. I was exhausted, my breath coming in short, painful puffs.

"Cease and desist or you will be shot!" I heard the voice bellow.

Another round of gunfire went off as the lights and sounds around me began to dim. My body rolled backward, my head cradled deep in water, affording a perfect view of a brilliantly lit night sky. From what seemed like a million miles away, cannons went off. I turned my eyes in time to see Mick's boat explode not once but twice into twin fiery balls, whose smoke clouded the extraordinary moon and hid all the beautiful stars.

"That was for MeMoe," I said to the universe without remorse, snuggling back into my wet sarcophagus. When death came, there was no anxiety, no judgment, no last wish, and no pain as the tsunami from the explosion hit me like a ton of bricks.

48

How much time had passed was anyone's guess. It could have been minutes or centuries, but suddenly I was back in the school yard at Clarksdale Elementary. The sun was hot, and it was a hazy Mississippi day. We were at break, all of us kids, playing softball.

Lance Mingledorf was teasing me again. "Turtle face, turtle face, Terry is a turtle face. Turtle Terry."

"I'm not either!" I shouted at him.

"Yes, you are. You're Terry turtle face. Turtle Terry. Ha-ha, Turtle Terry."

"You take that back, or I'll see you after school!"

Lisa Morgan was snickering into her hand, but Molly Langford was shouting to everyone to leave me alone. She couldn't stand to see people fight.

"Ha-ha, ha," Lance snorted. "I'm not afraid. We can fight now if you want. What? You gonna boohoo hoo?" He picked up a fist-sized rock from the dusty ground and threw it, hitting me dead center in the chest. It knocked the wind from my gut.

"Ooof!" I cried and rushed him, but my feet were rooted in place. I fought for breath.

He hurled another rock, and it hit dead center again, the shock of the blow going straight to my teeth.

I started bawling. "That hurts! Stop it!"

I could feel hard ground beneath me. When did I fall?

My eyes filled with tears, and I felt water gush from my mouth—or was it blood? I coughed and coughed and coughed some more.

"Sir? Sir? Can you hear me?" It wasn't Lance Mingledorf. It was a man I didn't know.

Something plastic was covering my nose and mouth. It was keeping me from breathing. I yanked at it. A hand stopped me. "You're OK," a voice said.

I opened my eyes. "Waa? What?" My lids were weighed down—so heavy. I was lying on a stretcher on the hard floor of a ship. A young man with short, curly red hair, dressed in a blue jumpsuit, was standing over me. "He's back," the man announced to a bunch of faces surrounding me. There was a flurry of activity that I couldn't really comprehend. I saw the moon and the stars and wondered what in the world was going on. "Don't worry. We'll get you all patched up so you can be good as new before you have to go to jail."

Jail? Oh, hell no! I began to fight.

"You're OK," the man insisted. He had to yell to be heard over all the ambient noise. Wherever I was, it was really loud. I reached for the annoying face mask again.

"You're going to be just fine," he reassured me, nodding to another man dressed in blue.

I stopped fighting at the sound of a helicopter circling low overhead. What was the use anyway? Evidently I was headed to the pen again; for what this time, I had no idea. Another man in an orange jumpsuit and life preserver put on his helmet and hooked my stretcher to four long cords. He gave a thumbs-up, and instantly we were lifted high into the air, all the way up to the chopper, where someone pulled us inside. The man in the helmet told me we were headed to the mainland. I wasn't completely sure at that point what a mainland was or when, in fact, we had arrived at this place. Everything was pretty much a blur of people telling me to stay awake, relax, move, don't move, breathe in, breathe out, this is going to hurt, and so on. Up until that point, I really had not been on the receiving end of acute trauma care and certainly never had to be rescued, so there were no expectations on my part. I do distinctly remember them sewing up my bum in the emergency department, however, and worrying about not being able to feel my jewels when they gave me the local, but luckily that all worked itself out. Finally, they allowed me to sleep.

49

When I awoke to my full senses, it was Sunday morning, but I didn't know that. I was in a hospital room. I was attached to a heart monitor, a blood-pressure machine, an IV, and, to my chagrin, a urinary catheter, which I would shortly demand to have removed. Lloyd was asleep on a chair at the foot of my bed. What was he doing here? What hospital was this? Lloyd stirred and jerked awake. He jumped out of his seat and came to my bedside.

"Hey. How you feeling?" he asked.

"Good," I said but didn't really mean it.

"Are you in pain?"

My chest hurt like hell, but I shook my head. "Where am I?"

"Miami."

I was silent and then asked, "So is this the prison hospital?"

"No...do you even remember what happened?" he asked carefully.

"I was out in the ocean." I struggled to recall. "They said I had to go to jail."

He laughed. "Yeah. The Coast Guard had you mistaken for a smuggler but couldn't figure out why your hands and feet were tied. I had to talk them down from that hill. It wasn't easy, but when the feds got here, we finally got it all cleared up."

"First a murderer and now a smuggler," I said without much emotion.

"It was all a misunderstanding, but it was good that they saw you floating around out there and fished you out. You were DOA. They had to shock your heart to get you back."

"At least it wasn't death by croquet wicket," I said tonelessly.

Lloyd gave me a questioning look.

"Mick McCrory," I said. "It's a long story." My memory was slowly returning. "What happened to them?"

Lloyd rubbed his crew cut. "Mick McCrory got blown all to hell. Went up like a powder keg—boom! Probably guns and ammo on board. The other thug was able to jump overboard but got some pretty bad burns. One guy they found swimming toward the keys."

"Really? What about the other three guys? The ones in the speedboat."

"Four," Lloyd corrected. "One was shot, and the others gave it up."

"Four?" I only remembered three.

"Yep, four. Your man Delmár was on the little boat. He was the one who wouldn't give it up. He's stinkin' up the city morgue as we speak."

Mick's thugs must have picked Delmár up somewhere after they dropped me off on Mick's boat.

"So that's it?" I asked.

"Pretty much," Lloyd said. "Thanks to you and Big Al, the feds got the break they needed in this case."

"Were they watching me?"

"No, but when you gave Big Al the idea about Mick McCrory, he started putting two and two together and sent over a dump truck to collect garbage from Mick's warehouse. Interesting what you can find in other people's trash."

"The dump truck was Big Al's?"

"Yeah. Anyway, he called me to come over and take a look at what he'd found. Immediately, I called Reardon, and he contacted the feds. I tried calling you but kept getting your stupid voice mail, and finally your overprotective nurse broke down and told me where you were. We just knew you were onto something, so the bureau made a beeline down here, and me too. We told the Coast Guard to keep a lookout 'cause it was pretty clear there was some serious smuggling goin' on."

"Yeah," I said, "guns."

"Guns and coke. My man, you cracked open a major gun-and-drug-running operation all by your lonesome. Guns were probably ending up with terrorists in the Middle East, and drugs, of course, here in the United States. They haven't gotten to everyone just yet. They all crawled back into their cracks like roaches, but you can bet your bippy this threw a huge monkey wrench in their apparatus."

"Good." I fiddled with the button to raise the head of my bed.

We were silent for a long while. Then I said, "You know Mick killed Simone, right?"

Lloyd shook his head. "No, I didn't."

"The son of a bitch told me all about how it went down before he had me hog-tied and thrown overboard. On top of being a two-bit criminal, the man was a butcher."

I must have had a sour look on my face, because Lloyd asked, "You wanna tell me about it?"

"Not right now. Suffice it to say, I'm glad for humanity that he's dead." I sighed. "I wonder, though, how I'll ever totally clear my name in Simone's killing. Mick told me how it went down, but people might think I made that up just to clear myself. My name'll be forever tainted," I despondently concluded. "Unless Delmár's sons start talking."

"I wouldn't worry too much about that," Lloyd said. "Those boys are still kids. They'll start squealing. Sooner or later, they all do. Jail's a mean place."

"I guess." I plucked at my sheet, not making eye contact.

"There's something else?"

"Maybe."

He waited.

I looked at him. He was a good friend to come all the way down here to sit with me in the hospital.

"I didn't see a light, Lloyd."

He folded his arms. "What do you mean?"

"When I died, there was no light...no tunnel either. I'm pretty sure Father Euclid promised us that, didn't he?"

Lloyd puffed his cheeks and blew out. "Well...personally I wouldn't put too much stock in what old *Father* Euclid had to say about lights and all that. With all the booze he had in his system, there's no telling what he was seeing. 'Sides, the Good Book doesn't say anything about seeing a light."

"Other people say they saw a light."

He rubbed his chin and thought about this for a moment. "Well, maybe you didn't actually die...die."

"They had to shock my heart, Lloyd."

"No, that's not what I mean. Maybe the higher-ups knew you weren't staying and didn't have any complaints about your life, so maybe they didn't feel you needed any kind of take-home message, you know? Maybe those other folks who saw a light did."

I wasn't convinced about what Lloyd was saying, mostly because I couldn't imagine the higher-ups approving of how I was living my life. Perhaps a change in my life's perspective was in order.

"Hey, at least you didn't see brimstone and fire," Lloyd mused.

I scrubbed my scalp. "Yeah, I guess it's better to live with uncertainty than be absolutely sure you're going to end up in line to meet the devil."

Lloyd laughed. "I'm heading downstairs to get a burger. You want something?" He hurried to the door.

"Won't they bring me food in this place?"

"I guess. For the prices they charge these days, you oughta get lobster."

"Yeah," I agreed, but as he headed for the door, I called after him, "Better bring me one, maybe two."

"Sure thing."

The phone next to my bed rang. Reaching for it reminded me of the trauma my backside had suffered at the hands of Mick McCrory. "Hello," I said into the mouthpiece.

"Oh my God!" It was Abigail. "It's Terry!" I heard her say to someone in the background; then I heard a sob.

"Abigail?"

She was crying. "Are you OK, sweetie?" she asked, sniffling.

"I'm alive," I responded plainly, not knowing what else to say or what else to feel.

"We just heard from Detective Reardon what went down. Oh my goodness, we were so worried about you. We called and called and kept getting your voice mail. I went by your place, and you weren't there. I even called the vet and asked if you'd picked up MeMoe; then I called your office, but they were already gone for the weekend. It's so good to hear your voice." Abigail's words came out in a torrent.

"Is Monique there with you?" I asked.

"Yes, she's right here, sitting right next to me. We were so worried."

"Well, ask Monique if she knows a Mick McCrory."

I heard Abigail ask; then she said, "She said hell yeah. He used to hang out at Sleep-Out Louie's all the time when she and Simone were there."

"Tell her it was him. He killed Simone."

I heard Abigail tell Monique.

"No!" Monique cried out in disbelief.

I continued, "Abigail, he would never have stopped until Monique was dead. He knew that she would figure it all out sooner or later. He was even going to come after you."

Abigail told Monique this, and I heard Monique gasp.

"But tell her it's all over now. It's OK. He's dead. He'll never bother her or any of us again."

"Oh, Terry!" It was Monique on the phone. "I would have never in a million years guessed it was him. He was so...so clean cut and nice."

"Yeah, he was nice all right, right up until he cut your heart out."

She was at a loss for words, and I heard her say, "Shit" as she handed the phone back to Abigail.

"So when will you be back in Memphis?" Abigail asked me.

"Soon, I hope."

"We have some talking to do when you get back," she said quietly.

"OK," I replied hesitantly.

"Nothing bad, and it can certainly wait. I'll see you soon, OK?"

"I'll call when I get back in town."

"Bye now."

"Bye." As I hung up the phone, I had a bad feeling that this wasn't just your run-of-the-mill *à bientôt* but a final *adieu pour toujours*.

50

A few days later, Lloyd and I were on the road home. He drove the entire way while I slept. Now, that's a really good friend. I was undeserving but thankful. The two of us were forced to drive because it seemed that expensive excursions were off the table for a while until the numbers in my bank account drifted into the black again. After the past few months and now with the cost of my rescue and hospital bill, it was down to eating beans and rice for a couple of months, especially if I wanted to keep my condo and all their high HOA fees and pay to keep my membership at the U Club.

We stopped at the pet emergency clinic to pick up MeMoe. My heart soared at the sight of this little furry creature who had stolen my heart. He was wearing an enormous white cone around his neck, his usually feathered plume of a tail as bald as a rat's. The good news was that it was still flying high, and there appeared to be no sag to his swag. The vet said we could expect to have a full tail of fur by the next year's dog show. MeMoe hopped and ran around in a little circle, delighted to see me. He'd been worried that I'd forgotten about him, but I assured him that he was the only thing on my mind when I drowned. That was a huge boost to his ego. He puffed out his chest, let out a couple of happy yelps, and thoroughly marked his territory on the fake rubber tree in the waiting room.

Lloyd dropped us off in front of my place. He wouldn't hear of letting me help pay for his gas but told me I could buy him a beer at the Red Eye whenever. Mangrove Island Resort had agreed to return my rent-a-car and forward my clothes, cell phone, keys, and wallet that I'd left behind in the room. They would charge my credit card for all of that, of course. Henry, the doorman, who was just arriving to start his shift, greeted me enthusiastically. You had to admire the tenacity of this old man who was within spitting distance of the century mark and still insisting on contributing to society. What a dude. It was good to be back home and back to normal. I was thankful to be alive, and believe it or not, I was taking my death to heart. My focus in life was about to change even if there is no light.

MeMoe tugged on the leash, trying to reach the green strip next to the sidewalk. A bright red Mazda Miata roadster squealed to a halt at the curb and parked. Abigail jumped out and ran around to where we stood. Monique was on the passenger side, looking a little worse for wear but beautiful nonetheless. Abigail gave me a big bear hug and a very long kiss on the lips and then squatted to greet MeMoe.

"You're looking good, buddy," she cooed. "Those tail feathers'll grow back soon." She was baby talking to him, and he was eating it all up.

I approached Monique and leaned in for a kiss, an offer she didn't refuse, although hers was a little shorter and cooler than Abigail's. "Glad you're alive," she said.

Abigail grabbed both of my arms and turned me around. "I have something wonderful to tell you!"

She did a little excited jump. "Guess what." I looked at her and then Monique. They were both smiling coyly. Abigail took both my hands in hers. "Guess!"

She was dressed in tight jeans and a scooped-neck sweat shirt that bared both of her shoulders. Her blond hair was giving off silver sparkles in the sunlight. I couldn't help but brush it back and then pull her close, so she could feel my aroused manhood. "Another ménage à trois? I can do either or both, whatever floats your boat, baby," I whispered to her, forgetting all about my promise to God to work on changing my life.

Abigail pushed away and then slugged me on the shoulder. "No, silly, not that." She laughed, embarrassed. "It's something amazing!"

The three of us or even just Abigail and me up in my bed was the most amazing thing I could come up with. "What?"

She held up her left hand, wiggling her fingers. Her ring finger bore a small diamond.

"We're getting married!" She jumped up and down with glee.

I stared at the ring and then searched Abigail's face. I didn't remember proposing to her. Had she met another man? "Who's we?"

"What'd you mean, who's we? Monique and me, of course."

Wham, boom, pow!

"What?" I shouted.

"It's in two weeks. Monique asked me a few days ago, and I said yes." She covered her nose and mouth with both hands in excitement. "Isn't it great news?"

Great news? This was horrible news. This gave a whole new meaning to erectile dysfunction. It was the coup de grace for my manhood, a chopping off at the knees, a punch in the puss. I was speechless.

Her smile faded, and she began to toy with a rock on the ground with the toe of her shoe. Monique turned and faced forward in the vehicle, not wanting to hear this part of the *really good news*.

"Well, what about me?" I finally blurted out.

"What do you mean?" Abigail asked, her face quite serious now. She squinted up at me against the late-afternoon sun.

"Well, me…us!" I moved my finger in a circle to indicate my full willingness to allow Monique into the mix if that was the way Abigail wanted it.

"Us?" Abigail asked, looking truly baffled. "There never was an us—I mean, not really. Was there?"

"Well, yeah, there was!" I shouted again. "I always thought so, any-way...well, kinda...sort of...maybe. It was always a possibility...an op-tion," I vehemently argued.

"An option?" She shook her head slightly, hurt written all over her face. "Terry, I don't want to be somebody's option. I want some-one who loves me, not just physically but all of me, all of the time. Monique does, and I...I feel the same way about her."

I couldn't speak.

She was quiet.

Monique was silent in her contemplation of the dashboard in front of her.

"What're you thinking?" Abigail finally asked. "Terry, please say something."

Shrugging, I backed up a couple of paces out of her reach. What was there to say? That I was hurt? That I'd been a fool and missed my chance? That I felt guilty for stringing her along all these years? Abigail deserved better. She knew it, and I knew it. I looked into her pale-blue eyes, now welling with tears.

"Will I ever see you again?" I asked, my insides lying on the side-walk between us.

She swiped at a tear. "Of course. You still mean a lot to me."

I took a deep breath. After the ocean incident, it still hurt to do that but even more so now.

She put both hands in her jeans pockets. "I was going to ask if you'd walk Monique and me down the aisle. Neither of us has anyone to do that."

I watched MeMoe, who was staring at Abigail in disbelief.

"Will you do it? Please?" she pleaded.

I sighed, looking over her shoulder and across the street at noth-ing in particular. "I guess," I agreed without much enthusiasm.

"Thank you." She kissed me lightly on the cheek. "It'll be fine; you'll see."

"Yeah, right—it's all good," I said sarcastically.

"OK then, I'll call you with the details about your tux and all that, OK?" She walked back around to the driver's side, got in, and fired up the roadster.

"Hey," Monique turned to me and said, "for what it's worth, thanks for taking care of you know who. I'm really glad you're OK."

"Yeah, well...no good deed goes unpunished, does it?" I said crossly.

"Aw, come on. Don't be like that, Terry."

"You stole my girlfriend, Monique; how should I feel about it? I damn near died, and for what? For whom?"

"I'm sorry. I almost died too, remember? This was something in the stars. We didn't plan this. If it weren't for you and Simone, I would have never met Abbie. It just happened." She paused. "Terry, we both love you very much; we do, and we want you to still be a part of our lives—just not like before, you know? Different but better."

I looked off toward the west and the setting sun. "Whatever." What else was there for me to say?

"OK, so give me a kiss for good luck." She reached out both arms, and reluctantly I complied.

"We'll meet this weekend to talk about the plans. OK? See you then!" She waved as Abigail put the car in gear and pulled away from the curb.

MeMoe and I stood staring down the street long after the red Miata had disappeared around the corner.

"What now, buddy?" I asked him sullenly.

His wise brown eyes studied me from the depths of his cone. He too was taken aback by this unexpected play that had ended up with the other team winning and the two of us being the big fat losers, but like a seasoned football player, he shook it off. For him it was *c'est la vie*, water under the bridge, life's too precious, and all that. He walked around in little circles until he was off the curb where the Miata had been parked, and then he squatted for business in the middle of the road. Live and let live was his advice, and good advice it is. We should all try to be more like MeMoe.

"So what do you want to eat tonight?" I asked him.

He barked twice.

"Steak, really? How about a burger? We can't afford steak right now. We can stop by Big Al's. They have a pretty good selection."

MeMoe thought about this and then agreed but only if the burger was well done. Eating raw meat's barbaric.

I punched in Big Al's number. "Hey, I'm back, I'm alive, and apparently I'm free again."

Big Al chuckled. "Glad you're alive, my man."

"Thanks. MeMoe and I are coming by tonight. Got any girls down there who want to meet a lonely, nondrinking, available orthopedic surgeon?"

The End

ABOUT THE AUTHOR

 Terry Canale has spent more than forty years working as an orthopedic surgeon for the Campbell Clinic in Memphis, Tennessee. In addition to his successful medical and academic career that has seen his leadership in a multitude of national and international orthopedic organizations, he is an accomplished author and editor, having published numerous journal articles and book chapters in the field of orthopedics. He is currently the editor of a book that has become known as the bible of orthopedics.

A Wicked Wicket is Canale's debut novel, a murder mystery that offers glimpses into the real—*or not so real*—life of Terry Canale. Besides writing, he enjoys painting and spending time with his wife, Sissie, at their home in Memphis. They have two children and five grandchildren.